D0810461

MYSTERIES *of* MARTHA'S VINEYARD

MYSTERIES *of* MARTHA'S VINEYARD

Wider Than an Ocean

BETH ADAMS

Guideposts
New York

Cover and interior design by Müllerhaus
Cover illustration by Greg Copeland, represented by Deborah Wolfe, LTD.
Typeset by Aptara, Inc.

Printed and bound in the United States of America
10 9 8 7 6 5 4 3 2

CHAPTER ONE

Priscilla couldn't believe the color of the sky. She thought by now she'd have grown used to the way the light here on Martha's Vineyard seemed to shimmer, the way it cast everything in a gorgeous, glowing radiance. And yet, as she came over the rise, the beauty still took her breath away. The vibrant sky was somewhere between robin's-egg blue and a deep, rich cerulean. The tidal marsh, surrounded by trees stripped bare by the long winter, appeared both beautiful and haunting. Priscilla slowed—a luxury she could afford in mid-March, when the island was down to just the hardiest of locals—and took in the vista. The contrast between the stark, barren tree limbs and the luminous blue of the sky struck her with awe.

Soon, she rounded the bend, and the marsh disappeared, replaced by woods on both sides of the road. Priscilla drove along, humming a hymn they used to sing at her church back in Kansas. She was headed out to Menemsha, on the western part of the island, to meet Gerald at the Coast Guard station, and she always forgot how rural this part of the island was. It was hard to believe she was only a few miles from Tisbury, the bustling village near her lighthouse-cottage home. She passed a few houses, set back from the road and surrounded by stacked stone fences, and a convenience store cloaked in wooden shingles and green shutters, making it the most attractive gas station she'd ever seen. Then, nothing but trees again, and another marsh, filled to the brim with glistening water. The tide was in.

She tried to keep her mind focused on the beauty around her, but inevitably her thoughts wandered, settling on the long list of things she had to do. She'd agreed to help Gerald organize an Easter egg hunt for the community; there were all the little details for Rachel's wedding she needed to check on; her best friend from home, Ruth, was about to have another granddaughter and she still needed to finish the blanket she was making for her; and...

Something caught her eye and pulled her out of her mental list making. A plane. A small plane, flying low in the sky above her. She slowed again, trying to get a good look at it. It was silver, with some blue on the tail and—was that a trail of smoke coming out of the back?

Priscilla didn't know much about planes, especially not small ones like this. "Flying tin cans," Gary had called them when he saw them cruising low over the cornfields of Kansas. But she was pretty sure they weren't supposed to be wobbling like that. Its wings shifted up and down as the pilot fought to keep the aircraft level over the marsh.

The day was still. Calm. It wasn't the wind causing the plane to shake like that.

Priscilla pulled over and stepped out of her car. The low whine of the engine filled the air. She watched as the plane cleared the marsh and swayed back and forth, fighting to stay airborne. She could just barely make out the form of someone sitting in the cockpit. It looked like the plane was about to scrape the tops of the trees and was slipping lower every second.

Yes, that was definitely smoke coming out of the airplane, Priscilla saw now. Grayish-black smoke. And more of it was coming out every moment. She continued watching the craft as it disappeared beyond the horizon, skipping lower and lower over the treetops every second, until it fell behind the tree line, out of sight. She reached back into the car and grabbed her purse. She dug out her phone. Her hands shaking, she dialed 911.

"911, what's your emergency?" the dispatcher asked.

"Hi. I'm out on N Road, headed to Menemsha. I passed the Colonial Market a ways back, and I'm by a marsh?" Did they need all those details? She had no idea. The dispatcher waited, and Priscilla decided to cut to the chase. "I just saw a small plane flying really low, and there was smoke coming out of the back of it. I think..." She took a deep breath. "I think it's about to crash!"

Priscilla gave the dispatcher all the information she could, including which direction the plane had been heading and where she thought it might have landed—or, more likely, based on what she'd seen, crash-landed.

After the dispatcher promised to send an ambulance out, Priscilla climbed back into her car. She wrestled with the idea of going in search of the craft, to see if she could help in any way, but when she looked at her heels and the marshy reeds she'd have to wade through, she realized she wasn't equipped, in any way, shape, or form, to handle an emergency like this. But there was one thing she could do. She could pray. She closed her eyes and prayed for the pilot, that he had been protected from injury, and for the rescuers, that they would find the plane quickly and bring whatever help was needed. She prayed for God's peace and for miraculous healing for the pilot, who was probably not in great shape, even if he had survived the landing.

She opened her eyes and started the car but then waited a moment, shaken. Had she really just seen a plane falling out of the sky? It seemed so awful, so startling, that at first it didn't seem like it could be real. And yet, that was exactly what she'd seen.

She took a deep breath. There was nothing more she could do now. Help was on the way. Maybe she should call Gerald, but as it was, she was about to be late to her meeting with him, and she could tell him about it then. Slowly, reluctantly, she put on her blinker, checked her mirrors, and pulled back onto the road.

A few minutes later, she was checking in at the security desk, early after all. The US Coast Guard station's offices were housed in a three-story white clapboard building with black shutters and a cupola on top. Another tidy white building, which Priscilla knew was the barracks for the officers serving at the station, sat next to the main building, overlooking a small pond, just a short way up from the inlet by the boathouse. The main building's entryway had high ceilings and polished oak floors, and black-and-white photos of men in old-fashioned uniforms on antique Coast Guard vessels lined the walls. Priscilla asked for Gerald at the front desk, and a few minutes later, he came down to meet her. After pulling her in for a hug, he led her up the stairs to his office, passing a number of staff along the way. Having called 911 about the small plane, Priscilla decided she could wait for the right moment to tell him what she had just witnessed.

"Thanks so much for coming out this way," he said.

Priscilla smiled. "Considering this is where the Easter egg hunt will take place, I thought it made sense to get a look at the grounds."

After a couple of recent mistakes—one botched open-water rescue that ended in two near-deaths, and a Coast Guard boat that crashed against the Jaws Bridge at high tide, damaging its pilings and injuring three of the officers on board—the Coast Guard had faced some bad publicity. Those incidents had been followed by a string of articles in the *Martha's Vineyard Times* that claimed that many people on the island didn't even know what the Coast Guard did and found the station foreboding and off-putting. Some officers had pointed out that the Coast Guard had something of a public relations problem. Gerald, captain of the Menemsha station, hadn't been overly concerned—this was a military base, after all—but he'd been persuaded by his higher-ups on the mainland that his team should do more to interact with the local community. The idea of an Easter egg hunt, where families could come out and have fun and explore the base and get to know some of the officers, had been born, and Gerald had recruited Priscilla and one of the younger officers to head up the event with him.

"I appreciate your help getting this set up, Priscilla. Chloe is finishing up a phone call and will be here in just a moment." Gerald led her into the large, light-filled office. His desk was set against one wall, which was paneled in dark wood and hung with various medals, certificates, and plaques. She sat down in one of the leather chairs across from his desk and looked out the large plate-glass window toward the water far below. The sky was still that bright blue, and the water below a flat greenish-gray.

"That one's new, isn't it?" she asked, pointing at a framed copy of the words to the hymn "Eternal Father, Strong to Save" on his desk.

"Yes, Aggie gave it to me for my birthday," Gerald said, handing it to her. The words were superimposed over the image of a Coast Guard cutter surrounded by water.

"I've always loved this hymn," Priscilla said. She let her eyes run over the familiar words.

> Eternal Father, strong to save,
> Whose arm hath bound the restless wave,
> Who bidd'st the mighty ocean deep
> Its own appointed limits keep;
> Oh, hear us when we cry to Thee,
> For those in peril on the sea!

The choir director at her church back in Kansas had had a soft spot for the old hymn and often chose it whenever there was a baptism, based on some logic Priscilla had never quite worked out. Something about water, she supposed, though the whole thing had always seemed a bit foreign in Kansas. It made more sense here, in Gerald's office, overlooking the vast and raging sea. But she had one question.

"Isn't this the British Naval Hymn?"

Gerald laughed. "It's often sung in the States too. And it seems entirely appropriate for the Coast Guard as well. I've always thought so, anyway."

"That it does." She handed back the frame.

"How are you?" he asked as he sat down behind his desk. His leather chair squeaked as he lowered himself into it.

"I'm..." She hesitated. "I'm fine, mostly. But the weirdest thing happened on the way out here."

"What's that?"

She took a deep breath. "I think I saw a plane crash."

"What?" Gerald leaned forward, the springs on his chair creaking. "What do you mean?"

Priscilla told him about seeing the small plane skimming low over the treetops, its wings whipping up and down as it fought to stay level while it dropped.

"Where was this?" Gerald asked, his brow wrinkled.

She told him where she was when she'd seen it, and that she'd called 911 immediately. "But I am worried about the pilot, and I hope he's all right—"

"Hold on a second," Gerald said, pushing himself up. "Let me see what I can find out." He stepped out of the office. Gerald was in communication with just about every emergency response team on the island; he was probably checking to see if they'd found anything yet.

Priscilla sat and waited, thinking he would be right back, but he was gone longer than she expected. She looked over each of the certificates and plaques—awards for valor and for dedicated service. She knew Gerald's dress uniform was also decorated with many medals and stripes, reflecting a long and distinguished career.

Finally, he came back into the office. "I think I have some good news," he said.

"Did they find the plane? Is the pilot all right?"

"No. They didn't find the plane, and aside from yours, there have been no calls about it."

"Oh dear." Priscilla had a sinking feeling.

"The EMTs didn't get any other calls, but it's strange that there weren't any calls on the radio either. Usually, if a plane is in trouble, the pilot will radio for help on 121.5, the radio frequency used for emergencies."

Priscilla had only a vague understanding of how a cockpit worked, but she'd seen enough movies and news programs to know that a pilot communicated with ground control and other pilots using a two-way radio.

"But the stranger thing is that none of the airfields in the area knew about a small plane approaching."

"Okay..." Priscilla wasn't exactly sure what he was getting at. Gerald sat down behind the desk again. He must have seen her confusion, because he elaborated.

"If the plane was planning to land at the main airport, it would have needed to contact the control tower to let them know it was approaching and ask for permission to land."

Priscilla was pretty sure he meant Martha's Vineyard Airport, outside Edgartown, where flights from Boston and Providence and

New York landed. Gerald continued. "Then, depending on whatever other planes they had coming in around the same time, air traffic control would let the pilot know when it was cleared to go in for a landing."

"So you're saying that if the plane was planning to land at the main airport, they would know about it."

"Absolutely." He placed his palms down on the leather blotter on his desk. "And given where you think you saw the plane go down, that's the most likely place it was headed."

"But they *didn't* know about it?" Had she heard him right? It seemed like he was doubting that she'd seen a plane.

"Correct."

Priscilla tried to make sense of this.

"Maybe the plane had just taken off." The plane she'd seen had been going down, but maybe that hadn't been intentional. "Maybe it had engine trouble and was trying to get back to the airport."

He shook his head. "They know for sure no small plane had just taken off."

Priscilla wasn't seeing where this was going. "But I definitely saw a plane. So where could the plane have been heading, if it wasn't going to land at the main airport?"

"Well, there's Katama Airfield, out in Edgartown. It's possible it was headed there."

Priscilla didn't know what he was talking about. "Katama Airfield?"

"It's a small place. It's mostly used for those scenic biplane tours of the island. It started out as a training facility for pilots during World War II, and it's still kind of rough. It's right on the beach, so in the summer, plenty of private planes land there, but it's pretty quiet this time of year."

"And they didn't know of any planes that were planning to land there?"

"No. They had no notice of any plane coming in for a landing."

"Is it possible someone could have planned to land there and not let them know?"

"It's possible..." Gerald said. "But if the plane was flying as low as you say when you saw it, it wouldn't have made it all the way to Katama."

"I don't think it was flying that low *on purpose*," Priscilla said.

Gerald nodded. Something wasn't adding up. Why was he so calm about this?

"Is there anywhere else the pilot could have been planning to land?"

Gerald shrugged. "There's an airstrip out in Oak Bluffs on the Trade Winds Land Bank. But you definitely need to have permission to land there, and I just spoke with the director, who said they hadn't given permission for any planes to land today."

"Okay." Priscilla tried to wrap her mind around this. "So we don't know where the plane was planning to land, but it doesn't really matter, because I'm pretty sure it didn't make it to an airport of any kind. I definitely saw it going down. So we just need to find it, and—"

"The plane didn't show up on any radar, either."

"What?"

"Martha's Vineyard Airport and Katama Airfield have radar systems so they can monitor the skies above them. None of them picked up any sign of the plane."

Priscilla just looked at him, openmouthed.

He shrugged. "I don't know what to say, but there isn't any sign of a small plane being anywhere near here."

Priscilla didn't understand. Could he really not believe her? "What are you trying to say?"

Gerald hesitated, and then said slowly, "The emergency crews have been sent out and are searching for the plane, but so far they haven't found anything. I'm sure they'll keep looking. If the plane is out there, they will find it."

There it was again. Priscilla wasn't imagining it. *If* it's out there. He doubted the plane existed.

"What do you mean, *if* the plane is out there?" she said. "I saw it, Gerald. I saw it with my own eyes."

"I have no doubt you did," Gerald said, but his voice had taken on a soothing, calm tone that only made Priscilla more frustrated.

"Then why did you say that? Do you think I'm imagining things? That I didn't really see it?"

The look on his face was inscrutable. He was giving nothing away. But he didn't believe her. That was clear enough, and for a moment, Priscilla began to wonder if he was right. *Had* she seen something that wasn't really there?

But—no. She had seen it. She had definitely seen that plane flying low, the trail of smoke coming out from behind. She knew what she'd seen, even if, for whatever reason, he didn't believe her.

"You don't think I really saw it."

"It's not that, Priscilla."

A dozen emotions swirled within her, but she was more confused than anything else. She and Gerald had gotten to know each other pretty well. They'd spent a lot of time together, and sometimes she even thought—well, of course they weren't a couple in any sort of official way, but she'd thought they'd been headed that direction.

"I *saw* it, Gerald. It was there. It was about to crash."

"It's not that I don't believe you, Priscilla." His voice now took on an exaggerated calm, which only made her more upset.

"I know what I saw, Gerald. And I know—"

"Priscilla. Listen to me." Gerald pushed himself up and walked around his desk. "I believe you saw something. I just don't think you saw a plane."

Priscilla reared her head back. "What else would I have seen?"

Before she could stop them, thoughts about government conspiracies and little green men flashed through her head. She'd had an uncle who was convinced the government was involved in some sort of elaborate cover-up involving alien spacecraft. He had wild theories about Area 51 and the FBI and all kinds of odd things Priscilla had never given any credit to. But was Gerald now suggesting something of the sort?

"What do you think it was, then?" She forced her voice to remain level.

"More than likely, what you saw was one of our drones."

"Drones?" Priscilla had heard about them, of course. The remote-controlled flying robots had been gaining in popularity and were usually used for taking video footage, she thought. Though didn't the military use them for other purposes? She felt certain she'd read that the military used them in warfare.

She thought about this for a second, and then she shook her head. "I don't think so. I've seen drones, and they have four arms with propellers. This was nothing like that."

"What you've seen are civilian drones. Quadcopters, they're called. Not all drones look like that. Some look like... Well, some look remarkably like small planes."

Priscilla let that sink in for a moment. "Did you have a drone crash this afternoon?" she asked.

"All I know is that we were doing some test flights. I should be hearing the results from them pretty soon."

"No," Priscilla said, shaking her head. "There was a person in there. I saw a person inside the plane."

Gerald let out a long sigh.

"I'm not really sure what to say, Priscilla. I really don't want to—"

A knock at the office door interrupted them.

"Come in," Gerald called. The door was pushed open, and a young woman poked her head in. "Hi, Chloe. Come on in."

This was the officer who had volunteered to help mend the Coast Guard's relationship to the public, then.

"Hi, I'm Chloe Park," the young woman said, holding out her hand. She had a bright smile and shoulder-length black hair. "I'm sorry I'm late. I was on a call and couldn't get off." Chloe spoke quickly and seemed cheerful and pleasant, and Priscilla got the sense she would enjoy working with her.

"Priscilla Grant," she said, holding out her hand.

Priscilla understood that the discussion with Gerald regarding what she'd seen was over. But she couldn't stop running it back through her head, trying to make sense of what she'd witnessed, of what Gerald said.

Had she mistaken a drone for an actual airplane?

Had she mistaken a toy airplane for the real thing?

Priscilla really didn't think so. She knew what she'd seen. She'd seen the shadow of a person inside the plane. But Gerald didn't believe her.

Emergency crews were out looking for the wreckage, she reminded herself. If it was out there, they would find it.

If. She realized she had just thought that word too. She was so turned around by this conversation she couldn't even be sure what she'd witnessed anymore. Had she really even seen the plane at all?

CHAPTER TWO

Chloe sat down and smiled at Priscilla. "So. Let's get some Easter eggs going, huh?" She flipped open a folder in her hand to reveal a yellow legal pad.

"I think that's a very good idea," Gerald said, leaning forward. "Thank you both for coming. As you know, it's recently come to our attention that this Coast Guard station has sort of a . . . complicated perception among the general public."

"They're scared of us," Chloe confirmed with a nod. "Probably something to do with the Keep Out: Government Property signs and the chain link fencing around the station."

Priscilla stifled a smile. Part of her couldn't believe the young woman was talking to Gerald like this. If Priscilla was reading the patches on her uniform correctly, she was a Petty Officer, Second Class, which placed her far below Gerald on the Coast Guard hierarchy. But she wasn't afraid to speak her mind, and Gerald didn't seem to be offended.

"That might have something to do with it," he said wryly. "In any case, it has been decided that we will host an Easter egg hunt here on the station grounds. The idea is to give the public a chance to come onto the grounds, look around a little, and have some fun. To let them learn a bit more about what we do and to feel like we're part of the community. We want them to know that nothing separates them from us." A small smile curled up the corners of his mouth. "The chain link fence notwithstanding."

"That sounds great," Priscilla said. "I think it's a wonderful idea, and I really think people are going to enjoy seeing a different side of what you all do here."

"Priscilla, Gerald said you've organized Easter egg hunts before?" Chloe said, gesturing toward her.

"Oh yes. I used to help with the children's egg hunt every Easter back at my church in Kansas," she said. It had always been so fun to see the little girls in their patent leather shoes and frilly flowered dresses and the little boys in their neckties and loafers, hunting high and low for the eggs the committee had hidden.

"And Chloe has some unique organizational experience as well," Gerald said, trying and failing to hide a smile.

"I was the social chair of my sorority," Chloe said. "So I was in charge of the spring mixer each year. It was a big job."

"I imagine it must have been," Priscilla said as seriously as she could manage.

"We've set the date for a week from Saturday," Gerald said.

"The day before Easter," Priscilla confirmed. "That's not a lot of time. So, I guess the first thing to decide is how we're going to get the word out. We need to find out what public service websites we can use, and put public service announcements on the radio. Then, of course there's Facebook, Instagram, and other social media. I'm sure the *Martha's Vineyard Times* and the *Vineyard Gazette* will cover it for us."

"That all sounds good," Chloe said. "But I was thinking we should start by talking about prizes. We've got to get some good ones."

"Prizes?" Priscilla wrinkled her brow. "I was figuring we'd just fill little plastic eggs with chocolate and jelly beans. That's how we always did it."

"I mean, sure, we can do that for some of them," Chloe said. "But these days, it takes more than jelly beans to get people to come out. I was thinking we could get local businesses to donate gift certificates. Free Pilates classes and pizzas and gift certificates from local shops. That kind of stuff. That's what's going to motivate people to come out."

Pizzas? Pilates? What was wrong with plain old Peeps? She looked at Gerald, who glanced from Priscilla to Chloe and back again, and then shrugged and pushed himself up.

"I'm going to let you two work it out," he said. He picked up a folder from his desk and headed toward the door. "I'm afraid I have to run to a budget meeting. But whatever the two of you decide is fine with me."

Priscilla watched him go, stunned. He was leaving? He turned and waved, then disappeared into the hallway. Priscilla had agreed to help with the Easter egg hunt because she'd thought she'd get to work with Gerald to plan it. Was he really going to leave her and Chloe to plan it on their own?

"He's always got meetings," Chloe said. "He's usually running from one to the other. I guess that's what happens when you're the boss." She flipped to a new page on her legal pad. "So, how about you and I come up with a list of companies and stores to hit up for donations? We can divide it up, and then we can talk about food. I want to have lots of food. I love food."

Priscilla nodded, but part of her couldn't believe what was happening. She was still glad to help with the Easter egg hunt— she knew she had the right skills, and it was a worthwhile task. But the way Gerald had run out of here, just abandoned them to plan it, when she thought she'd be working with him...

Was she getting upset over nothing? Priscilla couldn't tell if she was still smarting from the plane thing, or even whether she had reason to feel slighted. Had she been silly to think that Gerald would be overseeing the details of an Easter egg hunt when he had an entire Coast Guard station to run? But then, why had he made it sound like they would be working together?

"Is that okay with you?" Chloe was looking at her, her head tilted. Priscilla realized Chloe was expecting an answer from her, and she had no idea what the young woman had just said.

"I'm sorry. What was that?"

"I asked if you could take charge of getting the prizes and the entertainment for the day while I focus on the food and the band."

Band? Entertainment? What kind of Easter egg hunt was this going to be? But instead of protesting, Priscilla just nodded.

"I'll take care of the Easter bunny photo op. They've got some killer backdrops and props these days to really make the pics memorable."

Priscilla would have thought a picture of a child sitting on the lap of a rabbit the size of a full-grown adult would be memorable enough.

"And Gerald said we could do tours of the barracks and some of the boats," Chloe said. "People always like seeing what the cutters are like inside. I can work with the captain to schedule those."

Priscilla nodded. "What do you think of having someone talk with the children about the real meaning of Easter?"

"You mean, like, the Jesus stuff?" Chloe wrinkled her brow.

"Yeah. The Jesus stuff. The whole Christ-resurrected-from-the-dead-to-save-us-from-our-sins stuff and all that."

"Hmm." Chloe tapped her pen against her legal pad. "I mean, this is government property, so I'm not sure how people would feel about that."

"Well, I feel pretty strongly that if we're going to celebrate Easter, we need to at least mention the real reason for the holiday."

"Okay..." Chloe looked like she wasn't sure how to respond. Apparently, that hadn't been on her list of priorities for the day.

"How about this. I'll talk to the new pastor at my church and see if he can give a short message to the kids."

Seeing Chloe's face, she continued. "What if we hold it under a tent off the government grounds? We won't mention it in the flyers, so it won't be misconstrued at all that the Coast Guard is sponsoring it. I'm sure my church would be more than happy to sponsor it and set it up."

"That's probably a good idea," Chloe said. "Okay, so you'll handle that. Will you handle buying the plastic eggs?"

After she and Chloe had divided up the list of tasks for the planning, Priscilla had hoped to say goodbye to Gerald, but she was told he was still in his meeting. She texted him to say she was leaving, and then she headed out through the tall gates and back onto N Road again.

They had a solid plan for how to proceed with the Easter egg hunt, but she wasn't thinking about that. She was thinking about Gerald—both the way he'd left her to work with Chloe on the egg hunt and what he'd said about the drone. About the way he'd doubted that she'd seen a plane.

Was he right? Had she seen a drone instead of a plane? She glanced up at the sky through the windshield, replaying what she'd seen in her head. It *had* been a plane; she was sure of it.

Up ahead, she saw flashing lights by the side of the road. She slowed as she realized they were emergency vehicles. West Tisbury EMT was written on the side of an ambulance, and the Tisbury and West Tisbury police force had both sent cars. Had they found the plane, then? Priscilla knew she should simply drive past. She knew the officials were busy and would not appreciate dealing with a bystander with questions.

But she wasn't just an average bystander, she thought. She was the one who'd called it in. She was the one who could offer them information if they were still looking.

She saw Officer Teddy Holmes standing by one of the cars. Well, it couldn't hurt to stop in and see what she could find out from him. As she approached, she pulled the car over to the side of the road, and Officer Holmes looked up. He didn't exactly smile as she stepped out of the car—it was more of a grimace, actually. But she didn't let that stop her, and marched right on over to where he was standing. She saw that he was writing in a small notebook, and another officer was standing on the far side of the car, looking down at his phone. She'd met him before but couldn't recall his name. A few EMTs were standing around the back of the ambulance.

"Hi, Officer Holmes," Priscilla said, stepping closer. "Did you find it?"

His brow wrinkled, and he looked up from his notebook.

"I was the one who called 911," Priscilla explained. "I saw the plane going down and called it in, and I was hoping to hear you'd found the crash and the pilot was okay."

She hoped for that outcome. But judging by the leisurely pace everyone here seemed to be maintaining, she suspected there was no patient in the back of that ambulance.

"You called it in?" Officer Holmes was now interested, and the other officer was walking around the car to where they stood.

"I did. Did you find it? I was so worried for the pilot."

Officer Holmes looked at the other officer and back to her, and then he shook his head. "Can you tell us what you saw?"

Priscilla got a sinking feeling in her gut. Would he be asking this if they'd found the wreckage?

"There was a plane, wobbling in the sky." Priscilla recounted the scene, including the trail of smoke and the glimpse of a person in the cockpit.

"And you're sure it wasn't a toy plane?" Holmes said. "They make some very realistic remote-controlled planes these days."

"It wasn't a toy." Priscilla's voice was firm. "It was a plane. A real plane. With a real person inside." She looked at the crews standing around. One of the EMTs was holding his phone out, and the ones gathered around were laughing at something on it. "Can I assume the wreckage hasn't been found?"

"We've looked the area over thoroughly," the other officer said. Priscilla squinted and saw the name *Denton* written on the brass name bar on his uniform. That was it. Brian Denton. "And there's no sign of anything like what you're describing."

"No parts, no broken trees, no fire…" Officer Holmes's voice trailed off. "If the plane was trailing smoke when you saw it, it's fair to assume there was a fire on board. But nothing on the ground caught fire, no trees—nothing."

"And no one called for help or reported a problem on board," Officer Denton said. Gerald had said the same thing.

"Maybe whoever was flying the plane couldn't call for help. Maybe he's…"

She couldn't bring herself to say the word. But they knew what she meant.

Officer Holmes shifted on his feet. "We'll keep looking. But so far, aside from your call, there's no sign of anything like what you reported. And the plane didn't show up on radar."

Priscilla looked out across the road at the naked trees. Their bare branches, which had seemed so stark and pretty earlier, now just seemed dead and depressing. It was already mid-March. When would the buds come out?

"I'm not sure exactly where it would have landed," Priscilla said. Was this even where she'd called the plane in? Or was this closer to where it might have landed? The stretch of road along here was so long, and there was little that was distinctive. She couldn't be sure. "But I think it was probably farther up that way." She pointed up the road. "I'm pretty sure I wasn't this far west when I called it in, and the plane was headed east."

Officer Holmes gazed out at the trees that stretched for acres on the far side of the road.

"We'll keep looking," he finally said again.

"And there are still officers from West Tisbury out there searching right now," the other officer said.

"They're more familiar with the territory," Officer Holmes added, by way of explanation for why he and Denton were standing around.

"Please do keep searching," Priscilla said, though the officers' tones communicated exactly how enthusiastic they were about the task. "Someone was in that plane. And they could be badly hurt."

"We'll keep looking," Holmes repeated.

Priscilla wanted to believe them. She really did. But would they search with the urgency she felt, knowing there was someone out there who could be injured? Judging by their seemingly laid-back attitude right now, she doubted it. Priscilla set her shoulders. There was only one thing to do.

"Thank you," she said, and walked back toward her car. She climbed in and gave a little wave as she drove off. She drove until the flashing lights disappeared from her rearview mirror, until the little convenience store was just ahead. She tried to picture the angle the plane was traveling and how fast it had been going. Why hadn't she paid more attention in trigonometry class in high school? She pulled over a few hundred yards past the store, at the edge of the marsh, and stepped out. She had no way of knowing if this was the right area, but this was her best guess. She exited the car, making sure she had her phone, and looked both ways before crossing the road. Then, she said a little prayer and stepped into the woods.

Priscilla had only gone a few feet before she realized she wasn't going to get very far. There was no trail here, and no way to track where she was going. It was just... trees. Stripped bare for the winter, they let more light filter in than they would have in summer, but they somehow kept most of the sunlight from reaching her. She walked a little farther, picking her way through the white oak and pitch pine trees, searching for... She wasn't even sure. Would she know what evidence of a crash looked like if she saw it?

Priscilla didn't know whose land this was, she realized. She had no idea whether this was state land or was owned by someone who wouldn't appreciate finding a random woman walking through the trees. Still, she pressed on, trying to pay attention to the path she took so she could find her way back. A few minutes later, though, she realized it was hopeless. Everything looked the same. If she continued on this way, she was liable to get totally lost, not to mention her shoes were now covered in muck and dead leaves.

She turned around, carefully retraced her steps back to the road, and let out a sigh when she found her way out safely. It was hardly a huge, vast wilderness—they were still on a relatively populated island, after all—but there had to be miles and miles of trees out there. As she climbed back into her car, she tried to be grateful. She was safe.

But what about the pilot of that plane? she thought as she buckled herself in. Was he okay? Would they ever find him?

And then, as she pulled back onto the road, she thought about what Gerald had said and about what Officer Holmes had said, and she wondered. *Could* she really have mistaken a drone for an actual airplane?

CHAPTER THREE

Priscilla pulled up in front of Joan's house a few hours later and stepped out onto the crushed-shell driveway. Her cousin's home was a beautiful cottage covered in wooden shingles and surrounded by gardens that bloomed all summer. Priscilla was pleased to see that the bright green blades of daffodil leaves were starting to push through the hard earth. It didn't feel like spring, she thought, pulling her jacket tighter, but spring was certainly on its way.

She knocked on the door, and a moment later Joan pulled it open. Her dog pranced at her feet, wriggling with excitement.

"Hi there," Joan said, ushering her inside. "Come in, before Sister has a heart attack." She looked up at the sky, still light even as evening crept closer, and sighed. "Isn't daylight saving time amazing?"

Priscilla nodded as she peeled off her coat. They had just switched the clocks forward an hour a week ago, and as always the first few days of extended evening light felt glorious, like there really was hope that the long winter would soon end.

"How are you?" Joan asked, taking Priscilla's coat.

"I'm all right," Priscilla said. She bent down and gave Sister a good head rub. As she straightened, she sniffed and picked up the scent of simmering meat and onions. "What smells so delicious?"

"I made beef stew. I hope that's okay." Joan hung the coat in the closet by the door and started to walk toward the kitchen. "I also got some asparagus at the market because I couldn't resist pretending it's spring. But it's still so cold that I thought a stew would be nice."

"Beef stew and asparagus sounds like a perfect meal to me," Priscilla said, following Joan into the kitchen. The whole place felt warm and comforting, with its sage-green walls, white wood cabinets, and butcher-block countertops. She pointed to a loaf of crusty bread sitting on a cutting board. "Please tell me you didn't bake that yourself."

"Oh, you know I like to bake," Joan said. "I find it relaxing. And this is a simple no-knead bread. You literally just mix it up and let it sit."

"You make me feel like a slacker," Priscilla said. Joan worked part-time at an ultrasound clinic at the hospital and still managed to make her home and gardens look like showpieces.

"Oh, hush." Joan dismissed the compliment with a wave of her hand. "You're actually doing something useful for the community in your spare time. I'm just making bread. Now, let me get this stew dished up, and you can tell me what's going on with the egg hunt."

Priscilla had recruited Joan to help with the Easter egg hunt as soon as Gerald asked her, and Joan had invited her over to share the information from her meeting today and offered to make dinner while she was at it. Priscilla loved spending time with her cousin. She was so grateful that the move to Martha's Vineyard had allowed Joan, as well as her other cousins Trudy and Gail, to be a regular part of her life again. A few minutes later, they were seated at the table, steaming bowls of stew in front of them, Sister at their feet under the table, and Priscilla was updating Joan on her meeting at the Coast Guard station.

"So you'll be working more with this Chloe person, not with Gerald himself?" Joan asked.

"It kind of seems that way," Priscilla said. "And don't get me wrong, Chloe is great." She also seemed quite enthusiastic. She'd already sent Priscilla three texts since their meeting this afternoon. "I really liked her. She's smart and organized, and it will work out fine. I guess Gerald's just really busy. And planning an Easter egg hunt isn't really his thing, you know? It makes sense."

"I guess so." Joan scooped up a spoonful of stew and held it in front of her. Steam rose off the surface in little wisps. "But it's not exactly what you signed up for, is it?"

Priscilla shrugged. "It's fine. It will be better this way, probably. I mean, can you imagine Gerald choosing between tablecloths and buying baskets?"

Joan laughed. "No, I suppose not." She spooned the stew into her mouth and chewed, and then said, "But that doesn't mean it's okay. And if you want my opinion, I think you should tell Gerald that it's not fine. That you agreed to work on this because of him, and that his shrugging it off hurt your feelings."

Priscilla looked down at her stew. "It's fine," she said again, softer this time.

Joan didn't say anything for a moment. Then, slowly, she said, "It's not really fine, you know. If you're in a relationship with him, you need to communicate with him. You need to be able to speak up about your feelings."

Priscilla could tell Joan wanted to say more, but she took another bite of stew instead. Then, after a drink of water, Joan's expression changed.

"So what's the plan?" she asked.

Priscilla wasn't sure whether to be grateful or dismayed that Joan was changing the subject.

"Chloe actually had some good ideas about how to get people out to the Easter egg hunt." Priscilla filled her in on the tasks she and Chloe had outlined.

"Prizes?" Joan asked, wrinkling her brow. "You mean, more than free chocolate?"

"I guess it's a good way to get people to participate," Priscilla said. "Kids will be excited for chocolate, but to get their parents to drive them all the way out there, it probably makes sense to offer more of an incentive."

"I guess so," Joan said. "All right. Well, if you need gift certificates, I'll do my best to get some for you. What else is there?"

Priscilla ran through the list of tasks, and Joan promised to help as much as she could. Then Priscilla asked about Trudy and Gail, and Joan told her Gail had taken her father Hugh in to the emergency room for what they thought might be pneumonia, but had turned out to be bronchitis. He was on the mend, apparently, and back to his old self.

But when there was a lull in conversation, Joan asked, "What's wrong?"

"What do you mean?"

"You're upset about something. What happened?"

Priscilla reached for the butter dish and pulled it close. She cut off a thick slice of creamy yellow butter and smeared it on the bread.

Priscilla hadn't intended to tell Joan about the plane, but now that she thought about it, she wasn't sure why. Maybe she was a little embarrassed, doubting what she'd seen after all.

"Something strange happened today," she started.

"What's that?"

"I was driving along N Road, headed to the Coast Guard station for my meeting, when I thought I saw a plane crash. Or, nearly crash."

"You saw what?"

Priscilla told Joan the story, and as she spoke, Joan set her spoon down and let her mouth drop open.

"Did they find the plane?" she asked.

"Not that I know of," Priscilla answered. It felt gratifying to see that Joan took her seriously, even if no one else had. "It didn't seem like they were making much progress when I went past the spot again. And those woods are pretty thick."

"There are a lot of woods out that way," Joan said. "But there aren't *that* many trees. It's still a small island, and there aren't many places a plane could have crash-landed without attracting a lot of attention."

"Which I guess is part of why they seem to think it might have been something else."

"Something else?"

Priscilla sighed. "Gerald said what I saw was more than likely a Coast Guard drone."

"A drone?" Joan pulled the butter toward her and cut off her own thick slab. "There's no way you mistook a drone for a plane."

"Gerald said they're designed to look like planes. So people don't realize they're drones, I guess."

Joan spread the butter on her bread. "There's no way a drone is big enough to be mistaken for a plane."

"I don't really know all that much about drones," Priscilla said.

"I don't either. But I know you, and I know that if you think you saw a plane, you saw one."

"But it didn't show up on the airport's radar equipment."

"Then the radar was wrong."

After being doubted by everyone else she'd told today, it felt good to hear Joan affirming her.

"But what would a plane have been doing out there anyway?" Priscilla asked.

"What do you mean?" Joan frowned, her knife hovering over her bread. "It was flying somewhere, obviously."

"But where?"

"I don't know." Joan finally got the butter spread out to her satisfaction, and she set her knife down. "But I do know that small planes are not at all uncommon in these parts. There are more in the summer, but it's not unusual to see one this time of year."

Were they that common? "I hadn't really noticed."

Joan let out a deep breath. "Priscilla, I don't know if you've picked up on this yet, but this island is made up of all different kinds of people. There are people with boatloads of money around these parts."

Priscilla laughed out loud. Martha's Vineyard was her home, and the community she was a part of was full of normal, everyday people, but it was true: the island was known as something of a playground for the ultrarich. Especially in the summer season, roads were often choked with high-end cars, people wore designer-label clothes, and yachts and other large boats proliferated in the marinas. "You don't say?"

"I know it's hard to believe, but it's true." Joan broke off a piece of her buttered bread. "And you know what ultrarich people hate more than anything?"

"Taxes?"

"Waiting. Which is why so many of them like to skip the hassle of sitting in traffic and waiting for the ferry, and instead use their own private planes to get here."

"Huh." Priscilla didn't have any personal experience with this, but after living on the island for a couple of years, she didn't have any trouble believing it.

"I mean, what's a better status symbol than a private plane?"

"I can honestly say I've never given it any thought."

"And that's part of why I love you. But trust me, it's a thing," Joan said. "Over in Cape Cod, there's even a whole neighborhood designed around a runway. If you buy a house in that development, you can land your plane, park it in your garage, and go in and eat dinner."

"No way." Priscilla couldn't imagine it.

"It's true."

"And I thought communities with swimming pools and tennis courts were high end."

"Oh, you want high end, we've got high end. And private planes are the pinnacle." Joan took a bite of her bread and chewed for a minute, and then she said, "Remember John F. Kennedy, Jr.?"

"Of course."

"Well, you weren't living here then, but you remember what a big deal it was when his plane crashed just off Martha's Vineyard."

Priscilla did remember. "Something about getting disoriented in the dark?"

"Exactly. It was tragic, of course, and it was an international news story because of who he was. But it's also a good example of what I'm talking about. It was his own small plane he was flying. And if it's good enough for the Kennedys…" She took another bite of her bread and chewed, then continued. "There was a big controversy a few years back. Something about how low and where people could fly their private planes and helicopters."

"Helicopters too?"

"Oh yeah. In fact, I think that was the main problem, actually. There was some lady who insisted on landing her helicopter in her yard, and it was driving her neighbors nuts, so there was a lawsuit."

"Imagine that. The neighbors didn't like a helicopter landing next door."

"I believe the court ruled she had to stop. But I think there was also some discussion about limiting how low private planes could fly over residential areas."

"So it must have been happening enough that people were upset," Priscilla said.

"I suppose so." Joan set down her bread. "I'm not sure exactly where that gets you, honestly. But there were articles about it in the *Times*. You might want to look those up, in case they offer some suggestions for why a plane would be flying low over that part of the island."

"I'll check it out." Priscilla ate the last spoonful of her stew, which was hearty and delicious. "So anyway. We've done nothing but talk about me since I got here. Tell me. How are you?"

"I'm good. Nothing as dramatic as all that."

"How are Sam and Alice? How's Will?"

Joan gave an update on her sons and daughter-in-law, and about the new dog Sam and Alice had gotten.

"You have a granddog," Priscilla said. She chuckled. "Sister is an aunt."

"I'd rather have a grandchild," Joan insisted.

Priscilla laughed. "How's everything else? Work? Church? I saw that you have some flowers starting to come up."

"Yes, thank goodness. The first sign of spring. I don't think I could take much more of this winter." She shook her head. "Church is fine, but work has been a real pain."

"How so?" Joan usually enjoyed her job.

"There's all kinds of new restrictions about everything, including who can be where when. It's like our every move is being tracked."

"What?" This didn't sound like a normal hospital situation.

Joan sighed. "It's all because of that medication that went missing. Did you read about it?"

Priscilla nodded. She'd seen the headlines in the paper the past few mornings. A massive amount of medication had been taken from the hospital over the last few months, including a very large theft of opioids last week that had the authorities investigating and hospital staff cracking down. The medication taken was estimated to be worth hundreds of thousands of dollars.

"It sounded like maybe more regulation was needed," Priscilla offered. "If so much medication was stolen."

"Yes, I suppose it's possible," Joan said. "But it's made things more difficult, that's for sure. It used to be, when I needed more ultrasound gel, I would just go to the supply cabinet to get it. Now I have to get a supervisor with a key and sign it out. And that's not even where the bulk of the medication is kept. There's just a few samples of opioids in there. The nurses who dispense actual prescription meds have to go through a huge rigmarole to get what they need." She was quiet for a moment and then said, "You're right that it's probably a good thing. But it's an adjustment, that's for sure."

"I'm sorry." Priscilla could see that Joan was frustrated, and it no doubt did make her job more challenging. "Hopefully it will get easier soon. I'm sure everyone is very concerned about it all right now, what with the thefts and all."

"I'm sure you're right." Joan gave her a weak smile. "Well, anyway. Tell me about Rachel. What's the latest on her wedding?"

Priscilla was happy to fill her in on the planning for her daughter's wedding. Rachel had moved to Boston a few months back and was engaged to A.J. Montgomery, an FBI agent who worked in the area. Priscilla was over the moon about the marriage and the fact that Rachel had moved closer, and she happily told Joan that Rachel had picked pink and mauve and rose for her colors. She showed her a photo of the dress, which was a gorgeous blush-white. Most days, nothing made Priscilla happier than talking about Rachel and her upcoming wedding, but even as she shared the details, her mind was elsewhere, thinking about that plane. Joan was right—she'd really seen it. She didn't care if no one else believed her. She knew what she'd seen. And that meant it was out there somewhere. Maybe the pilot was still inside, waiting for help.

Priscilla decided then and there that she would do whatever it took to find that plane.

CHAPTER FOUR

Priscilla couldn't sleep that night. Chloe had sent her half a dozen texts with pictures of caterers' menus and links to Pinterest pages she liked for decorations, and one that just said *Easter Eggs Rock!!* Priscilla finally turned her ringer off, but whenever she closed her eyes she kept thinking about that plane, about the pilot she knew she'd seen, and about the fact that no one else seemed concerned about it. Finally, just past midnight, she got out of bed and carried her laptop to the kitchen table. She pulled her robe tighter around herself and set the kettle on to heat. The calendar said spring was around the corner, but, tonight, winter still held the island in its icy grip. A few minutes later, she sat down with a mug of chamomile tea and opened a browser window.

Joan had suggested she look up articles about the controversy over helicopters and low-flying planes a few years back, so she typed in "Martha's Vineyard Times" and "helicopters" and found the series of articles easily enough.

Joan was right; the lawsuit had started with a complaint about one helicopter, but it had expanded to a larger fight about how low planes could fly over parts of the island. It was an interesting civics debate—the rights of pilots versus the rights of those who lived below—but she couldn't see how it was getting her any closer to finding answers about the missing plane. She needed a way to find out more.

Her hands hovered over the keyboard. What had Gerald called that place? Kataki Airport? She typed that in, and was pleased when the search engine pulled up information for Katama Airpark. Thank goodness for autocorrect, she thought, as she clicked on the link.

The place didn't seem to have its own website, but between Wikipedia and some websites directed at pilots, she gleaned that the airport was basically a small grass field with three runways. Grass? You could land a plane on grass? Priscilla shook her head. She had no idea how this all worked.

But as she studied the pictures of the tiny airport, she realized that she had a way to find some answers. She'd make a visit to the airpark the next day and see if someone there could tell her about small planes.

Finally, with a plan in place, she felt weariness overcome her. She would learn more in the morning. For now, she was going back to bed.

Tuesday morning dawned gray and cold, with a fine mist hanging in the air. It wasn't rain exactly, but it added to the chill. Priscilla pushed herself out of bed and patted Jake on the head. In the kitchen, she brewed some coffee. After her devotions, she scanned the paper while she ate a bowl of cinnamon-and-brown-sugar oatmeal. There was no mention of the plane crash, she noted, even in the police log section, which reported police activity on the island. There had been a car crash on Edgartown-West Tisbury Road in Edgartown, and a break-in at a home in Oak Bluffs, where electronics, jewelry, and prescription drugs had been taken. But no plane crash, and no mention of a search for one.

Priscilla cleaned up her breakfast dishes and checked her email, and then, after taking Jake for a walk on the beach, she climbed in the car and punched the words *Katama Airpark* into her GPS. It was a twenty-five-minute drive to the southern part of the island, and Priscilla listened to an audiobook as she drove. Rachel had turned her on to audiobooks, and now she found herself listening to them whenever she could. This one was a mystery novel set in Dublin, and Priscilla was so immersed in the story that she didn't even notice she was getting close until she saw the sign for the airpark.

Ahead of her was what looked like a couple of old barns and a cluster of buildings off to the side, and to the left she saw a red biplane parked by the fence. Other than that, it just looked like a field. Priscilla parked her car by one of the barns and a man came out of it.

"Can I help you?" He was probably in his fifties, and he wore baggy jeans, a fleece jacket, and a Red Sox baseball cap.

"Hi. I'm Priscilla Grant. Is this—" She gestured at the field. "Do airplanes really take off here?"

He laughed and nodded. "They sure do." The man extended his hand in greeting and said, "I'm Travis. Travis Williams."

Priscilla shook his hand and replied, "Nice to meet you, Travis." She scanned the area. The place looked nothing like any airport she'd ever seen. "So, what can you tell me about Katama Airpark? Where is the runway?"

"We've actually got three runways. It's kinda hard to see from here, but they make a triangle. Here." He gestured for her to step inside the barn, which she could now see was actually a hangar, and led her over to an aerial photo of the airpark. And there in the picture, she could see that there were indeed three long straight sections that looked like they could, maybe, be runways.

"Do people use all of them?"

"They do," Travis said. "Which one they use depends on the weather and where they're coming from."

She looked, and thought about how to phrase her next question.

"If a plane wanted to land here, how would that happen?" She gestured around. "I mean, there's no control tower, right?"

"There is a radio frequency pilots typically use to contact us to let us know they're coming in, but as this is an uncontrolled air-field, it's not required." He waited a moment and then added, "It would be really dumb not to let us know you're coming in, but technically it's not required."

"What if a plane was trying to go to another airport? A bigger one? Would you know about it?"

"Well, you would have to make contact with the control tower if you're hoping to land at Martha's Vineyard Airport, for sure." A slow smile spread across his face. "Would your questions have any-thing to do with that plane that supposedly went down over West Tisbury yesterday?"

Priscilla nodded. "I saw the plane going down and called 911, so I guess I'm curious. I'm just trying to understand how it all works."

Travis paused a moment, and then said, "Well, I'll just say this. If there's a plane out there somewhere, we all want to find it. And I think there very well might be."

It was tepid agreement, but it was something. She decided to push ahead. "Is there any way to know where the plane was when it went down? Or where it was headed?"

"We know he didn't radio on ahead here, but again, that doesn't mean he wasn't planning to come here. But we do know Martha's Vineyard Airport has no record of contact from him, so we can assume that he wasn't headed there either."

"And I'm told the plane wasn't picked up on the airport's radar?"

"That's correct. Which is strange, because we're close enough to a big metropolitan area that most of the area is covered by radar. That's how they were able to find John F. Kennedy Jr.'s plane when it went down, because most planes around here are visible to air traffic control."

"So how is it possible that it didn't show up?"

"Well…" He took a deep breath. "Given the low altitude that was reported, it is possible."

"It *was* going down when I saw it," Priscilla said. "But I wouldn't think it started out that low."

"If it didn't show up on the radar, it makes me think the plane was flying low on purpose. If it was flying below fifteen hundred feet, it wouldn't show up on radar. 'Flying under the radar,' if you will."

"Huh." She thought for a moment. "But don't pilots have to file a flight plan? So you know where they're planning to go?"

"Not for a plane of that size. I mean, if you're smart, you do file one—that way if something goes wrong, that's how they know where to look for you. But it's not legally required."

"Huh."

"There's that word again." He gave another knowing smile. "What does that mean?"

"If the pilot didn't file a flight plan and stayed under the radar and didn't radio for permission to land anywhere and didn't radio for help when an emergency happened"—she took a deep breath—"the plane either didn't exist, or else it did, and the pilot was trying to keep his trip quiet. I want to know why." She shrugged. "And I wonder if there's any way to figure out where he was planning to land, if not here and not at the big airport."

"Honestly?" He turned to her. "If the plane was real, my guess is a private airstrip of some kind. Or there are plenty of other places you can land a plane. Remember the pilot that landed that plane on the Hudson River?"

Of course she remembered that. "But that was an emergency. He didn't do that for kicks."

"No, true enough. But any flat, open field will do. And plenty of people have private runways. My guess is he was headed somewhere like that. Somewhere people wouldn't ask too many questions about what he was doing."

"Why would he do that?"

He tilted his head and gave her a grin. "Well, I guess that's the sixty-four-thousand-dollar question, isn't it?" He reached in his back pocket and pulled a business card from his wallet and handed it to her. "Here's my number...If you think of it, give me a ring if you stumble on any answers."

Priscilla climbed back into her car. She'd promised she would get started on collecting gift certificates for the Easter egg hunt, and even though she was dubious about the prospect, she might as well begin. She drove back to Tisbury and decided Candy Lane Confectionery was as good a place to start as any. At least there she could get a sugar fix to motivate her. She stepped inside and let the door fall closed behind her.

"Hi, Priscilla," Candy called from behind the counter.

"Hi, Candy." Priscilla walked up and studied the pastry case in front of her. "How are you?"

"Just great." Something about Candy's voice caught Priscilla's attention. She looked up and saw that Candy had set her hands on top of the pastry case, trying just a tiny bit too hard to make it look casual. Something was going on. Priscilla looked down at Candy's hands, and then she noticed something.

"Oh my goodness. Is that a wedding ring?"

Candy nodded, grinning. She and Beau Ortmann had gotten engaged last year, but the last Priscilla knew, Candy was too swamped at the bakery to plan a wedding. But now there was a thin gold band next to the solitaire engagement ring.

"When? How? Oh my goodness!"

Candy laughed. "We never quite got around to making plans for the wedding, and finally we just decided to skip the whole thing and elope. We went down to the courthouse on Saturday, just the two of us and Beau's parents, and it was the best decision ever."

"Wow. That's amazing. Congratulations." Beau's parents ran the grocery store in town. Priscilla imagined they must have been excited to see Beau finally married.

"Thank you." Candy laughed. "We're pretty giddy, to be honest. I don't know why we didn't do this a long time ago. I guess I couldn't get past thinking we had to do the whole big wedding thing, but after my mom passed away, I realized I just didn't want all the fuss, you know?"

"It's perfectly understandable," Priscilla said. "I think that's amazing."

"Thank you." Candy smiled. "Now, what can I get for you?"

"I'll take a chocolate croissant, please, and a coffee."

"Coming right up."

"And I also have a request."

"What's that?" Candy held a paper cup under the spigot of the coffee carafe, and the heavenly scent wafted out.

"I'm helping organize an Easter egg hunt out at the Coast Guard station a week from Saturday," Priscilla said. "As a way to help the public get to know the Coast Guard a bit better and to see a bit more of what they do."

"You mean to make people forget about the...*ahem*...missteps of the past few months?"

"Something like that." Priscilla grimaced. "They're trying to change their image. Appear friendlier. That sort of thing."

"That sounds like a good idea. And everyone loves an Easter egg hunt. Easter candy is the best. I just love those little chocolate eggs."

"I'm partial to jelly beans, myself," Priscilla said. "But we're not just stuffing these eggs with candy. We're also trying to make things a bit more exciting by including gift certificates from local businesses in some of the eggs."

"Well, that *is* different." Candy turned off the coffee and seemed to think for a moment. "How much?"

"How much what?"

"You're asking me for a gift certificate to put in an egg, right?"

"Right." Priscilla smiled. "I suppose I am."

"Of course I'm happy to contribute. But how much?"

"I don't know." Why hadn't she thought this through?

"How about fifteen dollars?" Candy suggested.

"That sounds great."

"Coming right up."

A few minutes later, Priscilla was walking out of the bakery with coffee, a croissant, and a gift certificate. There. That wasn't so hard.

A short drive later, caffeinated and sugared up, she walked into Ortmann's grocery store and walked out with a gift certificate. She had the same result at the Red Cat Kitchen. This was easier than she'd thought it would be. She would hit a few more places before heading home.

Priscilla was climbing into her car when her phone rang. She dug it out of her purse and looked at the screen. Gerald. Priscilla hated the little frisson of resentment that coursed through her when she saw his name, and she took a deep breath before she answered the call.

"Hello?"

"Priscilla? Where are you right now?"

"I'm in town. I just visited a bunch of businesses, soliciting prizes for the Easter egg hunt."

"That's great." He wasn't really interested in her answer, his tone made that clear. Priscilla tried not to let herself get frustrated again. She was doing this for him, after all.

"Where exactly were you when you thought you saw the plane going down yesterday?"

"I was on N Road," Priscilla said. They'd been through this yesterday. "I had just gone past that little market when I saw it."

"Is there any chance you were farther than that? Maybe a mile or two farther down the road?"

Priscilla thought for a moment. She'd had a hard time finding the spot again yesterday. She wasn't exactly sure where she had been, if she was being honest. "I guess it's possible. Why?"

Gerald didn't answer for a moment, and then, slowly, hesitantly, said, "I'm not sure it's anything, really. It's just some trees that look strange."

She felt the air go out of her lungs. Strange trees? That was it?

"There's a patch of treetops that have been . . . Well, honestly, it looks like they've been knocked off."

"Knocked off?"

"Or sheared off. By something heavy. Something moving very quickly."

She started to see what he was getting at.

"And just past that, there are several trees where there are broken branches. There's even a small patch that looks like it might have been singed."

"Gerald, you don't think . . . "

"I don't know what to think," he said. "But I thought, well, I wondered if maybe you might want to come out this way and take a look at where it is and see if it's at all possible."

He didn't have to say what it was that might be possible. He wanted to see if it might be possible she'd been right after all.

"Meet you at the convenience store?" she said.

"I'll be there in fifteen minutes."

Priscilla met Gerald at the market and climbed into his SUV. She smiled at him and discovered that some of the frustration she'd felt earlier had melted away. He didn't believe her, exactly, but he was open to the idea that she might have been right, and that was a start.

"I was definitely past here when I saw the plane," she said. "But it was traveling east, and I have no way to figure out how far the plane would have traveled before it went down."

"Based on the drone footage I saw, I think we need to go this way to find those broken trees," Gerald said, pointing east. He held up his phone and showed her a picture she assumed must be a still from the drone footage. It showed just what Gerald had described—a line of trees with the tops sheared off, and several trees just beyond that with broken branches. Priscilla thought she would have been able to see through the bare tree limbs to the ground, but there were more evergreens mixed in than she would have guessed, and there was enough green in the shot to make it impossible to see beneath the trees. Was there a plane down there?

"Do you know how to get there?" Priscilla asked. "This looks like any other patch of trees around here."

Gerald nodded. "The drones have GPS, so I know exactly where this shot was taken." He took his phone back, typed something on the screen, and set it on his dashboard. She saw that there was a map with a pin dropped a ways into the woods a couple of miles down the road. "I figured we could drive down here and park as close as we can, and then go for a walk in the woods to see if we can find any sign of it."

Priscilla nodded and clipped her seat belt into place, glad she'd worn her walking shoes today. Gerald looked both ways and pulled out onto the road, then drove back the direction she'd come. As they drove, she told him about her conversation with Travis Williams at Katama Airpark.

Gerald kept glancing at the GPS screen, and about two miles down the road, farther east than she'd thought to consider, he pulled over. There was a narrow strip of dirt and gravel at the side of the road, and he parked the black SUV there. They climbed out of the vehicle.

"How do we know where to go?" Priscilla asked.

Gerald was looking down at the screen again. "I guess we just start walking," he said. He looked up at her. "Those broken trees are a good distance in, it seems. Hopefully we'll be able to get a signal in there."

He started to thread his way through the trees, and she followed a step behind. There was no path, so they had to pick their way across the soggy, marshy ground around pine and cedar and oak trees. It smelled fresh under the trees, and the air was cooler.

"Whose land is this?" Priscilla asked.

"It's state conservation land," Gerald said. "It's managed by a nonprofit, but the state owns it."

Priscilla was glad to hear that they weren't trespassing on private land, though in this case that wouldn't have stopped her. She guessed not too many people came through here, which was no doubt the point. They walked in silence for a few more minutes while Priscilla turned over in her mind all that had happened. Gerald's drone had turned up evidence that she might be right after all. That was the part she should cling to, she knew. But she couldn't help wondering what else it might have turned up.

"Do you smell that?"

Gerald had stopped, and she stopped a step behind him. She sniffed, and she realized he was right. There was something different. The air here smelled a bit... She sniffed again. Was there a hint of smoke hanging in the air?

"How close are we to those broken trees?" Priscilla asked.

"They should be just up that way," Gerald said, pointing through the trees in front of them. He stepped around a boulder and over a fallen branch, holding out his hand to help her over.

"Oh wow."

Priscilla stepped around him and saw what he was looking at. There was the flash of something metal caught in the branches of a tree directly ahead of them. It looked like a piece of an airplane wing caught in the lower branch of a pitch pine.

"It's here," Gerald said, walking more quickly toward the metal. "It has to be just up this way."

Priscilla rushed forward, passing Gerald as she hurried toward what she knew must be there. The smell of smoke grew stronger as they got closer, mixed with some kind of oily metallic scent. And then, as she made her way through a grove of red oak, she saw it—an airplane tail. The silver metal flashed like a beacon, and she rushed closer.

"Oh my." Gerald came up beside her just as the plane itself came into view. "There really was an airplane."

CHAPTER FIVE

Priscilla tried to take it in. The plane no one had believed she'd seen was right in front of her. It was a small plane, one of those two-seaters, and it was silver and blue. Its nose was buried in the ground, and the blades of the propeller that had once been attached to the nose lay nearby. One of the wings had sheared off completely, but the other was still attached. The tail was caught in the lower branches of a pine tree, holding the plane at what Priscilla guessed to be about a thirty-degree angle. The pine tree's branches had been singed, and a few of them were black—burned, no doubt, from the fire that had caused the trail of smoke she'd seen. But the tree's moist needles seemed to have prevented the whole tree from going up in flames.

Gerald pulled out his phone and tapped the screen. A moment later, he was talking to someone—someone back at the station? A 911 dispatcher? Priscilla wasn't sure. She just knew he was telling whoever it was that they'd found a plane crash, and they needed help right away.

Gerald returned his phone to his pocket and picked his way closer to the plane. Priscilla followed.

"Hello?" Gerald called. "Hello? Is anyone in there?"

He carefully climbed up onto the remaining wing to get to the hatch-style door of the cockpit.

"Be careful!" Priscilla called. But with the tail caught securely in the tree, the plane seemed stable enough to hold his weight.

Gerald peered in through the window, and she could see him shaking his head. Oh dear. Had he seen—

Priscilla stood on the ground, craning her neck to see into the cockpit. "Is he there?" she called.

Instead of answering, Gerald wrenched the door open and scanned the area behind the two seats. He shook his head again and looked back at Priscilla. She had been preparing herself to find someone desperately hurt—or worse. She hadn't even considered the possibility that now presented itself.

"There's no one here," Gerald said.

"No one?"

"No one," he repeated. "Whoever was flying this plane must have made it out of here."

"Good!" A wave of relief coursed through her. "Oh, that's good news." He had survived! The pilot must have survived the crash and found a way to get help.

Gerald nodded slowly. "Yes," he said, but his relief was tinged with something else. Confusion? Doubt? "Yes, it is good news." He turned and held out his hand to her. "Here. Come see."

He helped her scramble up onto the wing, and she peered inside the small plane. The cockpit held two leather seats in front of a dashboard with two big screens, as well as all kinds of lights and buttons she didn't understand. And there was blood on some of them. It was smeared along the seat and on the airbags that must have deployed on landing and along the inside wall of the cockpit as well.

"He was hurt," Priscilla said.

Gerald nodded, and he scooted over so she could see into the back of the plane, which was just a cargo area. She moved closer to try to get a better look at the items scattered there. There was a small spiral-bound notebook, and a set of keys. She saw sunglasses, a pocketknife, and a pill bottle. And there was a box with bandages and ointments, most of its contents scattered around the back of the plane. There were drops of blood all over the place.

"He used the first aid kit," Priscilla said, noting the opened packets that had held gauze and bandages.

"But it can't have done all that much good, judging by the amount of blood here," Gerald said. "Band-Aids weren't going to fix that kind of injury."

Where had the pilot gone? Out in the middle of the woods, with what appeared to be a serious injury? Where had he—or she—disappeared to?

Priscilla pulled out her cell phone and took a picture of the cargo area. She wasn't sure why, exactly, and it felt a little morbid, but she had a feeling she would want to look back at this scene. Then she maneuvered so she could reach in, and took a picture of the keys. She reached for the pill bottle.

"Careful," Gerald said. "You don't want to contaminate the scene."

Priscilla stopped. She pulled her sleeve over her hand and lifted the pill bottle up. Gerald must be thinking this could turn out to be more than a simple plane crash.

"I'll put it back exactly where it was," Priscilla said as she took a picture of the pill bottle. It was a prescription for OxyContin, and there were two pills left inside. "If I don't do this before the police get here, I won't have a chance."

Neither of them said anything about the reason she might want to have pictures of the scene.

She kept her sleeve pulled over her hand as she took a picture of the pocketknife, and then she flipped through the pages of the small notebook. The first three pages were taken up by some kind of writing in blue ink, but the handwriting was so messy she couldn't make out what it said. She took a picture of the pages and set the notebook back down.

Gerald had moved back to the cockpit and was surveying the area while Priscilla took a few more photos of the back.

"Hey," Gerald said. "That's strange."

"What?" Priscilla turned so she could see what he was looking at. He had put a glove on and pushed something, she could tell, because the dashboard was lit up and the video screens were on. One showed a green and blue map of the area, and the other had a bunch of numbers and symbols she didn't understand. "What did you do?"

"The electrical system is working," Gerald said. He reached out and touched a button on what looked like a car radio. Immediately, it hummed with noise, chatter about runways and approaches, and something about Charlie Bravo.

"So why didn't he use it to call for help?" Priscilla asked.

"Maybe he did," Gerald said. "We'll need to check into that."

But he'd told her yesterday that there had been no call on the emergency frequency, and the tone in his voice now made it clear that he had doubts it had happened. Priscilla did too. She took a picture of the dashboard area, then climbed out and scrambled down the wing and back onto the ground. She took several pictures of the outside of the plane. There was a number on the back side and on the tail—she assumed it was a registration number.

She looked around at the ground under them. The plane had landed in a low spot, where the earth was moist, and she wondered if she could find any footprints to indicate which direction the pilot had gone. She walked around, peering down at the ground, and noticed something.

It wasn't footprints. What was that?

She bent down and studied the mark in the soil. It almost looked like...

"What are you looking at?"

She startled, not realizing that Gerald had come out of the plane. Now he stood beside her, squinting down at the ground.

"See this?" She pointed to a flat indentation in the soil. It was maybe a foot along each side, and judging by the impression it had left, it was heavy.

"What is that?"

"There's another one a few feet away," Priscilla said, pointing toward the impression she'd seen near an oak tree. They both walked over and studied it. The ground rose in those few feet, and the impression in the soil was shallower than the other print, but she was fairly certain the same object had been set down again. And a few feet beyond, she could see another imprint, very faint in the higher, drier soil. The box—or whatever it was—had been set down and then dragged.

"Did he carry something out of the plane?" Gerald asked.

"He had to have," Priscilla said. She looked around the last print, but the soil dried out, and the marks vanished. "Something he couldn't leave behind, even as he went for help."

"Or something he didn't want discovered."

Gerald had finally said what they were both thinking. This did not seem like a simple accident. This no longer looked like a pilot who had just gone for help. He hadn't used the radio to call for help or ask for clearance to land at any of the local runways as the plane went down, though he could have. He had clearly been injured in the crash, but hadn't called for an ambulance. He hadn't reported the downed plane but vanished, dragging something heavy along with him.

Whoever had been flying this plane, whatever had happened up there...it sure seemed like the pilot didn't want to be found.

"What do you think happened here?" Priscilla asked.

Gerald let out a long breath. "I wish I knew." He turned around in a full circle, taking in the whole area. "It seems like something went wrong with the plane, and he crash-landed here. Somehow, he survived, though he was injured, but instead of radioing for help, he took something heavy from the plane and vanished."

"That's what it seems like to me as well," Priscilla said. Neither one of them said anything for a moment. Off in the distance, she heard voices. The rescuers Gerald called must be getting close. "But where did he go?"

"I have no idea." Gerald shook his head. "And who is he?"

The voices were getting closer. In a moment, the rescuers would appear. Hopefully the police would be able to figure out what happened here. But Priscilla knew that as soon as they arrived, she would be ushered away, brushed aside so the professionals could search for answers to their questions. For just a moment longer, she savored the fact that this was their discovery. That no one else yet knew about this plane in the woods.

"I guess the most important question," Priscilla said, "is *why* did he vanish?"

CHAPTER SIX

As Priscilla had guessed, once the police and medical crews showed up at the crash site, she was shooed away. She got the impression Gerald would have been welcome to stay—the Coast Guard uniform made his presence acceptable—but Gerald graciously asked Priscilla to join him for lunch instead. They made the trek out to the road together, the sounds of shouting and police radios echoing behind them. Neither of them said much as they climbed back into their cars and drove to Tisbury.

Soon they were seated at a table by the window in the Nautilus Café. The restaurant overlooked the harbor and, sitting there, they had a wonderful view of the fishermen unloading their catch on the docks below. While Gerald scanned the menu, Priscilla watched some men tie up a seiner and unload the day's catch into barrels. The silvery fish tumbled and slipped over one another as they landed in the bins.

Gerald closed his menu and cleared his throat. Priscilla looked up at him.

"I wanted to say I'm sorry," he said. "For not believing you."

Priscilla felt something in her unhitch at his words. "Thank you." She hadn't realized how deeply his doubt had affected her until she felt tears start to well up. "I appreciate it."

"You were right. I should know by now you aren't one to imagine things that aren't there."

"It was kind of a difficult story to believe," Priscilla said. "A plane crashes in the woods and no one notices? It *does* seem farfetched."

"But it was true." Gerald pulled his napkin off the table and put it into his lap. "I should have taken what you were saying more seriously."

"Thank you." Yes, he should have, Priscilla had to agree. But that was neither here nor there at this point. "The question now is, how do we determine what happened to the pilot and why he vanished?"

"Who he was shouldn't actually be all that difficult to figure out, now that we have the registration number of the plane." Gerald adjusted the silverware so it lined up against the edge of the table. "It will take some time to search the FAA records, but that should be fairly straightforward."

"That's the number painted on the side of the plane?"

"Yes. The police are no doubt getting in touch with the FAA as we speak. It may take a day or two for them to pull those records, but maybe they'll be able to put a rush on it."

"What if the owner isn't the missing pilot?"

"Then hopefully the owner will know who was flying his plane. If not, the case gets more interesting, but I don't expect that."

"We should check the local hospitals, to see if anyone has shown up with injuries like you would get from a plane crash."

"I already checked with Hank Westin about that. They've determined that no one has appeared at any of the area hospitals with injuries that are consistent with a plane crash."

Priscilla thought of something else.

"You said it could possibly take up to a couple of days to get the name of the plane's owner. In the meantime, we could look into that pill bottle we found in the back." She pulled out her phone and opened up the picture she'd taken. She enlarged the photo so she could read the name on the label. "The pills were prescribed to a Dennis Reid. And the prescription was filled in Chatham, Massachusetts."

"That could be a possible link to the pilot." Gerald used both hands to smooth out the napkin in his lap. "But, Priscilla, I noticed you used the word *we*."

"Yes." She lifted her glass and took a sip of water to give herself a moment to think of how to respond. "Naturally I'm curious about what happened to the pilot. Given that I was the one to see the plane go down and everything."

"I get that. But the police are on the case now. We don't know anything about who this guy is or what he was up to. I hope you aren't thinking you would get involved in this investigation."

She took another sip of her water. The ice tinkled gently against the sides of the glass. She realized that her hand was shaking.

"I haven't given much thought to it," she said. It was mostly true. This was all so fresh she hadn't really had a chance to think about much of anything. "I'm just trying to think of ways to find the pilot."

"I know you are very good at this kind of thing," Gerald said. It was a compliment, she knew that, but somehow it didn't sound like it. "But please, for your own safety, I'm asking you to stay out of this one. Like I said, we don't know who this guy is or why he disappeared. We don't know if there was more than one person in that plane. Whoever it is, he's certainly hurt, and potentially dangerous. The police will have this one wrapped up shortly, so in the meantime, please don't put yourself in harm's way."

Just then, a waitress appeared and took their order. Priscilla appreciated the moment to figure out how to respond. Gerald asked for a burger, and Priscilla ordered the lobster knuckle sandwich. She loved the image of lobsters having knuckles.

Then, as calmly as she could, Priscilla said, "I promise I won't put myself in danger."

Gerald looked at her. He'd heard what she hadn't said just as clearly as what she'd said, and he seemed uncertain how to respond.

"Like you said before, the most important question isn't really even who the pilot is, but why he disappeared after the crash," Priscilla said.

The waitress put a ramekin of butter and a basket of rolls on the table, and Gerald reached for one.

"And that's something the police will certainly be looking into," he said.

Priscilla knew his motivations were good. He wanted her to be safe. He wanted to protect her from whatever dangerous secrets that plane contained. But couldn't he see that it was too late for that? She couldn't help it—she felt a personal responsibility for the safety of the pilot.

"You mentioned earlier that it seemed like there was something he wanted to make sure wasn't discovered after the crash."

Gerald ripped off the top of the roll and spread butter across it. "It's a theory." He cleared his throat and added, "And it's one I know the police will investigate."

There was a note of finality in his voice. As if he expected the conversation to be finished because he had declared it so.

Priscilla also reached for a roll, and she thought about everything she'd seen at that crash site. She thought about the way the pilot had vanished. About the things he'd left behind, and those he hadn't. About recent activities in the area.

"If he had something in the plane that he didn't want to be found, what do you think it could be?" Priscilla watched Gerald carefully as she asked the question.

"I would hate to speculate. I suppose it could have been anything."

Priscilla tried again. "It would have to be something light enough for him to carry, right? And small?"

"I suppose." Gerald set the roll down and gave her a strange look. "Why?"

"I was just thinking about that big theft at the hospital. The one that was in the newspaper."

Gerald didn't say anything for a moment. Priscilla watched as the barrels of fish below were carried into the fish market just outside the restaurant.

"The Coast Guard searches ships regularly, right?"

Gerald nodded. A large part of the Coast Guard's job was boarding boats and searching to make sure nothing illegal was being brought onto US soil.

"So what if you were trying to get something off the island without running that risk? Wouldn't a small plane like the one we found be a good way to go? Does anyone search planes regularly?"

The fishermen outside had finished unloading their cargo and were hosing down the empty bins.

"It's possible," Gerald said. But the way his head was nodding made Priscilla think it was more than possible she was right. "The Air and Marine Operations division of Customs and Border Patrol does inspect planes sometimes, but that's usually if they're crossing an international border. Moving from one part of Massachusetts to another, it's unlikely anyone would search a small private plane."

Priscilla took another roll and broke it in half. Small wisps of steam wafted up.

"Is there any way to know who's flying small planes?" she asked. "And where and when they're flying? Does anyone keep track of these kinds of things? Travis at the airpark said it's not a legal requirement to file your flight plan if you're flying a small plane."

Gerald waited a moment before answering. Was he trying to decide how much to tell her? "Pilots actually have a fair amount of freedom in the skies," he finally said. "If you're flying to a remote or private airstrip, chances are you could take off and land without anyone really knowing about it."

The fishermen outside were now piling the clean, wet bins back onto their boats.

"So you *do* think the pilot was planning to land on a private airstrip, then." Priscilla thought as much after her conversation at

Katama this morning, but it was interesting Gerald had never mentioned the possibility until now.

Gerald wiped his hands on his napkin. "Yes, most likely. If he hadn't contacted air traffic control about any of the public airstrips here, he must have been planning to land on a private runway of some kind."

Priscilla felt frustration rise up in her again.

"Yesterday you told me there couldn't have been a plane, because none of the airports were expecting a small plane to land. But now you're saying it was probably headed toward a private runway. You knew that was a possibility yesterday."

Gerald pressed his lips together. He let out a breath, and then said, "I'm sorry, Priscilla."

"It's because you didn't believe me." She tried to keep her voice level, and largely failed. "You thought I had seen a drone, not a plane, so you didn't take me seriously."

She bit down on her lip to keep tears from welling up.

"You're right." Gerald picked up his water and took a sip. "All I can do is say that you're right, and I'm sorry. I wish I had listened. If I had, I would have deduced exactly what you discovered, that the plane didn't have to be flying toward Katama or Martha's Vineyard Airport. There are, no doubt, many private runways. Or you can also land on an open field, or even the beach. There are plenty of places a small plane could have been aiming to land."

Gerald had known all this, but he hadn't said anything yesterday. Why? Was it that he didn't really trust her or think she was competent? He'd apologized, and she needed to let it go. She would...sometime. Right now, though, she had more questions.

"The beach?" Priscilla tried to imagine landing a plane on the rocky, uneven shoreline near her home.

"A long flat strip of sand is a fine landing place. The problem is trying to take back off. Sand is not always packed hard enough to allow you to get up the speed you need to get airborne."

Priscilla tried to absorb all this. "So what you're saying is that the plane could have been planning to land anywhere." Again, this was basically what Travis had suggested earlier, but the fact that Gerald also seemed to think it was possible made it more significant.

"Not anywhere. Only on long, flat surfaces with no obstacles around. But yes, there are plenty of those around."

"Is there any registry of landing strips? Any way to track all the places it could have been headed?" Priscilla asked.

"Not that I know of, unfortunately."

She thought about this for a moment. There had to be a way to figure that out. But her mind was already heading in another direction, to why the pilot might have disappeared.

"Okay. Let's say there were prescription pills on that plane when it went down. Pills stolen from the hospital, that he was planning to smuggle off the island. He had taken off from some private airstrip somewhere, but something went wrong before he got very far, and the plane started to go down. If the plane was loaded with stolen prescription pills, it would explain why the pilot didn't call for help or stick around to be found after the crash. And there's that prescription bottle we found in the plane."

"That's true," Gerald said, nodding. "Everything you're saying is true. And I will talk to the police about it. They've probably already thought of this themselves, but if not, I can make sure they do."

The waitress arrived with their meals and placed a plate in front of each of them.

"But if you're right, if this is somehow connected to the missing prescription drugs, that's even more reason for you to let the authorities handle it," Gerald said. He gave her a significant look.

Instead of answering, she picked up her sandwich and took a large bite.

"How's it going over here?" Tobin Worthington, the restaurant owner, appeared at the table. Tobin was a single man in his fifties. He was on the zoning board and very active in the community, an all-around great guy.

"It's wonderful," Priscilla said, happy to see him. She'd had lobster back in Kansas, but she'd never had lobster like this there. "This lobster tastes like it was just caught."

Tobin gestured toward the window. "Fresh from the sea this morning." He turned to Gerald. "And how's the burger?"

"Delicious, as always," Gerald said.

They talked with Tobin for a while, and the rest of the meal was subdued. She updated Gerald on plans for the Easter egg hunt and they chatted about his baby granddaughter, but when they finished, Gerald apologized and said he had to get back to work. He tossed down enough cash to cover both their meals, gave her hand a squeeze, and ran off, leaving Priscilla feeling…well, abandoned.

He had to get back to work, she knew. He had an important job, and he'd already been gone several hours. But it still felt abrupt. And on top of the way he'd treated her yesterday...She shook her head and pushed herself up.

Well, she didn't have to just sit here and stew. And she also didn't have to do every single thing he asked her to. Gerald had asked her to stay out of this investigation. To stay safe and let the police find the pilot. He'd also dismissed her when she came to him with her concerns and kept her in the dark for some reason.

She had no doubt that the police would be looking into the matter. But she was the one who had seen the plane. She was the one who believed when no one else did. She was already invested in this. She would let the police investigate, but that didn't mean she was just going to sit around.

As she made her way to the door, she smiled. She would be careful, like she'd promised. Careful, and competent.

CHAPTER SEVEN

The first thing Priscilla did when she got home was to take Jake for a long walk on the beach. So many emotions flowed through her—excitement, fear, frustration—and it calmed her to feel the salty sea breeze on her face and the soft sand giving way beneath her feet. Jake chased a seagull, which screeched as it flew away, and tugged at a piece of driftwood. Priscilla filled her lungs with the clean, crisp air and let it out slowly. It was no wonder doctors used to prescribe visits to the seashore for sick patients. The slow, rhythmic pounding of the waves against the sand and the briny, moist air always did wonders for her spirits.

Priscilla looked out to the spot where the sea met the sky. On a clear day, you could see Cape Cod, but today everything faded in a mist of gray. She turned around and looked up at the tip of the lighthouse, just visible over the craggy cliffs. A little thrill went through her, as it did whenever she looked at the lighthouse, the strong, solid beacon that had protected sailors for generations.

When Priscilla climbed back up the wooden steps to her house, she felt refreshed. After wiping Jake down with a towel, she stepped inside and hung up her coat. Then she set the kettle on and made a cup of tea before settling down at the table with her laptop and opening a search window.

She pulled out her phone, scrolled through the pictures, and found the shot she'd taken of the prescription bottle. She typed in "Dennis Reid" and clicked search. She found a singer by that name and a high school student in Akron, Ohio, and a few others overseas. But she also found a Dennis Reid who had placed second in a sailing competition at the Monomoy Yacht Club in Chatham, Massachusetts. The same place where the prescription had been filled. She narrowed her search, typing in "Dennis Reid Cape Cod."

This time, she found lots of interesting results. A photo of Dennis Reid wearing a hideous orange and black striped blazer in the Princeton alumni magazine. The photo showed an older man with white hair and a lined face. He wore a black hat with Class of '62 embroidered in orange, and he was surrounded by several other men in the same outfit. There was a list of donors to the Chatham Players Theater group. An editorial in the *Cape Cod Times*, arguing against wind farms off the coastline. As Priscilla read, she found herself developing a picture of Dennis. He was older, retired, wealthy. He was, she had to admit, exactly the kind of person who seemed likely to own a private plane. They were toys for the very wealthy, weren't they? Had Dennis flown his plane to Martha's Vineyard to smuggle prescription drugs off the island?

Priscilla was making assumptions based on stereotypes, she knew. But she knew that Dennis was tied up in this somehow. His name was on the bottle of OxyContin they'd found. That wasn't a direct connection to the opioids stolen from the hospital, but it did prove that he took the drug—or had taken it at one time. Had he gotten hooked on the painkiller and needed to find a way to get his hands on more?

Priscilla had heard news stories about the growing number of people addicted to painkillers, but she didn't know a lot about it. Were the drugs so difficult to obtain that this scenario might be plausible?

A quick search for "stolen opioids" turned up pages and pages of results—news stories about the growing numbers of people addicted, longer editorials about societal reasons the crisis was growing, reports on overdoses and how to handle them. Priscilla's heart broke as she read. There were many different kinds of painkillers that fell into the category of highly addictive opioids: oxycodone, the medicine she'd found, which was marketed under the brand name OxyContin. Hydrocodone, buprenorphine, methadone, and morphine, were among the others. They were sold under various brand names, but the chemical substances themselves all worked by disassociating a user from the pain they felt. She read that most people abusing the drugs had been prescribed the pills by their doctor for a legitimate reason, following an operation or major injury of some kind, and had been unable or unwilling to wean themselves off. She found that doctors often prescribed the drugs far longer than necessary, and that many people held the drug makers accountable, blaming their slick marketing campaigns, for the rise in prescriptions.

The people addicted to the drugs crossed all age, racial, and social class lines too, and—most heartbreaking—she learned that the number of deaths by overdose was on a steady climb. Once a person was addicted, they often turned to the black market to get their pills if their doctors wouldn't continue to prescribe them.

Priscilla hated to think about how many families were being destroyed by the epidemic. *Please, Lord, help them*, she prayed. *Give them a way out of their addictions and help them to find relief in You.*

Priscilla sat still for a moment. She didn't know how to help with that huge societal problem. She didn't know how to make it better. All she knew was that she wanted to talk to this Dennis Reid. If he was involved with smuggling stolen prescription pills off the island, she wanted to stop him.

An online search only took a moment, and she easily found the most recent address listed for Dennis Reid, in Chatham, Massachusetts.

She picked up her phone. Joan answered on the second ring.

"How'd you like to go to Cape Cod with me tomorrow?" Priscilla asked.

"You know I would."

Priscilla loved that Joan didn't even ask why. She was in, no matter what.

"Let's take the ten a.m. ferry," Priscilla said.

"I'll pick you up at nine thirty."

Priscilla said goodbye and hung up. She had no idea what they'd find, but hopefully it would bring them one step closer to finding answers.

CHAPTER EIGHT

On Wednesday morning, Priscilla read the newspaper as she sipped her coffee. The small plane crash was now front-page news. There was a photo of the downed plane, and the headline read "Small Plane Crashes in West Tisbury; Pilot Missing." She read the article carefully, but it revealed nothing she didn't already know. The article claimed that the plane had been discovered by law enforcement, she noted. Apparently, Gerald hadn't given credit where credit was due. Oh, well. All she was interested in was answers, and so far, it seemed they hadn't found anything useful—or at least anything they were telling the press.

Priscilla gave Gerald a call as she walked Jake along the beach.

"I'm afraid I haven't gotten any updates," he told her. "I did talk to Hank Westin yesterday, and he thought the idea of the plane being used to smuggle prescription drugs off the island was worth pursuing."

Priscilla smiled wryly, glad he couldn't see her. The police chief liked her idea then. And would no doubt claim credit for it if it panned out.

"And I believe they've located the man whose name was on the prescription bottle," Gerald continued. "They're going to talk to him this afternoon."

Priscilla thought it wise not to mention that she would be seeing Dennis Reid that morning. She didn't have to guess what Gerald's reaction would be to that bit of news.

"Oh, I had a question about the Easter egg hunt," she said brightly, changing the subject. "I was hoping to bring in someone to give a short Easter message to the children. Faith Fellowship could sponsor it, and we could hold it in a tent off the Coast Guard grounds. I really think it would be a good opportunity to make sure the children hear about the real meaning of Easter."

"I..." It seemed to take Gerald a moment to catch up with the shift in conversation.

"I was going to ask Pastor Lannister. Would that be all right? Chloe was worried because the egg hunt will be on government property, but, like I said, we could do it a ways off and make it totally voluntary and a separate event."

"I..." Gerald once again seemed to be having a difficult time forming words. "I guess that would be all right," he finally said.

"Wonderful. Thank you. I'll talk with Pastor." She decided to end the call before he could argue any more. "I'd better go. Joan will be here shortly to pick me up." Priscilla hit End Call and tucked the phone into her pocket.

She knew she probably should have told Gerald that she was going to see Dennis Reid. She knew he meant well and simply worried about her. If she was honest, she *had* ended up in some tricky situations in the past when she'd delved into mysteries.

But this wasn't like those other situations. She was just going to talk to Dennis. This was a genteel older man who golfed and sailed. He was more likely to bore her to death with his stories from the good old days at Princeton than threaten her.

Then again, maybe she should just let the police investigate this. In theory, she knew that was the rational thing to do. But something inside her wouldn't let it go. She'd known the truth about the plane, even when no one else had believed her, even Gerald. She'd seen the possibility of the link to the prescription drug theft before he had. And something told her not to leave this, as Gerald had urged, to the pros.

"Come on, Jake." She called to the dog, and he looked up from where he was digging in the sand. She hadn't been lying when she'd told Gerald she had to go. She really did need to get ready. "Time to go."

Jake bounded over, and together they climbed the wooden stairs up the cliff. A few minutes later, Joan picked her up, and not long after that, they had parked in the car deck of the ferry and were settled in seats at a table by the window, headed toward Woods Hole. Priscilla always enjoyed the ride across the Nantucket Sound, especially once the land disappeared behind her and all she could see was open water. The sky was gray, and the clouds hung low in the sky. She had filled Joan in on their task on the drive to the ferry, and Joan was excited about talking to Dennis Reid.

"I've been wondering something," Joan said.

"What's that?"

Joan had bought them each a cup of coffee from the snack bar on the first level, and now she wrapped her hands around the warm cup. She blew on her coffee, and small wisps of steam rose off the surface. "Why is the Coast Guard using drones? What are they doing with them?"

"I don't know," Priscilla said. "I've been trying to figure that out as well."

"There are companies who are talking about employing drones to make deliveries," Joan said, laughing.

"I've heard that. People could buy something online and it would be delivered to their house by a drone in just a few hours. No more waiting two whole days for something to arrive by truck. It sounds pretty great to me."

"It's a little too 'Jetsons' for me." Joan took a sip of the coffee and made a face.

"Not good?"

"Basically used motor oil."

"But it still has caffeine."

"Amen to that." Joan took another sip and set the cup down. "So the Coast Guard is probably not going to be using drones to make deliveries. But what, then? I've read about the military using drones to drop bombs. It's far safer for the military personnel to send a flying robot into battle than to use a person."

"I've heard about that too," Priscilla said. "And that seems to me like a really good use of the technology. If we have to go into battle, let's protect the troops first and foremost. But I really don't think that's what's going on here."

"I don't think it is either," Joan said. "The Coast Guard may technically be a branch of the military, but they aren't likely to be dropping bombs. They're more into protecting our shores. It seems more likely to me that they're using drones to predict weather patterns and look for people lost at sea."

"That's my thinking as well. It makes the most sense, given that Gerald was reviewing the footage the drone took when he saw the broken trees that led us to the plane." She took a sip of her coffee and nearly choked on the strong, bitter brew. "You weren't kidding about this stuff."

"It's pretty terrible, right? But what are you going to do?" She took another sip. "All these drones and surveillance makes me nervous, though. Not everybody uses them for good. I mean, I can see how they would really save time and money and manpower, when used by the good guys. Like you said, maybe they send them out to look for boats that need help, so they have a more precise location before they send out rescue crews. Or maybe when there's a hurricane they can send it right into the storm to track it and predict its course. But in the wrong hands—and it seems anyone can get one these days—it's just a scary thought that someone can spy on other people so easily."

Priscilla shook her head. "The whole thing is kind of creepy, isn't it? The idea of cameras flying around, recording everything in their path?"

"It's a violation of privacy, if you ask me."

"It sure is. The thought that anybody can fly a drone over my house and see what I'm doing?" Priscilla took another sip of the coffee. "I don't like that."

Joan leaned back on the bench. "I hope it doesn't hurt the Coast Guard's image on Martha's Vineyard for people to hear they use drones in their operations. You know how paranoid some people are."

"Tell me about it," Priscilla said. "All we need is someone like Eldora Preston to tell people the Coast Guard is spying on her. It would take a whole lot more than a few Easter eggs to smooth things over."

Joan nodded and took another sip. "In any case, I guess there was an upside to it all, in that it led you to the plane."

"True." Priscilla also settled against the back of the booth. She looked around. The main cabin was nearly empty on this cold Wednesday morning. A few men in business suits sat reading newspapers at tables by the bank of windows on the far side, and another group of people with large suitcases was gathered on the seats in the middle. They were all speaking in some language Priscilla didn't understand. Dutch, maybe? In any case, she was fairly certain they were on their way back from a visit to the island. She studied the group for a moment, and then she looked down at their suitcases.

"What is it?" Joan asked.

"I was just noticing the suitcases," Priscilla said.

"What about them?" Joan glanced over to see what she was looking at.

"No one searches them as you get on. They're not x-rayed or anything."

"No, it's not that formal around here. It's not like the airport." She took another sip of her coffee. "Why?"

Priscilla didn't answer for a moment. The boat pitched gently on the waves. Over the hum of the engine, she could hear snatches of excited conversation in whatever language it was. "I was just wondering why you would need to sneak prescription drugs on and off the island in an airplane. If that was your goal, why not simply pack them in a suitcase and bring them on the ferry? It's not like anyone ever checks to see what's inside the suitcases that come on board."

"It's not a bad point," Joan said. "Though I suppose they *could* check through your bag, and using a private plane eliminates that possibility. Plus, flying is quicker."

"I guess so." Priscilla looked out the windows on the far side and realized they were approaching the terminal in Woods Hole. She could see houses perched on the hills above the harbor.

"Bottoms up." Joan finished her coffee and held out her hand for Priscilla's cup.

"Thanks," Priscilla said. She put the lid back on and handed Joan the cup, still mostly full, and Joan stood and walked over to toss them in the garbage can by the door.

A few minutes later they were in Joan's car, pulling away from the ferry terminal parking lot and threading through the narrow streets of Woods Hole. Tall trees arched over the roadway and shingle-style cottages surrounded by small yards lined the road.

As they drove, Joan chatted about Sam and Alice, and then suggested that they canvass some of the more well-known businesses in Chatham to get prizes for the Easter egg hunt while they were in the area.

"Would anyone really come all this way to use a gift certificate they found in a plastic egg?" Priscilla asked. They were now cruising down the Mid-Cape Highway toward Chatham, which sat on Cape Cod's elbow.

"You've clearly never been to the Chatham Bars Inn," Joan said. "You'll see."

Priscilla was dubious, but agreed that since they'd come all this way, it couldn't hurt to stop in at the legendary hotel to ask. She sent a quick text to Chloe: *What do you think of a gift certificate from the Chatham Bars Inn?* A moment later, Chloe responded with a thumbs-up emoji, followed by a picture of confetti and, inexplicably, an electric guitar.

"A guitar?" Priscilla tried to make sense of it.

"Let me see," Joan said. Priscilla held it out so she could see the screen. "I think she's saying 'rock on.'"

"Rock on?"

"Trudy sends me that one sometimes."

"Ah."

They exited the highway and Joan followed the directions on her GPS to a side street off the main road. She followed it to the end and turned into a driveway flanked by brick columns and an open gate.

"What is this place?"

For a moment, Priscilla thought the two-story brick building must be Dennis Reid's home, but then she saw a brass sign planted in the grass along the curving driveway. Soundview Commons.

"What in the world?" Joan said.

But Priscilla had figured out what this place was. As soon as she realized it, it was obvious. Even the graceful mansard roofline and the black shutters and ivy climbing up the brick couldn't disguise it.

"It's a nursing home," Priscilla said. Her father had spent the last few years of his life in a place not unlike this, though judging by the outside, this was a whole different level of luxury. Priscilla's mother had been unable to give him the care he needed, and even though Priscilla tried to help as much as she could, in the end, the facility had been the best situation for him. But she still got a lump in her throat whenever she thought about that place, and she was grateful she'd been able to keep her mother at home and comfortable in her last days.

"Could a man in a nursing home have flown a plane?" Joan asked.

Priscilla shrugged. "I suppose it depends." Joan parked in the lot, which was surrounded by boxwood and rhododendron bushes, bright green with fresh new leaves. Priscilla opened her door. "Let's go find out."

They made their way up the bluestone path toward the imposing brick building. The glass doors swung open, and a woman at the desk inside greeted them.

"Hello. Welcome to Soundview Commons. How can I help you?"

She was young and pretty, her hair pulled back into a tight ponytail, and she wore black slacks and a cashmere sweater. Everyone at Dad's nursing home had just worn scrubs.

Priscilla noticed there were signs posted on the walls directing people to the Leonard Wing, the Adler Wing, and the Wallace

Wing. She guessed the different wings offered different levels of care, but she had no way to be sure. The floors were polished hardwood, and the walls were painted a soft gray and hung with black-and-white photographs of the ocean. But despite the tasteful decorations, the place still had that familiar smell common to all nursing homes.

"We're looking for someone I believe lives here," Priscilla said.

"Dennis Reid," Joan offered.

"Oh." The woman's smile faded a little. "Are you a relative?"

"No," Priscilla said. "We just want to visit with him." She couldn't exactly come out and say why they were really there.

"Is he around?" Joan asked.

"I'm afraid not," the woman said. "He doesn't live here anymore."

"He doesn't?" Had they come all this way for nothing?

"I'm afraid not," the receptionist said.

She looked like she wanted to say more, but didn't.

"Did he move to another facility?" Joan asked gently.

The woman hesitated. There was something in her eyes, some look Priscilla couldn't read.

"I'm not allowed to give out information about patients except to close relatives," she said.

Priscilla noticed a large diamond engagement ring on her finger, flashing in the overhead lights. Not even fluorescent lights—they were some kind of pleasant yellowish light from elaborate fixtures in the ceiling.

"When did he leave?" Priscilla asked. "I'm sorry, it's just that we've come quite a long way to speak with him, and we would love to be able to find him wherever he is now."

The woman pressed her lips together and then she let out a long breath.

"I'm afraid you won't be able to do that," she said.

"Because you don't know where he went?" Joan asked.

She shook her head.

She must mean—

"I'm sorry, but I can't tell you anything about where he went or when he left, but I will tell you that in his last few months here, he was living in the Adler Wing."

Priscilla had no idea what to make of that, but she could see that this was all they were going to get from her.

"Thank you so much for your help," she said.

The woman waved her hand. "Please, feel free to walk around the grounds and stretch your legs, especially if you've come a long way. It's a lovely place, and you're welcome to enjoy it."

"Thank you."

They walked back outside, and Joan looked at Priscilla. "So now what?"

"I have an idea," Priscilla said. "Let's take her suggestion and take a little walk."

"I'm all for stretching our legs for a bit. Besides, this place looks amazing." Joan was an avid gardener and was already bending over to examine a hydrangea plant that was just starting to send out tender green buds.

"Let's see what else there is." They headed down a bluestone path, and Priscilla thought through what the woman had said—and about what she had not said. They followed the path around to the back of the building, where a large lawn unfurled toward water, cut through with paths, and a garden with waist-high walls waited at the far end.

"Ooh. How beautiful." Joan was already walking toward the garden.

"Wow." As Priscilla got close, she saw the garden had climbing roses clinging to the walls. The stems were bare and brown, but in a few months, she imagined that they would be brilliantly hued and smell divine.

At the far end of the garden, a bench was built into the wall that looked out over the ocean.

"Nice place," Joan said, taking it all in.

"It really is," Priscilla said.

They walked along the brick paths across the garden toward the bench, and Priscilla stopped to take a look at a marble sundial in the center. It was lovely, with roman numerals carved into the stone. Around the edges, the words to a poem were etched: *Grow old along with me! The best is yet to be.*

"It's kind of morbid, isn't it?" Joan said. "Considering the setting?"

"I think it's lovely," Priscilla said. She recognized the line from one of Robert Browning's poems. It had been printed in the card Gary gave her for their tenth wedding anniversary. She had always thought she and Gary would grow old together. She'd never imagined he would leave her so soon, and she would be left facing the rest of her life without him.

Joan started walking toward the bench, and Priscilla waited a few more moments, picturing Gary, the way he'd looked on their wedding day, so young and eager. He was so different from Gerald. Not better or worse—just different. She'd been frustrated with her husband many times too, she reminded herself. Then she pressed her lips together, took a deep breath, and followed Joan to the bench. The sound of the waves far below was soothing, and the air smelled salty and clean.

"So what do you make of what she said?" Joan asked.

Priscilla knew she meant the receptionist inside, but instead of answering, she stood up.

"I want to check something," she said. She walked to another entrance to the building and pulled the door open.

Joan followed. "Where are we going?" she asked once they were inside.

"To find the Adler Wing," Priscilla said. They walked down what looked to be a central hallway, passing a set of large glass double doors with the words "Leonard Wing" in ornate letters on the transom. They turned a corner and found an identical set of doors, this time with the words "Adler Wing" written above. There was a plaque to the left of the doors, mounted on the wall.

"What does it say?" Joan asked.

Priscilla read in a hushed voice. "'This wing has been named in honor of Dr. Sonya Adler, founder of Soundview Hospice, which has done so much for so many families in Cape Cod and farther afield.' The Adler Wing is a hospice."

"Oh dear." Joan sighed. "So it appears that Dennis didn't move to another facility."

"Not likely. I think when the receptionist said he was gone, she meant he passed away."

"Well, I guess that answers that." Joan shook her head. "How awful. He's not our pilot after all."

Priscilla laughed. "It's bad for other reasons as well."

"Well, yes. Obviously. I'm sure his family misses him."

"But if he's not the pilot, how did his pill bottle end up in that plane?" Priscilla asked.

"Oh, that one's easy. Most likely someone took it from his hospice room."

"You think someone stole painkillers from a dying man?"

"It could have been after he died. It's hard to say. But it's becoming more and more common. Relatives swiping painkillers from patients who need them, or grabbing them after they've passed."

"That's horrible."

"Addiction is a terrible thing. It makes people do all kinds of things they wouldn't normally do."

Priscilla thought about that for a moment. It was a sad state of affairs, no matter how she looked at it. But she couldn't dwell on that. For now, she needed to focus on what was in front of her.

"So I suppose the best thing to do would be to figure out who might have gone into Dennis's room either before or shortly after his death."

"That's what I'm thinking," Joan said. "I guess that means we're looking at his family and friends. And also the staff of the nursing home."

Priscilla hated to think that the staff could have had something to do with this. But then she thought about the pills that had gone missing from the hospital back on Martha's Vineyard, and she realized Joan was right.

"Okay then." Priscilla started walking toward the main doors where they'd come in earlier.

"Are you going to ask if anyone on staff stole his medication after he died?" Joan's heels clicked on the hardwood floor as she followed Priscilla.

"I'll probably phrase it a bit differently than that." They walked around the corner and saw the front desk again. The young woman smiled as they approached.

"You're back."

"I have a quick question," Priscilla said. "We figured out why Dennis Reid is no longer here. We're so sorry about his passing."

The woman bit her lip and nodded.

"I just wondered what your policy is for disposal of medications when someone passes away."

The receptionist cocked her head and thought for a moment. "I'm not sure. My guess would be it was disposed of by the nursing staff." She paused. "I guess I can ask, but…honestly, I'd be surprised if that's information we give to just anyone who asks."

"If you wouldn't mind checking with someone and letting me know?" Priscilla smiled at her.

"I'll ask the nurses and the custodial staff." She took down Priscilla's information and promised to give her a call if she uncovered anything, but judging by the tone of her voice, she didn't seem to think it was likely.

"I'm sure a fancy place like this would have a policy about medication," Joan said as they walked back toward the car. "I know we have a strict procedure we have to follow when someone dies."

"It might not be as well-monitored in a place like this," Priscilla said. "When my mom passed away, the nursing staff told me that they accounted for the leftover medication and disposed of it. It didn't even occur to me to question what they said."

Joan didn't say anything for a moment.

"What?"

"I was just wondering if it was a cover-up. I mean, how easy would it be for a nurse to say they disposed of the medication but really they take it home with them? I wonder if someone who works here took his bottle of opioids."

"It's possible," Priscilla said. They were on the bluestone path close to the parking lot again. Priscilla could still hear the waves crashing far below. Perhaps she should have asked for a list of employees. But surely if they hadn't even been willing to tell her that Dennis had passed away, they weren't going to be free with that information either. "I'll do some digging and see what I can find."

"All right." Joan reached for the door handle. "That's a good plan. Now. I'm starving. Shall we get some lunch?"

"That sounds good." Priscilla buckled herself in and stared out the window as they wound through the quaint streets of the historic town. Boutiques, bookstores, restaurants, antique stores, and churches were all huddled together in clapboard and shingled buildings. A few minutes later, Joan pulled into a parking spot in front of a white wooden building.

"The Impudent Oyster?" Priscilla read the sign above the door.

"Best seafood in town. You'll love it."

Priscilla followed her into the restaurant, which had a lot of dark wood and big windows. A few minutes later, they'd ordered fried cod and clams and were enjoying hot tea.

"This place is great. How do you know this area?" Priscilla asked.

"Allan grew up here. His parents passed many years ago, but we used to come over all the time to see them." She wrapped her hands around her tea. "There are still a couple of cousins in the area, though I haven't seen them in years."

Priscilla hadn't known that. She'd never even met Joan's husband, who had passed away years before she'd moved to Martha's Vineyard. She had missed so much of her cousins' lives.

After lunch, they headed over to the Chatham Bars Inn, and as soon as they approached, Priscilla could see this was a different kind of place than she was used to. The hotel was set on a hill, and the circular driveway was surrounded by greenery and foliage. A valet approached the car as they pulled in. Priscilla's mouth fell open.

"Is there no self-park?" she asked.

"I don't think so." Joan smiled. "It's okay. We'll just see how the other half lives for a little while."

Priscilla thought it was all a bit unnecessary, but Joan gave her keys to the valet, he gave her a tag that she tucked into her purse, and they walked inside. As attendants in uniforms swung the big doors open, she could see dark wood floors, white walls, and big windows overlooking an expansive view of the water. Tasteful, understated leather chairs and couches were set in clusters around the high-ceilinged space. A few people were seated around the lobby, chatting, and Priscilla felt out of place immediately. These people all wore sleek, tailored clothing and just the right amount of makeup. She wondered if they could tell she didn't belong.

Joan strode up to the front desk and asked to speak to the manager. While she explained that she was soliciting donations for a community Easter egg hunt sponsored by the local Coast Guard station, Priscilla wandered over toward the windows along the far wall and looked out. The waves rolled in, one after the other, crashing gently against the shore.

There were answers out there, Priscilla knew. Someone knew how Dennis Reid's pill bottle had ended up in that small plane. Someone knew who the pilot was, where he'd gone, and if he was connected to the theft from the hospital. The answers were out there somewhere. She just had to keep looking.

"All set?" Joan appeared at her side, a wide smile on her face.

Priscilla turned to her cousin. "Were you successful?"

"They gave us a fifty-dollar gift certificate," Joan said. Her pride was evident. "To be redeemed at the restaurant, spa, hotel room, or whatever."

"My guess is that won't go all that far in a place like this," Priscilla said.

"No, you're right. It won't. But it's a nice prize nonetheless, isn't it?"

Priscilla nodded. She very much doubted she'd come all this way to sit by the beach and eat seafood when there were plenty of great places to do just that back home on Martha's Vineyard. But still, she knew Joan was proud of her achievement, and she felt sure Chloe would be pleased as well.

They walked back to the front, and Joan handed the valet the tag, along with a couple of bills, and a few minutes later they were heading toward Woods Hole.

They chatted the whole way, but Priscilla's mind was elsewhere, puzzling through the possibilities.

CHAPTER NINE

After they got off the ferry in Tisbury, Priscilla and Joan made one more stop before they headed home. They parked outside the Tisbury Police Station and marched inside. They crossed the small lobby quickly, and Gabrielle Grimes smiled as they walked toward the front counter.

"Hello there, Priscilla, Joan." Gabrielle's brown hair was pulled back into a french braid, and she wore thick-framed glasses.

"Hi, Gabrielle. We'd love to talk to someone about a clue we've uncovered about the plane that crashed over in West Tisbury," Priscilla said.

"Hmm." Gabrielle looked back over her shoulder, through the window that showed the back of the station. Usually there were people walking around chatting or hunched over desks, but right now Priscilla couldn't see anyone. That was odd. "I'm afraid they're in an all-hands-on-deck meeting at the moment. But I could have someone call you when they're free."

"An all-hands-on-deck meeting?" Joan cocked an eyebrow.

It sounded promising. They must have had some kind of breakthrough in the case. Had they found the pilot?

"Yes, about that big theft at the hospital. The chief is very motivated to get that one figured out quickly." Gabrielle glanced over her shoulder again, and then back at Priscilla and Joan. "The CEO of the hospital is a big booster of the police force," she said, her voice lowered. "And he's made it very clear he wants that solved, stat."

Priscilla tried to keep her face neutral. She knew the theft of the medication was important. The drugs were worth a lot of money, and there was no doubt lives were at stake, given the soaring rates of addiction. But she couldn't understand how that was an all-hands-on-deck scenario when there was a man missing—a man who had mysteriously vanished under suspicious circumstances. Shouldn't *that* be their focus now?

Then again, maybe they were focusing on that after all. Maybe the meeting was about the possible connection between the missing pilot and the missing drugs. She felt somewhat better at that thought.

"Do you happen to know if they've found a way to connect the missing pilot to the hospital theft?" Priscilla asked.

"I really don't know," Gabrielle said. Priscilla thought she was telling the truth, considering how open she'd been just a moment ago.

"Are you sure no one could spare a moment to speak with us?" Priscilla asked.

"I'm very sorry." Gabrielle's dangly feather earrings swung as she shook her head. "They're not to be disturbed. But I will pass your message along," she promised.

Priscilla looked at Joan, who shrugged.

"Okay," Priscilla said. "Could you please ask someone to call me?"

"Will do." Gabrielle took down her phone number, though Priscilla knew they had it on file, and Priscilla and Joan walked out.

"Well, that was disappointing," Joan said.

"I guess the missing drugs are a big deal..." Priscilla let her voice trail off.

"I'm guessing you've never met Bret Lauf."

"Who?"

"He's the CEO of the hospital. He's... Well, he's a man who's used to getting his own way." A gust of wind blew Joan's hair up, and she smoothed it down. "He's very powerful, and I can totally imagine that he's decided to make it challenging for the police force to focus on anything but that."

Priscilla sighed.

"But with any luck, they've made a real connection between the plane and the missing prescription pills," Joan said. "And they'll find a way to direct all of Bret's... enthusiasm... toward the missing pilot."

"Let's hope so."

"Would a stop at the Boardwalk make you feel better?" Joan asked.

Just the thought of homemade ice cream made Priscilla feel a tiny bit better already, even on this frigid day. "You might be able to talk me into it."

A few minutes later they were enjoying their treats at a small marble-topped table inside the little dining room at the ice cream parlor. In summer, patrons would spread out on picnic tables all around the lush lawn, but today they had the little inside room all to themselves.

By the time Joan dropped her off at home, Priscilla had to admit she was feeling better. It was midafternoon already, and she really should take Jake for another walk. She was getting low on groceries; she should make a list and go to the store. She should work on that baby blanket. She had a meeting at church next month about possibly continuing the congregation's homeless shelter through the summer that she should do some prep for.

Instead, Priscilla grabbed her computer and settled in on the couch. She pulled her phone out of her pocket and was about to set it on the coffee table when she saw that she had four texts from Chloe:

> *We're gonna have Peep wars!*
> *Do you think we could get some real bunnies for the kids to pet?!*
> *I booked food trucks! Ramen and dosas and buns and lobstah rolls!*
> *How's it coming with gift certificates?*

Each of the texts was accompanied by several emojis. Priscilla hadn't even known there were so many kinds of images to choose from. She wasn't sure what dosas were, and wasn't at all sure she'd want to eat "lobstah" from a truck. And she didn't even want to know what Peep wars were. She was familiar with the colored marshmallow treats that were inexplicably popular this time of year. They were revolting, to her mind, but that didn't mean they deserved to be sent to war. She shook her head. She'd worry about that one later. She responded to the texts:

I'm sure we could find some rabbits. Maybe contact the Nature Center in Edgartown? I believe they have programs for school-age children and have some rabbits for such purposes. I've gotten several gift certificates for local businesses and the Chatham Bars Inn came through. Gerald said it was all right to ask our pastor to give a children's message.

It took forever to type the message out on her tiny phone keyboard. No wonder so many people used abbreviations and made-up words when texting. But Priscilla couldn't bring herself to do so. There were reasons for the rules governing written communication. Priscilla sent the text and set the phone down on the coffee table, then pulled a wool blanket over her lap. Jake sat down at her feet.

She typed "Bret Lauf" into a search window and hit return. A short bio came up on the Martha's Vineyard Hospital page, along with a photo. He appeared to be in his mid-to-late forties, with receding blond hair and a wide forehead. The information below his picture said he was a graduate of Harvard and the University of Pennsylvania's Wharton Business School, and he had worked at a number of hospital systems around the country before moving to Martha's Vineyard to run the hospital and "live in the best place on Earth."

Priscilla had to agree with that last part. But that didn't make her like him. She thought about what Joan had said, that he was used to getting his way. Well, fine. If she couldn't talk to the police because they were focusing on his priorities, Priscilla would continue to do her own research.

She'd spent so much time researching Dennis Reid online. How could she not have known he was dead? Why hadn't an obituary, at the very least, come up? Priscilla opened a new browser window and typed in the words "Dennis Reid Obituary." This time, the search pulled up the obituary right away.

Dennis Reid passed away surrounded by family in Chatham, Massachusetts, on January 21, after a long and valiant fight against cancer. Born in Ithaca, New York, in 1940, Dennis attended Princeton University and then Harvard Law School before starting his own law practice, which he ran for more than forty years. While in law school, he met and fell in love with Susan Kolwicki. They were happily married until her passing in 2008. An avid golfer, Dennis also loved sailing and collecting antique cars. Dennis is survived by his son Malcolm Reid (Ginny), his daughter Marie Coombs (Paul), and five grandchildren, Jennifer Reid Isaacs, Carolyn Reid, Ryan Reid, Clara Coombs, and Luke Coombs. He was preceded in death by his son Louis. In lieu of flowers, donations can be made to the American Cancer Society.

There was a good chance the people listed as his survivors would have been there to visit him in his last days. She decided that was as good a place to start as any.

She first typed in the name Malcolm Reid. Dennis's son. She quickly discovered that he was a professor at a small liberal arts college in Connecticut. He taught applied mathematics. Whatever that was. She poked around on the college's website, reading up on his classes, his research, and what students said about him. Then she found his LinkedIn page and some articles he'd published in journals, which were incomprehensible to her. But nothing about a plane. Nothing to indicate he had any interest in flying. Or in selling prescription drugs, though she couldn't imagine what kind of evidence she'd find about that on LinkedIn anyway.

She decided to move on to Ginny Reid, Malcolm's wife. From what Priscilla could find about her online, she worked at a greenhouse growing organic produce and enjoyed boatbuilding in her spare time. Again, there was nothing to indicate any interest in flying private planes, or anything else. Did that mean she wasn't involved? Priscilla had no way to tell. She could have taken the pills from Dennis Reid's room.

With a growing sense of hopelessness, Priscilla sifted through the online footprints of Dennis's daughter Marie and her husband, but all she discovered was that they lived in Arizona and had taken a trip to Paris for their twenty-fifth wedding anniversary the past year. She was an elementary school teacher, and he was a lawyer. Nothing useful.

Priscilla moved on to the grandchildren, one by one. Jennifer Reid Isaacs worked in marketing. Carolyn Reid was an architect. Ryan Reid worked in IT. Clara Coombs was married and had two small children. She posted a lot of pictures of her kitchen and mugs of coffee to social media. Luke Coombs worked for a bank and liked to run marathons, and...

Wait a minute. What was this?

Priscilla clicked on a picture of Luke Coombs next to another man in a dark shirt. They were standing in front of a small plane. Priscilla enlarged the picture and studied the plane. This plane was white and red, so it wasn't the same one that had crashed on Martha's Vineyard. But...She looked at Luke's face, and the face of the man next to him. The caption next to the picture read *Me with my flight instructor Dave...just a week to go before the big test!*

Luke had been learning how to fly a small plane. And this picture, she could see, had been posted last summer. Presumably Luke had already taken the test then—the test to get his pilot's license, Priscilla assumed. And if he'd passed the test, then that meant...

Well, it meant she had to do some looking into Luke Coombs, that was for sure.

An hour later, she'd gathered as much information as she could about Luke. He was forty-two, married to a redhead named Heather, and had three children. He lived outside Manhattan in a tiny suburb and worked at a big corporate bank in mergers and acquisitions. He posted pictures of exotic vacations—India, Morocco, and Thailand, just in the past year—to his Facebook page, and also talked a fair bit about his marathon training. And, she discovered, he'd passed his pilot's training and had bought himself a Cirrus SR20 with his annual bonus. Of course, he'd also posted a picture of the plane, which was silver with an orange stripe. So, his wasn't the plane that had crashed, then. But he was a licensed pilot. Could Luke have been the pilot who'd vanished after the crash?

There was one way to find out. Priscilla easily found the main phone number for the bank where Luke worked, and it only took her a few minutes of patiently wading through the company's internal directory to get to a chirpy young woman: "Luke Coombs's office."

"Hello. Is Mr. Coombs there?"

"May I ask who's calling?"

"My name is Priscilla Grant." She debated about what more to say. "I'm calling from Martha's Vineyard about a plane."

There. She hoped that would be intriguing enough to get him to pick up.

"Let me see if he's in."

She recognized the standard assistant response. Whether or not Luke was actually in, the assistant would now check and see if he wanted to talk to her.

A moment later, she was back on the line.

"I'm afraid Mr. Coombs isn't available at the moment. Can I take a message?"

"Sure." Priscilla tried to hold in a sigh. "Could you ask him to give me a call when he's free?" She gave her number and hung up. She had located his home phone number as well, but given the assistant's response, she was fairly certain he was at the office and simply hadn't answered because he didn't recognize her name. She would wait and see if he called back before she tried calling him again.

She set her laptop to the side and closed her eyes. Luke Coombs was a solid lead, but there had to be more. She thought back over her search through the plane. The pill bottle had led her to Luke Coombs. But there had to be more clues in that plane. There had to be some clue she was overlooking. What was she missing?

Priscilla scrolled back through the pictures she'd taken inside the plane. There was the pocketknife. She studied it. Was there something special about it? She couldn't see anything that made it stand out, though she was hardly an expert. Surely the police would test it for fingerprints. Well . . . *hopefully* they would, anyway. Eventually. She scrolled to the next picture and studied the key ring. There were eight keys on it, but they all looked pretty standard. There were what seemed like home or office keys, and a car key, with a rubber cap. She enlarged the photo. The rubber had the Toyota symbol stamped into it. It felt like that should be helpful, but she couldn't for the life of her figure out how. How many millions of people drove Toyotas these days?

She scrolled to the next picture, which was a shot of the first page of the notebook that had been in the back of the plane. It was covered in blue ink, but the handwriting was so scrawled and cramped that she couldn't make anything out. This was in English, wasn't it? She enlarged the photo and realized she could make out a few words here and there. *The. That. His. Past.* She zoomed out, and then in again. Was that . . . *tablet*?

Tablet. Like medication? Her heartbeat sped up. This might very well be related to the prescription drugs, she realized. Could this be the clue they needed that linked the plane to the theft at the hospital?

She scanned the rest of the pages, but she couldn't make out anything more. Still, she felt certain the word *tablet* could be important. This might be exactly what they needed to prove a connection between the medication theft and the downed plane.

Her cell phone rang, startling her and Jake. She looked up and realized the shadows were gathering in the corners of the room, and the sky outside the window was a golden orange. What time was it? She grabbed her phone from the coffee table and saw that it was Rachel calling. She answered the phone and put it to her ear.

"Hi, hon."

"Hi, Mom. How's it going?"

When Priscilla first moved to Martha's Vineyard from Kansas, Rachel hadn't been thrilled. But she'd come around, in no small part due to meeting and falling for A.J. on a visit last year. After a few visits and a large number of lengthy phone calls, Rachel had moved to the Boston area and would marry A.J. in a few months.

"Things are fine." She realized Rachel didn't know anything about the plane and the missing pilot, but explaining that all seemed too difficult. "I'm helping organize a big community Easter egg hunt at the Coast Guard station."

"That's awesome. The kids will love it. I always loved the egg hunt you and Debbie Castleman put on after church when I was a kid."

"That woman seemed to take great joy in hiding the eggs where they'd never be found." Priscilla hadn't thought about Debbie for years. She'd run the junior high Sunday school with an iron fist, but she was kind and loving and always quick to laugh. She also made a famous cheese and onion dip that was the hit of every church potluck, and she'd never given out the recipe. She'd moved away from Kansas to be closer to her grandkids about a dozen years ago.

"Hiding them well was a way to keep the older kids busy so the little kids would find some eggs too, I guess." Rachel laughed. "Just make sure you put good candy inside the eggs. Mrs. Castleman always bought off-brand candy, and it was disgusting."

"I don't seem to remember that stopping you from devouring it."

"No way. I mean, candy is candy. But still. Kids notice."

"Well, these eggs will be filled with candy, but also all kinds of other things."

"Like what?"

Priscilla told her about Chloe and about soliciting gift certificates from businesses in town.

"Sounds like a good plan to me. Hmm. Maybe I'll even come myself if there's a Chatham Bars Inn gift card in the mix."

Priscilla smiled. It seemed Joan had been right about that.

"Hey, I have to run in a moment, but I wanted to let you know that the sample invitation came in from the paper store, and I wanted to show it to you before we approve it. A.J. is coming to Martha's Vineyard tomorrow, so I'm sending it with him. Can you get it from him and take a look and make sure you're happy with it?"

Ordering the invitations was one of a thousand details Rachel and Priscilla were tending to for the upcoming wedding. Priscilla was excited to take a look at the invitation—it would make the upcoming wedding feel real when those were printed. But that's not what caught her attention.

"A.J. is coming to Martha's Vineyard?"

"Yeah, he's got a case he's working on there. He says he'll probably be there for a couple of days. So can you find a time to check in with him and look the invite over?"

"Do you know what he's doing here?" Priscilla's radar went up.

"I don't know. He might have said, but all I heard was that he would be gone, and we'd have to move the premarital counseling session we had scheduled."

So the FBI was being called in, then. Bret Lauf must really want those prescription drugs found.

"Of course I'll meet up with him. I would be disappointed if he was here and didn't at least say hello."

"I'm sure he'd love to see you, Mom. I think he'll be pretty busy with work, but I'm sure he can find the time to see you. And, well, he has to, since he'll have the invitation."

"I'll give him a call," Priscilla said. "To arrange a time to see the invitation."

"Thanks Mom. I appreciate it."

Priscilla hung up and sat still for a minute, thinking through the implications of what she'd learned. The FBI was being called in. That must mean there was either a federal crime being investigated, or the scope of the investigation was beyond the abilities of the local police force, or... Well, now that she thought about it, there were all kinds of reasons the FBI might be called in. But A.J.

usually worked on counterterrorism stuff, didn't he? That was the impression she'd always gotten, but now that she thought about it, he never really said a lot about the specifics of his job. Was there a terrorism link in all this? What had that pilot really been up to? Or was the FBI, as she'd first suspected, being brought in because powerful people were demanding answers about those prescription drugs? She remembered reading about how the FBI had found and prosecuted the perpetrators in the largest prescription drug heist in history a few years back. So prescription drug theft didn't seem to be out of the range of cases they normally worked on. Finally, she realized she wouldn't figure out anything by speculating. She should go right to the source.

She scrolled through the list of names to find A.J., and pressed Call. She waited while it rang.

"Priscilla?"

"Hi, A.J. Do you have a moment?"

"Of course." There were some echoey thumps, and he sounded out of breath. "I was going to call you later this evening." Now the sound of a whistle screeched in the background.

"Where are you?"

"Sorry. I'm playing basketball with a few friends. Hang on. Let me get somewhere quieter."

She waited while he walked, breathing hard, and then the noise on the other end of the line died down.

"Sorry about that. So did Rachel tell you I'm coming out to your neck of the woods tomorrow?"

"She did. I'm looking forward to seeing you. What brings you out this way?"

He laughed. "Knowing you the way I do, I think there's a good chance you already know."

"I figure it has to either be about a big prescription drug theft or a small plane crash, or both."

"You know I'm not allowed to tell you anything, right?"

"I was guessing you'd say that."

"I love that you asked anyway."

Priscilla had liked A.J. for his dedication to an unsolved case when she'd first met him, and she'd grown very fond of him as he and Rachel had fallen in love. He was exactly the kind of man she'd always prayed for Rachel to find—stable, sensible, kind, and with a heart for the Lord. True, his job in the FBI involved a lot more danger than she would prefer for her daughter's husband, but Rachel seemed to be resigned to the fact that her life would never be boring, and Priscilla tried to feel peace about that as well.

"I was the one who saw the plane go down."

"What?"

She filled him in on the story, and he let out a low whistle. "I don't know how you do it, Priscilla, but you're always right in the middle of the excitement somehow."

"You're coming about the plane then."

He laughed. "If I were, what would you be interested in knowing?"

"I want to know who the pilot was and what happened to him."

"Well, that makes two of us. Given your track record, it will be interesting to see which of us finds him first."

Priscilla's heart swelled with gratitude. He was taking her seriously. "Gerald keeps telling me to stay out of it and let the pros handle it, but I don't know. For some reason I can't stop thinking about it. There's a real person out there. Someone who's obviously hurt and may need help."

"I know. And I appreciate that you know that too." He was quiet for a moment, his breathing slowing to normal. "But I wouldn't be so worried about this guy's safety if I were you. I think Gerald is smart to be concerned about keeping you out of this."

"What do you mean?"

Again, a moment of silence. "Let's just say this: they don't call me in to catch the good guys."

She let that sink in for a moment. "Why is the FBI being brought in? Is this just too big for the local police?"

"I can't answer that."

"Is the pilot involved in the prescription drug theft?"

"I really can't say."

Priscilla knew he was being careful, as his job required, but she wasn't ready to give up, not yet.

"Do you know who the pilot is?"

He laughed. "I can't say."

"Do you know why he vanished?"

"I can't tell you that."

He was good. Still, she pressed on.

"Have they figured out who the plane belongs to yet?"

"You haven't figured that out yet?"

"Gerald was looking into it and said it would take a few days to find out. Have they figured that out yet?"

A.J. hesitated. And then, "You said you saw the plane, right?"

Priscilla nodded and then realized he couldn't see her. "Yes," she said.

"You do know there are registration numbers on the airplane, right? Really big ones? I'm surprised you didn't use that to find the owner yet."

"I could do that?" Priscilla asked.

"Sure. That's all public record."

"It *is*?" Why had Gerald made it seem like it was something only official investigators could find out? Had he said that? Priscilla tried to remember. He'd made it seem that way, hadn't he? Or had she just interpreted what he'd said that way?

"You *can* find that information," A.J. said. "But that doesn't mean you should go chasing this person down yourself. Again, Gerald is probably right to warn you to stay out of this."

"Where would I look?"

A.J. let out a sigh. "I probably shouldn't have said anything."

"You certainly should have. Where is that information found?"

A.J. laughed. "My answer is, I can't tell you that."

"All right then, I'll just see what I can find."

"You know Rachel will kill me if you end up in danger because of something I said."

"You're probably right about that, sadly. I will do my best to keep you from that fate." After a moment's thought, she added, "And I promise I will do nothing that would interfere with the FBI's investigation."

"I hope that goes without saying," he said.

"It doesn't hurt to say it anyway."

A.J. was quiet for a moment, and she heard vague squeaks and whistles in the background.

"I guess I can't stop you from looking," he finally said. "But please, once you've figured out who the owner is, don't go after him yourself, okay? There's a reason the FBI was called in here."

"I understand."

"'I understand' is not the same as 'I won't try to catch him myself.'"

"You're a good listener. That will serve you well in marriage."

A.J. sighed. "Speaking of my marriage... When can I hand off the invitation? Rachel will kill me if you end up in danger, but she'll be *really* upset if we don't get these invitations approved and printed."

"I knew I raised that girl to have her priorities right."

They made a plan for A.J. to drop the invitations off the next evening, and then she let him get back to his basketball game.

As soon as she hung up the phone, Priscilla made a beeline to her computer. A quick search brought up the website for the Federal Aviation Administration, where she found a searchable registration database. How did she not know about this? She leaned back against her throw pillows. Gerald hadn't said this information wasn't available online. He'd just said it would take a few days for the authorities to look into it. Hadn't he? She closed her eyes and tried to remember how the conversation had gone. Did he really not know that she could have found this information herself? Or had he known, and tried to steer her away from finding it?

Priscilla didn't know. The last thing she wanted to think was that Gerald would keep something from her or mislead her. But was there any other way to interpret what had happened?

Gerald had said he just wanted to keep her safe. And A.J. had warned her that the people involved in this were not good guys. But was that all that was really going on here? Or was this more of Gerald not trusting her or thinking she wasn't competent?

She shook her head. She could worry about that later. For now, she wanted answers.

Priscilla found the photo she'd taken of the plane and zoomed in on the number painted on the tail. N6398.

She typed the number into the search field on the FAA website, and a moment later, there it was. The plane with that number was registered to an Eric Ivans, in New Bedford, Massachusetts.

It only took her a few minutes to come up with an address.

She glanced at the clock. It was nearly seven o'clock now. Too late to go today.

But tomorrow, she thought. Tomorrow, she'd find answers.

CHAPTER TEN

For the second day in a row, Priscilla found herself staring out the window of the ferry as it crossed Nantucket Sound. The day had dawned brilliantly clear, and the sky was a gorgeous shade of cerulean, but it was windy and frigidly cold.

"Boy, it sure doesn't feel like spring, does it?" Trudy stepped in from the observation deck, her blonde hair blowing every which way.

"No, it sure doesn't," Priscilla agreed. She sipped from the travel mug of coffee she'd brought along. She wasn't going to make that mistake twice. "That's why everyone else stayed inside." She gestured around the cabin, which once again contained just a few people who were mostly absorbed in their phones or newspapers.

"Oh, but you have to stand outside and watch as you leave the dock. It's required." Trudy flopped down on the bench across from Priscilla. "Still, it's nice to be out of that wind."

Priscilla laughed. Joan had to work on Thursdays, so she hadn't been able to come along with Priscilla on her trip to the mainland today, but Trudy had been up for the outing. Priscilla wasn't as close to Trudy as she was to Joan, but she loved Trudy's exuberance and her fun-loving nature, and she knew that having Trudy along was always an adventure.

"Does Dan stand outside and watch as he leaves the dock?" Priscilla asked. Trudy's husband worked at the Woods Hole Oceanographic Institution and rode the ferry to and from the mainland every day.

"No. He says it's the same view every day, but the newspaper always changes." Trudy shook her head. "Though how he thinks the view is the same every day is beyond me. The sky and the trees and the waves are different every time I look."

Priscilla laughed. Trudy's husband was her opposite—methodical, logical, and reserved—and they made a funny match, though they loved each other deeply.

"So. What's our plan?" Trudy pulled her own travel mug out of her bag, but the aroma wafting from it told Priscilla it held tea. "Are you going to just straight-up ask Eric what he's been smuggling?"

"I don't usually like to be that direct," Priscilla said. "I was thinking we could ask him about his plane and see what he volunteers."

"We need a story," Trudy said. "We can tell him we're interested in buying a small plane and want his opinion."

"I usually try not to make things up when I—"

"Or maybe we say we're from the insurance company. The plane must have been insured, right? We say we need to know more about the crash."

"I don't even know if he'll be there," Priscilla said. "He didn't answer the phone when I called, and if he is the missing pilot, he might be still hiding out somewhere."

"Or he might have injuries that will make it obvious he's been through a crash."

"Right." Truthfully, Priscilla didn't know what to expect. She had learned through her research that Eric Ivans was a professor of Management and Business Administration at the University of Massachusetts, Dartmouth, but she didn't know much else about him. She had no idea if he would be at home or at work, or if he would talk to them if he was. And she knew that neither A.J. nor Gerald would approve of the trip. But she had to see for herself. She had to try to find out if he was the man who had walked away from a plane crash and vanished.

"But most likely, he's not there, and this whole trip will come to nothing," she said.

"Way to think positive." Trudy sipped her tea.

"In any case, I'm grateful for the company."

"And I'm grateful for the chance to get out and do something interesting. This winter is never-ending, and I'm so tired of being cooped up in the house."

"At least there are a few signs that spring is on the way," Priscilla said. "I saw some snowdrops pushing through the soil yesterday."

"Speaking of . . . Did you see that there's a chance of snow coming early next week?"

"*What?*" Snow in March wasn't all that unusual around here, but it was still hard to bear when she was dreaming of spring. "Please say that's not true."

"I'm afraid that's what the weather report said this morning," Trudy said. They chatted for the rest of the ride, with Trudy filling her in on her uncle Hugh's romance with Marigold Townsend, and before she knew it, they were climbing into Priscilla's car and heading toward the Bourne Bridge, which soared high above the Cape Cod Canal. There was a seasonal ferry that went straight to New Bedford in the summers, but at this time of year, they had to go through Cape Cod to get where they were headed. The drive took them past charming homes and through historic downtown, but once they crossed over the bridge, they were on highways until the exit for the town of Dartmouth. Trudy kept up a constant chatter, and Priscilla appreciated the distraction, which kept her from worrying about how this meeting was really going to go, or what to do if Eric Ivans wasn't there.

The downed plane was registered to an address in New Bedford, but Priscilla guessed that a professor would be at work during the week, so they were starting out by trying to find him at his office on campus. They found parking on the campus easily enough and then studied a map of the school, which seemed to be arranged in a large circle.

"His office is in the business school," Priscilla said, scanning the map. She tapped her finger on the drawing of the long, boxy modern building. "Which should be right over there." She pointed across the quad. At one end sat a large building with all kinds of squares and pieces jutting out. The wind whipped around them, and they put their heads down and covered the ground as quickly as they could. Students walked past them, carrying books and lugging heavy backpacks.

They reached the door to the business school, went inside, and Priscilla pulled out her notes. "His office number is 213."

"Easy enough." Trudy made her way up the staircase directly in front of them, and soon they were wandering down the hallway looking for the right office. The building was bright and airy and modern—nothing like the dark wood and creaky floors and leaded glass windows she imagined for a college. "There it is."

213. Eric Ivans, Associate Professor of Business and Management, the nameplate read. The door was closed.

"Here goes." Priscilla took a deep breath and knocked.

She hadn't realized how much she was dreading silence until there was no response. Was he just elsewhere in the building? Was he at home? Or was he...gone?

"Come in."

Trudy's eyes widened at the voice from inside, and Priscilla heard herself let out a gasp. But then, slowly, she reached out and turned the door handle.

"Yes?" Eric Ivans was seated behind a large desk. He looked up from a computer as they stepped in. He had wavy brown hair and dark glasses, and he was handsome, young, and strapping. His brow wrinkled when he saw them.

"Hi. I'm Priscilla Grant." She stepped into his office, and Trudy followed a step behind.

"And I'm Trudy Galvin," she said. "Her cousin."

"You're not students." He had no visible cuts or bruises. No apparent broken bones. Could this possibly be the man who had walked away from a plane crash just a few days ago?

"You're right, we're not students," Priscilla confirmed. "We live on Martha's Vineyard, and we were hoping we could ask you a few questions."

Something flitted across his face when she mentioned Martha's Vineyard, but she couldn't read the look.

"Are you with the FBI?"

"No." Priscilla glanced at Trudy, who was trying to suppress a smile.

"Though we are flattered that you thought we might be," Trudy added. "Could be a good second career, right, Priscilla?"

"I don't know that they're hiring middle-aged church ladies, but it might be worth a shot." She kept her tone light and jokey, trying to disarm the sense of distrust she'd sensed as soon as she mentioned Martha's Vineyard. "But no, we're not with law enforcement."

She ran through the list of excuses she and Trudy had come up with in her mind, and decided the best course of action was honesty. "We're actually just concerned citizens, hoping to help. You see, I was driving along the road in Tisbury on Monday when I saw a small plane flying low and unsteadily. There was smoke coming out of it. It sure looked like it was about to go down." She watched his face carefully. A muscle worked in his jaw, but there was no other reaction. "Then Tuesday, my friend and I found the plane in the woods. The pilot had vanished, and I haven't been able to stop thinking about what might have happened to him.

I found your name registered as the owner of the plane, so we're here to try to find out if you're okay, or if you know what happened to the pilot."

He didn't answer for a moment, so for good measure, she added, "I understand that no one has appeared at a local hospital with injuries consistent with a plane crash. Anyone who survived a plane wreck like that no doubt needs medical attention, and every day that passes makes it more dangerous for them."

Still, he said nothing, though his eyes slid from Priscilla to Trudy and back. Priscilla took in the bookcases lined with thick books and the window that looked out over the trees. His desk was clear, the office meticulously clean.

"I'm not really sure who you are or what you're really hoping to find out here," he finally said. "But I'll tell you what I told the FBI when they showed up here yesterday."

Priscilla waited, holding her breath.

"The plane is mine, as you already know," he finally said. "But I was not flying it when it crashed, as you might have guessed." He held up his arms to show that he was fit and healthy. "Flying is a hobby of mine. The plane is hangared at New Bedford airport, and I don't have a clue how it ended up on Martha's Vineyard."

New Bedford wasn't far from here, along the southern coast, and there was a small airport there. It sounded plausible that he would keep the plane there, she supposed.

"Someone must have taken the plane, and they did so without my permission. I don't have any idea who it could have been."

"You're saying someone stole your plane and flew it to Martha's Vineyard without your permission," Trudy said. The tone of her voice conveyed skepticism that matched Priscilla's.

"That is correct." He nodded. "Now if you'll excuse—"

"How would someone have access to your plane?" Given how tight security was at airports these days, Priscilla couldn't imagine they simply let anyone waltz into a hangar and take a plane.

"I don't know. I guess that's a question for the staff at the airport. I know it's certainly one I'll be asking." He pushed his chair back and rose. "I have to get go—"

Priscilla looked around, desperate to find something that would keep him engaged. Her eyes lit on a framed picture of Eric and three other men, all in military uniforms, standing in front of a small plane, their arms around each other's shoulders. The frame around the picture had the words "Air Force" on the top, "United States" running down the left side, "Aim High" running down the right side, and "77th Fighter Squadron 'Gamblers'" on the bottom. "Oh, were you in the military, Professor Ivans? My father-in-law was a pilot in World War II. Where did you serve?"

His eyes followed hers to the picture. "My buddies and I flew F-16s in the Middle East." His voice softened. "Only two of us in that picture made it back home."

Before Priscilla could respond, the mood was broken, and he was almost out the door. "I'm afraid I really have to go. I have a class to teach in a few minutes."

Priscilla wasn't sure what else to do, and, a moment later, she and Trudy were in the hallway, alone.

"Well," Trudy said.

"Well, indeed," Priscilla said. He'd closed the door to his office behind him. Not that she would have gone in and looked around without his permission, exactly, but, well... In any case, that wasn't an option.

She couldn't see what else to do, so she and Trudy headed back down the hallway and down the stairs, out of the building.

"Do you believe him?" Trudy asked as they walked back across the quad.

"Not entirely." Priscilla shoved her hands into her pockets, fighting against the frigid wind. "It's obvious he wasn't flying the plane. He doesn't seem to have any injuries."

"I agree with that," Trudy said. "Unless by some miracle he walked away without a scratch."

"There was blood all over the cockpit. Whoever was flying that plane was hurt, badly."

"Okay. So we agree he wasn't flying it," Trudy said. "But I find it hard to believe his story that someone took the plane without his permission. How would that happen? Did someone just steal a spare key and take it for a joyride? Do planes even use keys to start?"

"I have no idea." Priscilla shook her head. "But I did notice one thing."

"What's that?"

"He said the plane was taken without his permission. And he said he was going to ask the airport employees how that happened. But he didn't say he'd reported the plane stolen to the authorities."

"He didn't, did he?" Trudy said. "We don't know when he discovered the plane was gone though. He didn't answer that question. It's probably not like a car, where you use it every day and would notice right away if it was gone. He might not have known it was missing until the FBI showed up asking about it."

"True," Priscilla said. "And if that's the case, he obviously wouldn't have known to report the plane as stolen. But if he'd somehow realized the plane was gone before the newspapers reported it Wednesday morning, and hadn't reported it stolen, that's a different story."

"But we don't know which story is true."

"No. We don't." Priscilla felt frustration rising. "My gut says there was something he wasn't telling us."

"My gut says there were plenty of things he wasn't telling us."

Priscilla dug her hands deeper into her coat pockets. What was it that he wasn't saying? How was he involved in all this? Who was flying the plane, and what, if anything, did he know about them?

"Do you think A.J. was one of the FBI agents who met with him yesterday? Would he tell you what happened?"

"I think it's fairly likely A.J. was one of the officers who talked to him yesterday, but I don't think it's likely he'll be able to tell me what Eric said."

"Too bad." They passed a group of students walking together, all looking at their phones. "I think Eric knows something."

Priscilla agreed. But what did he know? And why wasn't he saying it? She had so many questions.

But what she said was, "Do we have time to make a quick stop before we head back to the ferry?"

Fifteen minutes later, they were driving alongside the chain link fence that separated the New Bedford Regional Airport from the service road. Small planes were parked alongside hangars that looked little bigger than sheds.

"It's not a very big place, is it?" Trudy asked.

The main building, redbrick, with large windows, was two stories tall and smaller than many of the houses on Martha's Vineyard. There was a circular driveway in front of it. Beside that stood a restaurant and a playground situated next to a small parking lot with room for a couple dozen cars. That was about it.

"Should we go see what we can find out about the planes?"

Priscilla pulled over by the hangars where the small planes were kept. The car was out of the way here, and she would only be a moment anyway. She and Trudy hopped out, and they walked toward the fence.

"Look over there." Trudy pointed at a sign at the corner of the fence that said Sandman Air.

"Let's check it out."

Priscilla followed Trudy down a paved path and into the small building made out of what looked like corrugated metal. A man stood behind a wooden counter and smiled when they came in. There was a computer on the counter, and a framed aerial photograph of the airport from above hanging on the wall behind the counter.

"Hello, and welcome to Sandman Air. How can I help you?" The man was thick around the middle, with curly brown hair and a genuine smile.

"What..." Priscilla thought about how to phrase her words.

"Who owns all these planes?" Trudy jumped in, pointing out the window to the dozens of propeller planes around them.

"Oh, all sorts of folks. The main building houses the commercial flights, but these aircraft are all privately owned. We have a wide clientele, and we are known for our high level of service. We have hangar space for rent, but we also offer fuel, maintenance, you name it. Are you in the market?"

"No," Priscilla said. "We're trying to find out about a plane that's kept here."

"Ah." The man adjusted the strap of the black plastic watch on his wrist. "And is the plane yours?"

"No," Priscilla said.

"Are you with law enforcement?"

"No." Priscilla shook her head.

"I think I know which plane you're asking about, but I'm afraid I can't divulge anything about it unless you're with the authorities."

"So we're not the first to come here asking about the plane that belongs to Eric Ivans, then?"

He grimaced. "I really can't say. Privacy is of the utmost concern for many of our clients, and we pride ourselves on maintaining the highest standards."

Priscilla stifled a groan. They weren't going to get anything out of this guy. "We understand," she said.

"But you must keep records of which planes are taken out and by whom," Trudy said.

"Even if we had such records, I'm afraid I couldn't share them."

"Wait," Priscilla said. "You really don't keep track of who is behind the controls when someone takes one of these planes?"

Priscilla couldn't believe it. She'd thought Eric was misleading them when he'd said someone had taken his plane without his permission. How could such a thing be possible? But now she was beginning to see that it might not be so crazy. There was a door at the rear of the small building that led directly out to the blacktop where the planes were parked.

"I didn't say we don't have records." His voice was getting tight. "It is our job to make sure the planes are kept safe. But we don't monitor usage." A few beads of sweat appeared over his lip.

"So you don't keep track at all?" Trudy looked as perplexed as Priscilla felt. "Wouldn't that mean that anyone could just waltz in here and steal a plane?"

"I merely said our records are not available to the public," he said with a vehemence that made Priscilla doubt him all the more. "And I assure you, it's not that simple to steal a plane."

"How *would* someone steal a plane, if they were so inclined?" Priscilla asked.

He gave her a sharp look. "I'm afraid I can't help you with that. Is there anything else you need?"

"Do you have any sort of security here?" Priscilla didn't see any scanners or x-ray machines. No conveyer belt to place a person's shoes and coat and luggage on.

"I assure you, our security is among the highest in the business. I—"

"But you don't, like, check to see what everyone brings onto the planes, right?" Trudy placed her arms on the counter and leaned forward. "No TSA agents looking through your underwear and whatnot?"

The man didn't seem to know how to respond. "No, we do not look at our customers' underwear."

"So people can bring whatever they want to on their planes?"

"That's one of the many benefits of flying private," he said simply. "Now, if you'll—"

"Can you tell us who took Eric Ivans's plane last Monday?" Priscilla asked.

He sighed. "I'm afraid I can't do that. Now, if you'll excuse me, I must get back to work." The man turned and disappeared through a door behind the counter.

Priscilla looked at Trudy. She was craning her neck to try to look at the computer screen. "Should we just poke around and see if we can find anything?" Trudy nodded at the screen.

"No, probably not," Priscilla said. "That's probably illegal."

"Boo."

Priscilla sighed and turned back toward the door. "Well, if nothing else, this seems to make Eric's story seem more plausible." She pushed open the glass door and stepped out into the cold air.

"Right," Trudy agreed as they got back into the car. "I don't know whether they keep records or not, but in either case, the security isn't as high-tech as I would have guessed."

"You're sure right about that." Both car doors shut, and Priscilla started the car and pulled back out onto the narrow road that circled the small airport.

She hated to leave without the answers they sought, but as they drove back toward the Cape, she realized how little the answers would help her. Even if she did find out that someone had taken Eric's plane, it wouldn't get her any closer to knowing who might have done so. She believed that Eric was the only one who could answer that question.

Besides the injured pilot, of course.

CHAPTER ELEVEN

When they got back to Martha's Vineyard, Priscilla dropped Trudy off and then headed to Faith Fellowship Church, where she had an appointment to meet with Curt Lannister, the new pastor. Priscilla had spoken with Curt a few times and liked him a lot. He'd only been at the job a few months, since Pastor Katie had left to take a job closer to her aging parents in upstate New York, but Curt was friendly and approachable, and so far she'd found his sermons to be insightful and grounded in Scripture.

She parked in the lot at the side of the brick building and went in through the doors that led to a small foyer. Ahead was the sanctuary, and to the left were stairs that led downstairs to the fellowship hall, the Sunday school classrooms, and the small church office. She knocked on the door to the pastor's study.

"Come in!"

Pastor Lannister—Curt—smiled as she walked inside. Though her instinct was to use the more formal term, he'd asked to be called Curt, and she tried to remember that.

"Good afternoon, Priscilla." He gestured for her to sit down in the chair across from his desk. Curt was in his late thirties and had receding brown hair and a slight paunch, and today he wore a dress shirt with jeans. "Welcome. Have a seat."

"Thank you." She sat down and smiled. "How is everything going so far?"

"Really well. People here are so friendly," he said. "And we're loving living here. I've heard it gets crazy in the summer, but for now we really appreciate the laid-back pace."

Priscilla laughed. She didn't think of Martha's Vineyard as laid-back, but then the Lannister family had moved from Brooklyn, where he'd been the associate pastor of a church of urban professionals, so maybe it was laid-back compared to that.

She eyed the titles in the bookcases behind the desk. There were a lot of theological books, as well as titles by some Christian authors she'd heard of. She also noticed a number of figurines, which she recognized as Lord of the Rings characters.

"I'm glad you're settling in. And believe me, I understand what it's like to be new around here, so let me know if there's anything I can do to help."

"You've been here for a while now, right? And isn't your family from here?"

"Yes, but that only counts for so much. You'll always be new if you weren't born and raised on the island."

He laughed and shook his head. "Well, I guess I have to admire that kind of pride of place."

Priscilla noticed there was a framed picture of his wife Heidi and their two boys hanging on the wall. Heidi was blonde and very pretty, and when she'd first met her, Priscilla had been delighted to find she was witty and well read.

"So," Curt said. He leaned back in his chair. "What's this about an Easter egg hunt?"

Priscilla quickly explained what she was planning, and asked him to come and share a short message about the real meaning of Easter with the children.

"The Coast Guard is okay with this?" Curt raised his eyebrows.

"We'll have to hold it off-site, but as long as it's not seen as a part of the hunt itself, or advertised as such, they're okay with it," Priscilla said.

"Well, in that case, I'd be happy to," Curt said. "It would be an honor."

"Thank you," Priscilla said. "And of course your children would be welcome to participate."

"They will love it," he said.

Priscilla chatted with Curt for a while longer, asking him about Brooklyn and his hobbies. She found out he liked to hike and was a huge J.R.R. Tolkien fan, which she'd already surmised. The topic turned to local news, and Curt said he was saddened to hear about the plane crash he'd read about in the newspaper.

"We're praying that the pilot is found quickly, and that he's all right," he said. Priscilla agreed, and thought for a moment about whether to say anything more. Surely it couldn't hurt to tell a pastor what she suspected, so he would know how to pray for resolution. But she decided to hold her tongue, and she stood and thanked him for his time, then headed back to her car.

When she got back home, she found a pink gift bag sitting on the doorstep. She opened it up and saw that it was the sample invitation, along with a note from A.J.

> Priscilla,
>
> Thanks for taking a look at the invitation. Sorry I missed you, but I know Rachel is anxious for you to see this, so I'll leave it here and check in when I get a moment.
>
> Thanks again,
> A.J.

Priscilla appreciated that he'd taken the time to include a handwritten note. Many people would have simply dropped it off or sent a text to let her know it was there. She thanked God once again that Rachel had found someone as thoughtful as A.J.

She carried the bag inside and set it on the table. She took the invitation out of the bag and pulled off the outer envelope. The paper was thick, in a creamy ivory color. She opened the inner envelope and slid out a thick card embossed in a glossy black.

Priscilla's eyes filled as she read the words. She could hardly believe it. Her baby was all grown up and getting married. She'd prayed for the man Rachel would marry since the day her daughter was born, and now here it was. In just a few short months, it would be real.

She took a deep breath, trying to hold back the tears. Priscilla was glad to be able to help Rachel have the wedding of her dreams. But she couldn't help thinking her own name looked just a little lonely up there on the invitation. Gary's name should have been there too. How he would have loved to see this. How much he would have loved to see his daughter married.

She set the invitation down and pressed her lips together. Sometimes she was still taken by surprise by how much she missed him, by how raw the pain still sometimes felt.

Gary would have liked A.J., she was certain of that. He would have loved that A.J. would protect and cherish their daughter, and that he was a good, honest man. Rachel had chosen well. They had raised her well. Gary had lived long enough to know that for sure.

Slowly, she slid the invitation aside and looked over the reply card and the return envelope. They all looked nice, Priscilla thought. She would call Rachel later and let her know.

In the meantime, she was antsy. She set the invitation back into the pink bag and looked around. She still had to run to the grocery store, and she could tidy up a bit here or do some laundry. But even with everything else going on, she couldn't stop thinking about that plane.

She was missing something, she was sure of it. But what? There had to be some clue she was overlooking, some hint she wasn't seeing. But as she thought back through the morning's events, she couldn't figure out what. Eric was hiding something, it was clear. But what? How could she figure that out?

She took Jake down to the beach for a walk, but the icy wind drove them back pretty quickly. The sun was hanging low in the sky when she stepped back inside and set the kettle on the stove. A hot cup of tea would warm her up, and maybe the caffeine would help her figure out what it was she was overlooking.

She set an Earl Grey teabag into a pretty teacup, and after she let it steep, she added a splash of milk and a spoonful of sugar. Then she curled up on the couch under a wool Pendleton blanket and picked up the novel that was sitting on the table next to the couch—a charming story about three reunited friends who were opening an inn together. She could read for a while; let her mind get lost in a story and stop racing around and around this whole plane thing. But as soon as she picked up the book, her mind drifted back to the plane and to her trips to the mainland the past two days. She sat thinking, watching the wisps of steam curl up from the surface of the tea.

She hoped the FBI was coming up with more than she was. Surely they must be, now that A.J. was on the case.

Still, though. With a sigh, she set her book down and stood up to grab her phone and laptop. She took a sip of her tea, and then she opened up a browser window and typed in "Eric Ivans." She'd run this search last night, and hadn't found anything useful. She'd found out where and what he taught, but aside from the information she found on the university's website, there wasn't much. The problem, she realized, was that she didn't even know what she was looking for. Google couldn't tell her what secrets he was hiding.

Priscilla closed her eyes and tried to think. Searching for information about Eric Ivans wasn't getting her anywhere. But she still hadn't gotten in touch with Luke Coombs. She set her laptop to the side and unlocked her phone. Three more texts from Chloe. She'd look at those later. She dug up the phone numbers she'd found for Luke and tried them again. She wasn't any more successful at getting through his assistant to speak with him directly at work, but someone did pick up at the home phone number.

"Hello?" It was a woman's voice, but Priscilla would put money on it not being the pretty young redheaded wife. This woman sounded older, and she had some kind of an accent—Jamaican, maybe, or somewhere thereabouts.

"Hi. Is Luke Coombs available?"

"I'm afraid he's not in right now. Can I take a message?"

"Sure." Priscilla thought quickly. "My name is Priscilla Grant, and I live on Martha's Vineyard. I was calling about his plane."

"Is something the matter with the plane?" the woman asked.

"No, it's nothing like that," Priscilla said. "Can I ask, is this Mrs. Coombs?"

"No, I'm the nanny," the woman said. "But I'd be happy to let Mr. Coombs know you called."

"I would appreciate that," Priscilla said and gave her phone number. "Can you tell me, has Mr. Coombs taken any trips recently?"

There was a pause, and then the woman said, "I'm afraid you'd have to ask him about that. I'll give him the message."

She was good at her job, Priscilla thought as she hung up. If the nanny had given out Luke's personal information, she'd more than likely be jeopardizing her job. Still, that made it difficult for Priscilla.

Now, unsure of what else to do, she scrolled again to the photographs she'd taken at the crash site and studied them. She stared at the photographs of the notebook pages, but the scribbles refused to form themselves into words. She looked at the picture of the keys again, then the pocketknife. Had the police been able to lift any fingerprints from any of the objects? She just didn't know.

She jumped when the phone in her hand rang. The green bar that appeared at the top told her Rachel was calling.

"Hi, kiddo," Priscilla said.

"Hi, Mom. Did A.J. bring you the invitation?"

"Yes, he left it here. It's beautiful."

"Do you think it'll work?"

Priscilla heard the hope in her daughter's voice. She wanted her mom to be pleased.

"I think it's perfect."

"Oh good." Rachel blew out a breath. "Should I tell the printer to go ahead with the order, then?"

"You get a green light from me."

In the silence, Priscilla heard Rachel's relief. "Your father would be proud," she said.

Rachel sighed. "Thanks, Mom." And then, after a beat, "I miss him."

"I do too. There is nothing he would have loved more than to walk you down the aisle."

"I would have loved that too."

They were both quiet for a moment.

"A.J. called today and said it looks like he'll be on Martha's Vineyard through the weekend at least. I was wondering, would it be all right if I came to visit while he's there? Then I could see him when he's not working. And of course, I'd love to see you too."

"Of course." Priscilla was always glad for a visit. "You're welcome any time."

"Awesome. I'll take the ferry over after work tomorrow then."

"I'm looking forward to it."

Rachel asked how things were going, and Priscilla wasn't quite sure how to answer. "It's going okay. Keeping busy."

"I bet," Rachel said. "A.J. told me you found a plane that crashed?"

Priscilla told her about finding the plane and trying to figure out what happened to the pilot. "But I'm not getting anywhere," she said.

"Mom," Rachel said firmly. "You know how I feel about your getting involved in these dangerous crimes."

"I'm not really 'involved,' per se." Priscilla didn't want Rachel to stress out when there was no reason to worry. "I'm just doing some minor sleuthing. Internet searches, a couple of visits to a nursing home and a university. What kind of danger can I get into at a nursing home?"

"Well, if you're sure you're staying out of trouble..." Rachel paused. "What kinds of clues do you have to work with?" she asked.

"Right now I'm looking at the pictures I took at the crash scene, trying to figure out if there's something in them I missed."

"What are they pictures of?"

"Here. I'll send them to you." Priscilla put the phone on speaker, opened the photo app on her phone and selected the pictures, then sent them to Rachel.

"Oh wow. That's a lot of blood," Rachel said.

"Sorry."

"No. It's...wow. And you think the pilot walked away from this?"

"Either that or he vaporized. He's gone. We're trying to figure out where and why. Well, that's what I'm trying to figure out. I'm not sure what A.J. knows."

Rachel was quiet for a moment.

"These notebook pages are crazy."

"I know. I made out a few words, but I can't read most of it."

"Bronze and gold," Rachel said.

"What?"

"I think that's what's on this first page. The third line down says something about bronze and gold."

"Really?"

Priscilla pulled up the picture and tried to make the words come into focus. "Oh yeah...I guess that could be what it says."

"And farther down on the page. I think it says 'necklace.'"

"Where do you see that?"

"Let's see...one, two...ten lines down."

Priscilla looked at the scribbles and tried to make them form into words. "I guess so?"

"That's what it looks like to me," Rachel said. "But it would take forever to decipher the rest of this."

"You made out more than I did," Priscilla said. "All I got was 'tablet.'"

"Tablet? Like an iPad?"

"No, I think it's more like prescription drugs."

Priscilla explained about the drug thefts and her suspicion that they were connected to the missing pilot. "Which would explain why the FBI is involved, I guess. I think it was extremely valuable medication that was taken."

"Huh."

"Huh?"

"I mean, it makes sense. The FBI would only get involved in a case where it was something major that was taken."

"But...?" Priscilla heard the hesitation in her voice.

"But it's not usually the kind of thing A.J. is involved with," Rachel said. "He can't really tell me much about the cases he works on, but I don't think that prescription drug theft is really the kind of case he typically works on."

Priscilla turned this around in her mind. "He's counterterrorism, right?"

"Mostly. But I guess he does other stuff too. Maybe they needed someone and he was available. Or maybe there's a terrorism link to the prescription drugs somewhere."

Priscilla thought about this for a moment. "Do you think there's any chance the drugs are going to be sold to fund terrorist organizations?"

"I have no way to know, Mom. I'm just trying to work out what makes sense."

"What would we have to do to get him to tell us about this case?"

Rachel laughed. "You mean, what would it take to get him to violate his professional ethics, breach his security clearance, and put his job and our national security at risk?"

"When you say it that way, it doesn't sound like such a great idea."

"Ya think?" Rachel laughed.

Priscilla sighed. "Well, I guess it's back to trying to figure it out on my own."

"What about these keys?" Rachel said. She must have scrolled to the next photo, so Priscilla did too. "I guess the pilot drives a Toyota."

"I got that far. But I have no idea how to use that."

"Can the manufacturer trace the car using the key?"

She hadn't thought about that. Was that possible? "I don't know."

"And that looks like a security box key there beneath it."

"Oh yeah." She zoomed in on the short, wide key. "I guess you're right."

"I don't know what good that does you," Rachel said. "Because I can't figure out any way to tell where that security box is. But maybe that could lead to something once you figure out who he is."

"Maybe." Priscilla's mind was racing. Could the key be to a box where the stolen drugs were being kept? There had to be some way to figure out where the box was. If there was a box.

Rachel looked through the other photos, and Priscilla told her about finding the owner of the plane and tracing the name on the pill bottle.

"So the pilot is definitely not Dennis Reid?" Rachel asked.

"Not unless he came back from the dead."

"Ooh. A ghost plane. That would be an interesting twist."

Priscilla laughed. "Based on the amount of blood inside that plane, I can only assume the pilot was very real."

"Sounds like it." Rachel blew out a breath. "Well, remember, Mom. I'm trusting you not to do anything dangerous. Any clues you find you should turn over to the police and let them do the dirty work."

"I'll keep that in mind." It sounded like Rachel was preparing to get off the line, so Priscilla was surprised when she asked, "So how's Gerald?"

"What?"

"Gerald? You know, your boyfriend?"

Priscilla felt a bit strange using the word *boyfriend*. It made her feel like some lovestruck teen, not a woman her age nearing sixty. But wasn't that what he was?

"He's fine."

"Mom. What's going on?"

"What do you mean?"

"Well, you haven't mentioned him in this phone call yet, and usually you can't stop talking about him."

"I don't—"

"It's okay. It's cute. But you haven't brought him up at all this time. Is everything all right?"

Priscilla paused to figure out what to say.

"It's fine," she said.

"Mom. What's wrong?"

"Nothing is wrong." It was true. Nothing was wrong, really. Not technically. "It was just kind of frustrating that everyone kept trying to convince me I hadn't seen a plane about to crash, when I knew I had."

"Everyone including Gerald."

"Yes. He said it was a Coast Guard drone."

"Did he apologize once he realized you were right?"

"He did. But I don't know."

"What else?"

"Well…" Priscilla felt a bit bad talking like this. But why couldn't she talk through her feelings with her daughter? "He really wanted me to stop investigating the missing pilot."

"Of course he did. He wants you to be safe. If the FBI is involved, he's probably right to worry."

"But it wasn't so much that. It was more like he thought I couldn't handle myself. I'm not dumb. I'm not going to put myself in a dangerous situation."

"I don't know, Mom. Your track record there isn't so good."

Priscilla didn't say anything. Okay, so maybe she had gotten into a few scrapes investigating mysteries. She'd always come through just fine, hadn't she?

"Then there's this whole Easter egg hunt thing," she said instead of answering.

"What do you mean?"

Priscilla explained how he wasn't actually involved in the planning like she thought he would be.

"Have you talked to him about any of this?"

"What do you mean?"

"I mean, have you told him how you feel? How frustrated you are?"

"Not really. I mean...I don't..."

"Mom. You have to tell him."

Tell him? She made it sound so easy. "It's not that simple."

"Why not?"

Priscilla tried to work out how to answer. Rachel and Gary had been very much alike. Both loved a good argument; both never shied away from confrontation. She'd never felt fully equipped to go into battle with either one of them. Rachel just didn't understand. Plus, Rachel and A.J were engaged. There was a formal commitment there. Priscilla and Gerald were just dating. It was a different relationship dynamic.

"It's just different."

"Mom. Don't do this again."

"Do what?"

Rachel let out a sigh. "You disagreed with Dad, but you always just let him get his way. You never told him how you really felt."

"That's not true." Priscilla felt herself bristle. "I just don't like to argue."

"I know you don't. And I'm not saying you should. With Dad, you always bit your tongue, and he was so oblivious he never even seemed to notice. But you don't have to do that here. You don't have to keep your mouth shut when something is bothering you. Gerald is different than Dad. I bet he would be open to hearing how you're feeling."

A thousand thoughts zoomed through her head. Rachel was making her sound like some weak pathetic wife who went along with whatever her husband had said. But it hadn't been like that. She'd just learned early on in their marriage to pick her battles.

Gary, for all his kindness, had a bit of a temper and liked things a certain way, and she'd learned how to manage that. So maybe she hadn't always given voice to all her thoughts. So what? Wasn't that what love was? Wasn't biting your tongue a part of any relationship? Since when did true love mean you uttered every thought that came into your head?

"Mom?"

Had she kept silent too often? Had she kept quiet about how she felt more often than not? It was hard to say. Maybe, she realized. Maybe she had. But did she think she'd done anything wrong in that? She couldn't say.

"I mean, think about the time Dad had to have that new top-of-the-line tractor. We couldn't afford it, and you tried to convince him not to get it, and he bought it anyway."

"No one could have stopped your father when he went into a John Deere dealership."

She meant it as a joke, but Rachel didn't laugh.

"We nearly lost the farm over that."

"As you say, I did try to stop him. I did speak up."

"But what he wanted always won out. And what about my school?"

"What *about* your school?"

"Even as a kid I knew you wanted me to go to the Christian school in town, but Dad wouldn't have it. Not when public school was free. But you didn't even fight for what you wanted."

"No, I tried to avoid fighting with my husband. That's how we stayed married for so long."

"I know you did. I *never* saw you guys fight. Which was great. I had so much security in knowing our family was safe. But now I wonder if it was because you avoided conflict and let Dad have his way."

"You had a great education at the public school."

"Of course I did, Mom. I'm not saying I didn't. I'm just saying, even as a kid I could see that Dad was going to win that one, because you wouldn't stand up for yourself and tell him how you really felt."

Priscilla didn't answer for a moment. She knew she had to choose her words carefully here.

"The thing is, it's not about winning," she finally said. "Marriage is about making the best decision as a family, for the family. Sometimes that means you don't get your way."

"I know that." Rachel took a deep breath. "I'm just saying that you seemed to always defer to whatever made Dad happy instead of what you wanted, instead of the other way around. And that's fine sometimes. But I wonder what would have happened if you'd spoken your mind more often."

Would things have been different? She hadn't felt oppressed, not by any means. And if she'd had to go along with choices she wouldn't have made sometimes, well, again, wasn't that what marriage was?

"Mom?"

"I'm here."

"I didn't mean to hurt your feelings."

"I know you didn't." She wasn't sure what else to say.

"I'm just trying to say, every relationship is different. And you don't have to defer to Gerald all the time if you don't want to. I think he would totally respect it if you told him that you felt hurt because you thought you'd be working with him on the Easter egg hunt. That's all."

Was she right? Priscilla didn't know, and right now her head was so confused she wasn't sure what to think.

"I'm sorry if I upset you," Rachel said.

"You didn't upset me. You've made me think."

"Okay then. Well, take my advice or leave it, but I had to say it."

The conversation moved on to wedding details, but Priscilla couldn't stop thinking about what Rachel had said. She thought about it the rest of the night. Was Rachel right? Had she bitten her tongue too much with Gary? Should she have confronted him more? How much was too much? Priscilla wasn't even sure how you were supposed to decide about such things. And more importantly, she didn't know what it meant she should do about Gerald.

CHAPTER TWELVE

Priscilla slept restlessly Thursday night, and when she dragged herself out of bed Friday morning, she was still bleary-eyed. She scanned the newspaper headlines and saw that the plane crash and the missing pilot was still front-page news. She read the article, but there was nothing new in the piece. Apparently the police had been flooded with tips. People reporting seeing a man with a gash across his forehead on the ferry or with a broken arm in the grocery store. But so far none of the tips had played out.

There was also an article reporting on the continuing search for the prescription pill thief, but despite the massive amounts of manpower the Tisbury police had poured into that investigation, they had made little progress.

After a walk on the beach and two cups of coffee, she felt a little better, so she got dressed and headed into town. Joan was coming over this afternoon to help her get started on stuffing plastic eggs for the Easter egg hunt, but Priscilla had the morning free, and she had a plan.

She parked in front of the brick-and-clapboard building that housed the Tisbury Public Library and walked inside. She stood in the airy room, with its high ceilings and wooden floors, and the portrait of her ancestors Llewellyn and Elodie Latham over the checkout desk, and looked around. Now that she was here, she wasn't really sure where to start.

"Hi, Priscilla." Clara Lopez emerged from the stacks and strode toward her. Her dark hair was pulled back into a low ponytail, and she wore a thick cable-knit sweater over dark pants. "You look lost."

"I am searching for something, and I'm not quite sure where to start," Priscilla admitted.

"Maybe I can help. I love a challenge."

Priscilla considered how much to disclose to the friendly librarian. "I have a few words I'm trying to make sense of."

"A few words?"

"I know, it's not much to go on. But I'm hoping to find a connection between the words 'tablet,' 'bronze and gold,' and 'necklace.'"

"Huh." The look on Clara's face said it all. "You took me at my word when I said I love a challenge, didn't you?"

"I was hoping you would see some obvious connection I was missing."

Clara smiled. "Well, the most obvious connection is between 'gold' and 'necklace.' Is there any chance this is referring to jewelry of some kind?"

"I wondered that," Priscilla said. "But I don't know. I'm pretty sure the word 'tablet' is referring to medication, but I don't know what that has to do with the other words."

Clara considered. "Well, you've stumped me."

"Do I win a prize? Stump the Librarian?"

"I'm afraid I would be giving out a lot of prizes. You should hear some of the questions I get asked around here." Clara laughed.

"In any case, if it were me, I'd start by searching through the online catalog of newspapers and magazines about jewelry. Maybe something will come up." She shrugged. "Then you could check out the medical books to see if there's some connection between gold and bronze and medicine?"

Clara sounded like she was grasping at straws. Well, so was Priscilla.

Priscilla sat down at one of the computer terminals and opened the program that searched back issues of newspapers. She tried every combination of the words she could think of. She learned that gold had been ingested in small doses throughout history as a way to treat conditions as varied as arthritis and skin conditions, but that was the closest she came to finding anything she could use. After perusing every shelf of books she thought might be even slightly useful, she left the library, no closer to finding answers than when she started.

She decided to cut her losses and run a few errands while she was in town, and she finally went to the grocery store and to the pet store to pick up more food for Jake. Then she went to the discount store and bought out their whole stock of plastic eggs and more Easter chocolate than should be legal.

Buying loads of plastic eggs, Priscilla texted to Chloe.

Chloe immediately responded with a string of emojis that seemed to indicate she was excited.

Then, she headed home. After a quick turkey sandwich and soup, she took Jake for a walk and was back by the time Joan rang the doorbell.

"Hi there," Priscilla said, ushering her cousin inside.

"Hello." Joan held bags of Easter grass and several jumbo-sized bags of jelly beans. "I'm ready to stuff some eggs."

"I'm glad to hear it." Priscilla ushered her in, and together they set up the table as a kind of assembly line. Priscilla would reserve some eggs to stuff with the gift certificates to add to the mix just before the event, but filling the bulk of the eggs was one task that could be done in advance, so they wanted to get it out of the way.

"How many of these are we doing?" Joan asked as she filled a pink plastic egg with jelly beans.

"I have about six hundred of these." Priscilla held up a plastic egg. "And that's not all we need to do. Chloe and I figure we'll need at least fifteen hundred to be on the safe side. Each child should be able to find at least five eggs."

"Oh boy."

Priscilla filled an egg and then she pulled out her phone to take a picture of it.

"What are you doing?" Joan asked.

"Making sure this meets quality control standards," Priscilla said, snapping the photo. She sent the picture to Chloe with the question, "Does this look okay?"

Immediately, three dots began to dance underneath her text. Chloe was writing back. That girl was always on her phone.

SO CUTE LOVE IT, the reply came, followed by emojis of a heart, a rainbow, and a rabbit.

"Do we have permission to proceed?" Joan asked.

"Permission granted." Priscilla held up the phone so Joan could see the reply.

"Thank goodness. I've been stuffing Easter eggs for decades, but it's good to know I'm doing it right."

"Hey, now." Priscilla gave her cousin a look. "She's just doing her job."

"I know." Joan closed the egg she was working on and set it aside. "And I'm glad you have more patience with her than I would."

Priscilla shrugged. "She just has a lot of enthusiasm."

"And a vast library of emojis at her disposal."

"That she does."

They each filled a few more eggs, setting the finished products into plastic bags, before Joan said, "Something interesting happened at work this morning."

"Oh?" Priscilla placed a couple of jelly beans in a lavender egg and then dropped in a foil-wrapped chocolate. "What's that?"

"You know how I mentioned there are all kinds of new rules about accessing the medication cabinet?"

Priscilla nodded.

"Well, I was going toward the supply closet to get more rubber gloves this morning, and I saw my coworker Michelle come out of the medication closet."

"What's so odd about that?" Priscilla set the top onto the egg and pushed it closed. "She probably needed something for one of her patients."

"But that's just it. She's not a nurse or a nurse's aide. She's a receptionist, so she wouldn't have any reason to be in that closet.

And the way she acted when she saw me made me think she was up to something she shouldn't have been."

"How so?"

"Well, she was just coming out when I turned the corner, and when she saw me she put her hand behind her back and looked panicked, like I'd caught her doing something she shouldn't."

"What did you do?" Priscilla set the finished egg into the plastic bag.

"I asked if she needed help, and she just turned and hurried down the hall."

"Huh."

"Then she left work right after that. Said she had to pick up her son from school, or something like that."

"She wasn't scheduled to leave early?"

Joan shook her head. "It wasn't on the schedule. She doesn't report to me, so obviously she doesn't have to tell me when she needs to leave, but I don't know. After what I saw, it just seemed . . . strange."

"Strange is right." Priscilla was moving faster now, filling eggs more quickly as she talked. "What kind of medication is kept in the closet? Is there anything in there that she could want?"

"We don't keep tons of medication on hand, but we do get samples from pharmaceutical companies all the time," Joan said. "That's how they get doctors to prescribe their medication. The sales reps come in with samples and hand them out. The radiologists then prescribe them to patients sometimes, if they're called for. But the samples are there in the closet."

"So someone could feasibly come in for an X-ray or ultrasound, and be sent home with a sample of some opioid painkiller?"

"It doesn't happen very often, but it's theoretically possible," Joan said. "So if a prescription painkiller was what Michelle was after, she would have been able to find some in the cabinet."

Priscilla thought for a moment. "Do you think that's what she was after?"

"All I know is that it seemed really strange to me, and given your theory that the missing pilot was involved in ferrying drugs off the island, I thought it was worth telling you about it."

"I'm glad you did," Priscilla said. "But how would she be connected to the pilot?"

"I have no idea." Joan shrugged. "She might not be. That's for you to figure out."

"Did she have anything in her hands?"

"I don't know. Like I said, she put her hand behind her back. And she was wearing scrubs, like we all do at work, so it's hard to say if she had anything in her pockets."

"Hmm." Priscilla had been to Joan's office before, and she tried to picture the receptionist. She vaguely remembered a woman in her forties, with brown hair and a round face. "Has she been working there awhile?"

"Five years or so." Joan was carefully sorting jelly beans and including one of each color in the egg she was assembling. "She's really sweet. She has two boys. Middle school, or somewhere thereabouts. Her husband is a firefighter. She doesn't seem like the kind of person who would take medicine without permission."

Priscilla believed Joan. But she also knew from her research that opioid addiction affected all kinds of people. That was part of what made it so dangerous. It seemed no one was immune.

"Do you know if she takes any medications?"

"I don't know," Joan said. "We're friendly at work, but we're not close enough that she tells me about her medical needs." She put the lid on the egg she was working on. "I hate to suspect her if there's nothing wrong. But since you asked, I just thought…"

"It can't hurt to do a little research on Michelle," Priscilla said. "We'll be discreet. There's probably no connection to the missing pilot, and then no one will ever know we looked into it."

"You're right," Joan said.

"What else can you tell me about her?"

"She eats a ham sandwich every day for lunch."

"Not sure what I can do with that."

"She wears a lot of dangly jewelry. She has hand cream that smells like lemons."

"Anything a bit more personal?"

"Hmm." Joan thought for a moment. "I know she's working on a children's book. She's a great artist, and she makes these really beautiful watercolor paintings. She's trying to learn about how to get such a thing published, and I think she's good enough."

"Hmm." A children's book. Priscilla could work with that.

"What are you thinking?"

"I'm thinking I need to pay Michelle a visit."

"Oh dear."

"I take it that means you're not interested in coming along?" Priscilla smiled at her cousin.

"I think I'd better sit this one out."

Priscilla understood completely. It could make work awkward for Joan if Michelle figured out the real reason for the visit. "That's fine. Do you have any idea where she lives?"

"There's a staff directory. I can look it up tomorrow."

"Perfect." Priscilla felt better already. Finally, a new clue to this puzzle.

CHAPTER THIRTEEN

By the time Priscilla showed up at Michelle Goldstein's door Saturday morning, she had a story prepared. Rachel had arrived on a late ferry last night, and she was sleeping in while Priscilla made this visit. She took a deep breath, rehearsed her spiel once more in her head, and then stepped out of her car. Michelle lived in a ranch-style home at the edge of Tisbury, in a neighborhood of modest homes. The houses were small and well-cared for, but Michelle's was different, Priscilla saw as she drove up. The dirt on one side of the house had been dug up—heavy machinery had to be involved, she was sure—and the outer wall of the house had been removed. The studs were covered in plastic sheeting. It was an odd time of year to be doing major renovations, Priscilla thought.

She walked up the cracked concrete driveway and saw that there was a brand-new SUV parked in the open garage. It was so new the license plate still bore the name of the dealer.

Home renovations and a brand-new SUV at the same time. Michelle must have come into some money.

She rang the doorbell and heard footsteps coming toward the door. It opened, and a preteen boy with sandy hair and braces stared at her.

"Hello, I'm Priscilla Grant, and I'm looking for Michelle Goldstein." She pasted a big smile on her face and tried to look friendly.

She was about to launch into her speech about why she was interested in Michelle, but the boy just turned and yelled, "Mom!" and walked away. Priscilla stood there, unsure what to do, until a moment later a woman in yoga pants and a baggy sweatshirt walked up.

"I'm so sorry," she said, shaking her head. "I swear I've tried my best to teach that kid manners, but it sure doesn't seem like it, does it?"

Priscilla smiled. Michelle seemed warm and friendly. She had shoulder-length brown hair and brown eyes, and she was probably in her late forties, if Priscilla had to guess.

"That's quite all right. I've raised a teenager myself," Priscilla said. "You can't make them do anything they don't want to do."

The woman laughed. "Isn't that the truth?" Then she gave Priscilla a quizzical look.

"I'm Priscilla Grant." She held out her hand. "I'm sorry to interrupt your Saturday morning, but I'm organizing an Easter egg hunt over at the Coast Guard station. In addition to the actual egg hunt, we wanted to have some activities for the kids."

It wasn't untrue. Chloe had wanted entertainment. Priscilla had run the idea of bringing in Michelle past Chloe last night and gotten an enthusiastic text back, with lots of exclamation points and a whole line of brand-new emojis. Priscilla took that to mean she liked the idea of an art demonstration for the children.

"Michelle." She stuck out her hand, and then gestured for Priscilla to come inside. Priscilla stepped in, and she saw that the kitchen, just off to the left, was also under construction, with cabinets half-assembled and plastic over the appliances.

"I'm sorry for the mess. We're in the middle of a renovation, as you might have guessed."

The new kitchen would have white wood cabinets and granite counters and stainless steel appliances, Priscilla saw. By contrast, the rest of the house looked a bit worn and tired, with stained carpet and furniture.

"That's quite all right. It looks like you're adding on to the house?" Priscilla said.

"Yes, that's the plan. Though I wouldn't recommend starting a project like that in March." She shook her head. "This is when the contractor was available, but I don't know. I think we're spending most of our renovation budget on heating at the moment."

"It's a big project," Priscilla said. She watched Michelle carefully.

"Yes, it is, but it's very much needed. We've been wanting to do this for a long time. With the boys getting bigger, this house is just too small for all of us."

"I'm sure it will be wonderful when it's all done," Priscilla said, and Michelle sighed.

"If we make it through it all, yes." She laughed. "Anyway, what can I help you with?"

Priscilla launched into her speech about wanting children's activities at the egg hunt and how she'd heard from her cousin Joan that Michelle was an artist who was working on a children's book. "I checked out your website, and your watercolor pictures are really beautiful," she said. "I was wondering if you might be willing to give a short art demonstration to the kids."

"Me?" Michelle seemed confused. "My children's books haven't been published. Wouldn't you want someone who's gotten their books published?"

Priscilla smiled. "From what I can tell, your art is wonderful."

"You are too kind." Michelle hesitated before asking, "Would you like to see my art in person before you decide?"

"Sure." Priscilla felt disingenuous, knowing there was no decision to be made. If Michelle was up for it, the gig was hers. But she followed Michelle into a small dining alcove off the kitchen. The area had a formal dining table and chairs, but they were pushed to the side, and most of the space was taken up by an easel and paints. Thick watercolor paper was scattered everywhere, depicting colorful paintings in various stages. Beyond the dining room was a living room, where the teenage boy was now sprawled on the couch, the television blaring some show that seemed to involve home videos.

"These are lovely!" The paintings showed cherry blossom trees in full bloom, some gathered around a pond. "That's Washington DC, right?"

"Exactly." Michelle nodded. "They're based on photographs I took during a trip a few years ago. We arrived at peak cherry blossom season."

Priscilla had never seen the district's famed cherry blossoms herself—and hadn't been to Washington DC since a school trip in eighth grade—but she knew they were an attraction that brought thousands to the nation's capital every spring.

"How did you get them to look so real?" Priscilla leaned in and studied one of the paintings. The tree branches, heavy with pink blossoms, almost seemed to come off the page.

"A lot of patience." Michelle laughed. "I add some paint, I wait for it to dry, I add more paint, I wait for it to dry."

"Well, it's beautiful," Priscilla said.

"And this is a series I was working on last week," Michelle said, indicating a stack of sheets of watercolor paper. The top painting was of a craggy gray mountain, surrounded by tall green trees.

"This is gorgeous."

"Thanks. These are based on old family photos my dad took on a trip to the White Mountains when I was a kid. I found the old slides recently and thought they were so pretty, I decided to try painting them." She shrugged. "And here are some pictures for the children's book I'm working on." She pointed to a series of pictures of a brown rabbit hopping through a beautifully detailed garden.

"After seeing this, I'm even more hopeful you'll come and do a demonstration at the festival," Priscilla said.

At first this had just been an excuse to get inside the house, but now that she'd seen how beautiful Michelle's artwork was, she really was hopeful she would come to the egg hunt.

"Really?"

"Really. The kids would love it."

"Let me talk to my husband," Michelle said. "Can I let you know?"

"Of course."

Priscilla thought quickly. Now that they had that out of the way, there was no reason for her to stick around. But she hadn't found out anything useful.

Michelle started to lead Priscilla toward the door, but Priscilla stopped in the entrance to the kitchen. "What a project," she said. She stepped into the kitchen and looked around. "It looks beautiful. Are those custom cabinets?"

One thing she'd learned through the years was that most people were happy to talk about their renovation projects—usually much more than most others wanted to hear about them.

"No, we got them at a great cabinet store in Hyannis," Michelle said. "They're even cheaper there than at the big box stores."

"I love white cabinets. And this granite is gorgeous." It was onyx, flecked with shades of gray and white. "I've been wanting to do some updates in my cottage, but it's ridiculous how much these things cost."

"Yes, it is really crazy," Michelle said. "We've been wanting to do this for a while, but we couldn't figure out how to make it happen." She ran a hand over the smooth granite countertop. "But my dad passed away last year, and I got a modest inheritance. I wanted to put it away for the boys' college, but my husband insisted that we needed more space if we were all going to survive the years until they go away to school, and I can't say I disagree."

"It looks like it's going to be beautiful." Priscilla spotted a stack of mail on the counter. Magazines and bills, it looked like.

"I sure hope so." Michelle gave her a smile. She looked at Priscilla, no doubt wondering what she was still doing here. Priscilla pretended not to notice.

"How long have you worked at the clinic?" She kept her voice upbeat, as if this was a totally normal visit between friends, not a desperately pathetic attempt at gathering intel.

"Over five years now, I guess," Michelle said.

"Do you like it?"

"Most of the time." Michelle leaned back against the counter. "Of course, what I'd really love to do is sell my book and quit my job, but until that happens, it's a fine job. The people are nice."

Based on what Priscilla had heard about publishing, she thought it was unlikely Michelle would be able to quit her job even if she did manage to get her book published, but she didn't say that. Instead, she said, "Joan really likes it too. Although she's been sort of frustrated recently. She said something about new rules for accessing the medicine cabinet making things difficult."

"Oh yes," Michelle said. Did she flinch? Priscilla was certain she saw something flit across Michelle's face, but she wasn't sure how to read it. "It's added an extra step. But it's necessary, I think, given the situation."

"You mean the big theft of medicine from the hospital?"

"That, and just the cost of drugs these days. It's insane. People get desperate. And then some of them are so easy to get hooked on…" Something passed across her face again, but Priscilla couldn't read it. "You have to be careful."

Was she speaking from experience here? Was that what she meant?

Just then, she heard a door open, followed by a childish voice. "—and one of the guys said there was blood all over everything but nobody was there!"

A boy of about ten came in wearing a soccer uniform, followed by a man.

"Hello," the man said, smiling at Priscilla.

"James, this is Priscilla." Michelle gestured at her. "This is my husband and our son Miles."

"Nice to meet you." James held out his hand. "Miles and I were just discussing that downed plane they found this week. Seems the kids on the soccer team have their own theory about what happened. I think it mostly has to do with a lot of knives and maybe a ghost or two."

"Dad, you don't know, it could be true." Miles spotted his brother on the couch and hustled to plop down beside him.

"How was the game?" Michelle asked.

"They lost. Otherwise, he'd still be talking about it," James said.

Michelle laughed. "I'm not surprised the kids are making up their own versions of what could have happened to the pilot of that plane. The police don't seem to be any closer to knowing anything."

James put the soccer ball he'd been carrying on the kitchen counter. "If you ask me, I say they should be looking for someone who was a pilot in the military. It took a lot of skill to crash-land a small plane and be able to walk away from it." He turned to his wife. "I'm gonna catch a shower, then how about we hit Bobby B's for lunch?"

Priscilla could see that she was in the way, and she couldn't think of any other way to stay without coming across as really invasive. "I'll get out of your hair," she said, and started to move toward the door. "But let me know about the Easter egg hunt."

"I will. Thank you." Michelle walked toward the front door, and Priscilla had no choice but to follow her. She said goodbye and then headed back to her car and started for home. She thought through the conversation as she drove. Was Michelle involved in the medicine theft? Even if she was, did that mean she was tied up in the smuggling? Priscilla had no idea. She replayed the conversation the whole way home, thinking it through from every angle, and came to the conclusion that she'd learned nothing.

Well, it hadn't been a complete waste of a morning, Priscilla realized. If nothing else, she might have a wonderful artist to do a painting demonstration at the Easter egg hunt.

When she got home, Rachel was awake and on the phone with the caterer for the wedding, talking through appetizer options. Priscilla let her be and did some chores around the house, and then when Rachel went for a run, she got to work on a Bakewell tart. Gail was having the cousins over for dinner that night, and Priscilla had promised to bring dessert. She'd seen this tart on the *Great British Baking Show*, and had wanted to try it for herself, so she spent the next few hours making an impossibly complicated series of jams, frostings, and pastry. When she finished, she had to admit that the pink and white design she'd made on top didn't look quite as nice as the one they did on the show, but overall the tart didn't look bad.

"It looks great, Mom," Rachel said. She was eating a container of yogurt, and nodded encouragingly at Priscilla's attempt at dessert.

"It's a little lopsided," Priscilla had to admit. "But hopefully it will taste good."

After she'd cleaned up the kitchen and changed, she still had a while before they needed to head to Gail's. Her mind wandered back to the mystery of the missing pilot. It felt like there were so many pieces that didn't fit together to make a complete puzzle. What did Eric Ivans know about who had taken his plane? How had Dennis Reid's pill bottle gotten into the plane? What did the words in the notebook mean—and what were the other words she couldn't make out? Was Michelle involved in all this? And—most importantly— what had happened to the pilot, and why had he vanished?

Priscilla was just going around in circles. Maybe the FBI had come up with answers. She would ask A.J. when she saw him tonight. Gail had invited him and Rachel to join in the gathering, since they were in town. She doubted A.J. would be able to tell her much, though, even if he had found anything.

Priscilla sat down on the couch and thought through her visit to Michelle's this morning. She played back every part of the visit again, trying to figure out if there was anything she'd missed. Was Michelle somehow connected with all of this? As she went back over everything in her mind, she realized something. She hadn't figured out whether Michelle was involved in taking prescription medication, but there was something she'd heard there that maybe she could use.

James had said that the downed pilot had probably been in the military. She had some names that she could check—and she already knew that Eric Ivans flew planes in the military. He couldn't possibly be the injured pilot, but... What if one of his buddies in the picture in his office was?

She grabbed her computer and opened up a new browser window. She pulled up Dennis Reid's obituary again and wrote down his grandsons' names: Luke Coombs and Ryan Reid. If those names didn't produce any clues, she'd look up the granddaughters. Nobody said the injured pilot was a man.

Priscilla had just typed Luke's name into the browser when there was a knock at the door. A.J. must be here. She would need to find out more about the grandsons later. For now, she grabbed a jacket and the tart, called for Rachel, and headed for the door.

Gail had made spring pea tarts for dinner, declaring them aspirational at this point in the year, and after a loud and boisterous meal, the whole family was gathered in the living room, balancing plates of Bakewell tart on their laps. Gail's living room was crowded but comfortable, stuffed with lots of furniture including her mother's player piano and her grandmother's rocker, in which Priscilla now sat.

"This is really good," Gail said to Priscilla. "Thank you for bringing it."

"Thank you for having us all over."

"Thank you for coming," Uncle Hugh said. He was sitting on the couch with a wool blanket over his legs. He looked tired, and Priscilla wasn't sure how long he would last tonight. "It's nice to have company."

"It's nice to not have to cook," Trudy said.

"It's nice to not have to eat your cooking," Trudy's husband, Dan, said wryly.

They all laughed. Trudy gave Dan a good-natured elbow to the ribs, and then conversation turned to what had brought A.J. to the island.

"You're investigating that plane, aren't you?" Trudy asked.

"I'm not at liberty to say." A.J. must get tired of giving that same answer, but he didn't show it. He had a smile on his face.

"Do you know what happened to the pilot?" Gail asked.

"If Priscilla doesn't know yet, the FBI doesn't know," Uncle Hugh said. "She's always smarter than the authorities when it comes to stuff like this."

A.J. laughed again, and she was grateful for his easygoing nature.

"Uncle Hugh," Priscilla admonished him, "you know that's not true."

"I'm afraid I'm not at liberty to say anything about the pilot," A.J. said.

"What can you say?" Dan said. "There has to be something you can tell us."

A.J. cocked his head, thinking for a minute, and then said, "I can tell you they've determined the plane went down due to mechanical failure. It looks like something went wrong with the engine."

This was news. "Really?"

"That's what was determined today." He shrugged. "That's not classified though. You'll probably read it in tomorrow's paper."

Priscilla mulled that over. A.J.'s next words brought her back to the present.

"I also wouldn't get in trouble if I tell you the plane is being removed tomorrow," he said. "That's not classified information either."

"How in the world will they do that?" Hugh asked.

"A really big crane?" A.J shrugged. "I'm not sure, to be honest."

"How in the world would you even get a crane back there?" Trudy said.

"They don't make cranes that big," Dan insisted.

Priscilla laughed as her future son-in-law deflected more of their questions, but her mind was elsewhere again. If the plane was being removed in the morning, she thought, that meant she was running out of time.

It was late when A.J. dropped Priscilla and Rachel back off at her cottage. The house was still, and you could hear the waves crashing

against the rocks along the shore far below. The rhythmic turn of the strobe from the top of the lighthouse lit up the yard for moments at a time, and then, between each turn, the area descended into darkness again.

Rachel yawned and headed directly into the guest room. Priscilla knew she should get to bed too. She had church in the morning. The Palm Sunday service was always well attended, and she would be too tired to enjoy it if she didn't get to bed soon.

But she also knew she wouldn't be able to sleep until she knew more about Dennis's grandsons. So Priscilla sat back down on the couch with her laptop and pulled the wool blanket over her. Jake down next to her, and within a few moments, his soft breathing was the only sound. She'd already learned a fair bit about Luke, so now she did a search for the name Ryan Reid, and she clicked open the first link, which was a profile on a career site.

Priscilla stared at the screen. She couldn't be seeing that right. She blinked and then held the screen closer.

She was seeing it correctly. And she couldn't believe it.

CHAPTER FOURTEEN

Sunday morning, Priscilla got up just as the sun rose over the horizon. The morning was cold and the air was clammy, so she put on her thickest wool sweater and pulled on her heavy jacket. Rachel was still sleeping. Good for her, Priscilla thought. Let her enjoy it before the whirlwind of the wedding. Priscilla didn't disturb her, and after a quick breakfast, a cup of coffee, and some time in prayer, she took Jake for a short walk on the beach. The sea was moody and gray, reflecting the hazy gray of the low sky. She'd just gotten Jake settled in the house and grabbed her jacket when Rachel came out of the guest room. "Mom? You going somewhere?"

Priscilla smiled at her groggy daughter. "I thought I'd head out to see the plane one last time before they cart it away."

Rachel's eyes widened, and she came to life. "Count me in— just give me a couple of minutes, and I'll be ready."

"If you're sure," Priscilla said doubtfully. "You'll need to wear boots or some sturdy shoes. Did you bring any?"

Rachel rolled her eyes. "Mom. Please. I'm a Kansas farm girl. Do you even have to ask?"

Priscilla laughed. Sure enough, it was only a couple of minutes before Rachel was by her side, boots on and travel mug of coffee in hand. Priscilla knew she'd raised that girl right.

They climbed into her car and headed west, toward the wooded marshy area where she and Gerald had found the plane.

Rachel took a swig of her coffee. "So, Mom, what're you hoping to find out here? Anything in particular you're looking for?"

Priscilla thought about the question. What *was* she looking for? She wasn't sure exactly what she was hoping to find. In the five days since the plane had been found, there had no doubt been dozens of police officers, FBI agents, reporters, and curious onlookers in the area around where the plane had crashed, all of them looking for clues about the missing pilot. She knew the chances were minuscule that she would find something that had been overlooked by the others.

She shook her head. "I guess I'm not really sure. Maybe I just need to see it again, to remind myself that it's real. That, after all the searches I've done and the places I've been, there really is a plane that crashed and a pilot who vanished. That all of this isn't one big figment of my imagination."

She parked at the bend in the road where she and Gerald had parked before. This time, there were plenty of tire marks and patches of flattened grass to mark the spot. She pulled her coat closer, tugged her hat down onto her head, and she and Rachel stepped out of the car. It wasn't hard to find the trail. What had been a GPS-guided trek through the trees was now a defined path, and after a ten-minute hike, they easily found the plane.

There it was, just where it had been. The nose was digging into the ground, the propeller was snapped off. The tail was still caught high in the trees. The whole area was cordoned off with caution tape. She wondered how they were going to get the thing out of here.

Rachel whistled. "Wow. You weren't kidding, Mom. How could a person just vanish after crashing like that? No wonder you want to find the pilot."

"It seems unbelievable, doesn't it?" Priscilla felt a bit of vindication from Rachel's words, and was glad she'd wanted to come.

"Can we look in the cockpit?" Rachel was standing on her tiptoes, trying to see as much of the plane as she could.

"No, we better not. We shouldn't cross the crime tape. Besides, with my luck, I'd get stuck up there, and they'd have to use the crane to get *me* down."

Rachel laughed. "I guess we'll just have to stay on the ground, then."

Priscilla said a silent prayer for the pilot, whoever he was, and turned to look around the scene. What had been a patch of wooded forest a few days ago had become ground zero for the search, and there were footprints in the spongy earth fanning out in all directions. She and Rachel circled the site, dodging around trees to take in the glistening silver skin of the aircraft. Priscilla walked around the plane to study it from the other side, but nothing revealed itself.

She stepped around a tree and ventured a few feet into the forest on the far side of the plane, away from the road. She was sure the entire area had been canvassed, but she walked a few feet into the trees anyway. Pines and oaks stood tall and proud, mixed here and there with beech and maple. She walked for a few minutes, searching for...she didn't even know what. There were footprints in the soft soil, but there was no way to know who they belonged to. Probably investigators, she thought.

She then turned back around and made her way back to the plane, and then stepped out in a different direction, wandering a few feet into the forest. She stepped over roots and ducked under branches, but after a few minutes, she turned around and headed back. If any clue had been left behind, it was long gone. She made her way back toward the plane, but as she got closer, something in one of the trees caught her eye. A flash of white, caught on a branch. A bud?

But no, Priscilla realized. That was an oak, not a magnolia or cherry tree.

"Rachel," she called. "Come look at this."

It was probably nothing. But still, Rachel joined her, and they moved closer to take a look. They stood under it, as close as they could get.

Rachel tilted her head. "It looks like a piece of paper."

Priscilla thought so too. "It does. But what are the chances it has anything to do with the pilot?"

Rachel grinned at her. "There's only one way to find out."

Priscilla stood under the tree, weighing their options. The scrap was caught most of the way out on a branch at least ten feet in the air. She looked around. There was no ladder, no stepstool. Rachel was right. If they wanted to check it out, one of them was going to have to climb.

Priscilla walked to the tree trunk.

"Mom! You can't possibly think I'm going to let you climb that tree." Rachel was gaping at her. "You're almost sixty years old! You'll break your neck."

Priscilla frowned at her. "I'll have you know I've climbed many a taller tree. I spent half my childhood swinging from trees around the farm. My muscles will remember what to do. Besides, you have a wedding coming up. Can't you just see yourself on crutches, with a big ol' cast on your leg, walking down the aisle to A.J.?"

Rachel clamped her mouth shut, intertwined her fingers, and held out her hands to give Priscilla a boost.

Pricsilla set her foot in Rachel's hands and reached for the lowest branch. It was still more than a foot above her head. She wrapped her arms around the trunk and used her legs to push herself higher. She shimmied up a little way, and then she was finally able to reach for the low branch.

"I'm glad it's only you seeing this display," she gasped to Rachel as she used every ounce of strength in her arms to pull herself up so the top of her body hung over the branch. Then, steadying herself carefully, she pulled her feet up, reached up for the next branch, and pulled herself up. There. The paper was caught halfway down this branch.

"You're doing great, Mom. Please, be careful."

She glanced down at Rachel, and the ground swayed beneath her. Goodness. She was never afraid of heights as a child, but apparently more than her body had changed since then. She forced herself to keep her eyes up, and slowly, painstakingly, edged her way out toward the paper. The branches were sturdy, and though the one she was on bent under her weight, it wasn't going to snap. At least, she didn't think so.

"After all this, that paper better have some connection to the plane," Rachel said.

She was...almost...There. She grabbed for the paper, managed to snag it with two fingers, and then moved herself back toward the trunk of the tree.

"Way to go, Mom!" Rachel cheered. "Hopefully another clue."

Well, yes, but first, Priscilla had to get down from this tree without killing herself. She tucked the paper into her jacket pocket and carefully reached down for the branch she was standing on. She lowered herself until she was sitting on it. She'd forgotten that getting up was the easy part. Getting down was always trickier.

She edged her way out a few feet, and then, slowly, she gripped the branch with all her might and swung her body down so she was hanging from the branch. She hung only a few feet from the ground now, and, with a quick prayer for safety, she let go.

She hit the ground hard. She'd be sore tomorrow, for sure.

Rachel ran up to her. "Why didn't you tell me you were going to let go? I was going to help you! Are you all right? Did you break anything?"

Priscilla stood up...very slowly. "Yes, I'm fine. No, I didn't break anything. And the important thing is, you will walk down the aisle with all your limbs intact and working."

She pulled the paper from her pocket and smoothed it out.

Right away she noticed one thing. This paper was the same size as the pages of the notebook she'd found in the plane. It was lined the same way, and the ragged edge made it seem as though it had been torn from a spiral notebook. It was worn, as though it had been outside for a while—which she supposed it had, whether or not it was associated with the plane. But when she unfolded it, all it had written on it was an incomprehensible string of numbers.

Rachel was looking over her shoulder and read them off. "41.387258 -70.470207. What is it, a math problem?"

"I have no earthly idea. But look, the numbers are written in the same shade of blue as the other pages, and the handwriting looks the same."

"Is this something you'll have to give to A.J.?"

"Yes, I'm sure I'll have to turn it over to someone."

"Let's take a picture of it first. Do you have your phone?"

"Excellent idea, honey!" Priscilla pulled her phone out of her pocket and took a picture of the paper. "I knew there was a reason I brought you along." She grinned at Rachel, who wrinkled her nose at her in return.

She knew she would need to turn the paper in to the authorities. And she also knew once she did, she wouldn't see it again. Well, there was no cell signal out here to tell anyone about it. It would have to wait until she got to the car.

Priscilla tucked the paper back into the pocket of her jacket and she and Rachel made their way back through the woods, following the now-worn path. When they made it back to the car, she pulled her phone out again and looked at it.

"Who are you going to call?" Rachel asked. "Did you decide who to give the paper to?"

Priscilla's fingers hovered over her phone. "I'm just not sure if I should call Gerald or A.J. or the police." Her first instinct was to call Gerald. But she was still nursing a bit of hurt where he was concerned and didn't want to hear what he thought of her snooping around the crash site. Maybe she should tell A.J. first.

"It's Sunday morning," Rachel pointed out. "Surely they won't do a whole lot about it until later today anyway."

Priscilla looked at her phone a moment longer and then decided Rachel was right. She'd worry about it later. Besides, she had something else in mind for today . . . and it didn't involve anyone who wanted her to leave it to the professionals.

A few hours later, Priscilla and Rachel made their way up the aisle and out the doors of the sanctuary into the church foyer, where Pastor Curt waited to greet everyone who walked out.

"That was a wonderful service," Priscilla said, shaking his hand.

"Thank you." He gave her a warm smile. She wanted to say more, like how much she appreciated him agreeing to tell the Easter story at the egg hunt, but there was a line of people behind her, so instead she simply said, "This is my daughter, Rachel."

"Rachel. Delighted to meet you," Curt said. He shook her hand.

"It's great to meet you. That was a beautiful service," Rachel said.

Priscilla and Rachel headed down the stairs to the fellowship hall. It *had* been a lovely Palm Sunday service, focusing on Jesus's triumphal entry into Jerusalem, and they'd sung some of Priscilla's favorite hymns, including "All Glory, Laud, and Honor" and "Lift Up Your Heads, Ye Mighty Gates." And now, Priscilla could see, the children were continuing the annual Holy Week tradition of batting each other with palm fronds.

Rachel went off to get a cup of coffee, and Priscilla spotted Joan on the far side of the room, chatting with Teresa Claybrook. Priscilla started toward her but was stopped when Gerald appeared at her side.

"Hi," he said. He gave her a smile, wide and genuine.

"Oh. Hi, Gerald."

"How are you?"

"I'm all right." Priscilla wasn't quite sure what to say, but he didn't seem to recognize her hesitation. "And you?"

"Just fine. I spent time with Aggie and her family last night. Ava is saying a few words, including Pop Pop." He was beaming, just thinking about it.

"That's wonderful. It must have been fun to see them."

"It sure was. But seeing you is just as nice." She couldn't detect any hesitation or reticence in his voice. "That is a lovely dress."

"Oh. Thank you." Was she imagining it? Did he really not feel the tension between them? Or was he just doing a good job of ignoring it, of trying to get past it? "It's an old one." She held out the skirt of the sprigged green and white dress. Wearing it made it seem like spring, even if the thermometer didn't agree.

"Well, it's lovely." He looped his arm through hers. "Now, do you have any plans for brunch? I'd love to take you and Rachel out."

Priscilla hesitated. Usually, after-church brunch with Gerald would be the highlight of her week. But today, she had other plans.

"I can't today," she said. "I'm sorry."

A look of confusion crossed Gerald's face. "You have other plans?" The fact that he seemed so surprised made her sure he hadn't picked up on the fact that she was upset.

"I'm afraid we do." At the wounded look on his face, a part of her wanted to explain, but she knew he wouldn't approve, would probably try to stop her, and she wasn't going to let her plan get derailed today.

"Oh."

She felt a twinge of guilt, seeing how disappointed he was. But frustration, hurt, and disappointment quickly crowded in, and she couldn't find the words to explain the emotions that had characterized their interactions the past few days.

"Dinner, then?"

He looked so hopeful, and if she was honest, a part of her wanted to say yes. To have dinner plans to look forward to, and spend some time with him tonight. But Rachel had decided to stay the night and leave on the first ferry out in the morning, so she'd invited A.J. over to have dinner with them.

"How about lunch tomorrow?" She had thought the offer would be a way of making him realize she still wanted to see him, but she could see that it had the opposite effect.

"Sure," he said. He was smiling, but his eyes told a different story. *Crestfallen* was the word that came to mind. She felt bad... But she also felt frustrated. What did he expect? He'd not believed her. He'd asked her to work on the Easter egg hunt with him and then handed it off to a twenty-something sorority girl to organize. He'd undermined her investigation. He'd claimed he was just protecting her, but didn't he see how belittling it was to treat her as if she was so vulnerable all the time? To assume she couldn't take care of herself?

Her frustrations from the past week all came rushing back. She was sorry if he was hurt that she had plans today, but she wasn't going to go along with what he wanted just to make things peaceful. Rachel would be proud of her, Priscilla thought.

"Great. Tomorrow, then," she said, and smiled again. "I'm sorry to run, but I need to get going."

Gerald nodded, and she hurried off across the room, threading her way toward her daughter. Rachel, who had been caught by Eldora Preston, was looking around the room, a little bit wild-eyed, searching for an escape.

"Ready to go, Rachel?" Priscilla came up to her.

"Looks like I have to run," Rachel said to Eldora. "It was nice talking to you." They stepped away, and as soon as they were out of earshot, she whispered, "Thank you."

"Eldora is lonely," Priscilla said, though that still didn't excuse her habit of spreading nasty gossip about people. "But my interruption wasn't entirely selfless. We need to hurry if we're going to catch the ferry."

They climbed into the car and drove toward the ferry, and she mentally calculated whether they had time to stop to give A.J. the piece of paper she'd found in the plane, but decided they didn't.

A.J. would be at the crash site all day, and that was in the opposite direction. She would deliver the paper later. She felt just the tiniest twinge of guilt that she hadn't given the paper to Gerald, but managed to convince herself that church wasn't the place to discuss his work. They made it to the ferry, got their tickets, and got seats only minutes before the boat pulled away from the dock.

On the now-familiar ride across the Bay, Rachel read a book, just like she'd done every spare moment when she was a child. The girl had always kept the local library in business. Priscilla had a book in her purse, and she thought about pulling it out, but she was distracted. She thought through everything she knew about Ryan Reid, and she became even more convinced that she was headed in the right direction. When she'd pulled up Ryan's profile on that site last night, her heart had just about stopped. He was a veteran. An air force pilot. Flew F-16s. In the Middle East. And his squadron was the Gamblers, aka the 77th Fighter Squadron. So now the question in her mind was, how far would a man go to help his buddy?

When the boat docked in Woods Hole, she and Rachel got the car out and drove up through the Cape and over the bridge again. This whole journey was becoming familiar. Rachel helped her navigate once they got off the main highway in New Bedford, and a little while later, they pulled up in front of a house on the outskirts of town. Priscilla hadn't spent much time in the old whaling city, but much of it looked like it had seen better days. The downtown was populated by a number of old brick buildings that must have once been magnificent but now seemed down at the heels. The address she'd found for Ryan took them to a duplex along a street of identical houses. His half was painted gray while the other side was painted a bright yellow. Priscilla climbed the narrow concrete steps and rang the doorbell. She held her breath, but there was no answer. She rang the bell again. There were no lights on inside.

"It doesn't look like he's here," Rachel said, pointing to the mail box, which was overflowing with magazines and envelopes.

"Hello?" Priscilla called, this time rapping on the glass of the small window in the door. "Ryan?"

Still there was no answer. Had she come all this way for nothing? Priscilla leaned forward and peered in the glass. There was a small living room with clunky furniture, and what looked like an efficiency kitchen down the hall.

"He's not there."

Priscilla leaned back and turned to see a woman about her age standing in the open doorway of the other side of the duplex. She wore sweat pants and a Patriots sweat shirt, and her hair was dyed an improbable shade of platinum. She held a lit cigarette between her fingers.

"Is this where Ryan Reid lives?" Priscilla asked.

"Yep. But he's not there." She looked at Priscilla, then at Rachel. "Ain't been around for nearly a week."

"Oh." Priscilla did the mental math. She'd seen the plane go down on Monday. The timing worked. "Do you have any idea where he might have gone?"

"Nope. Sorry. We mostly keep to ourselves around here." The woman now looked Priscilla up and down. "Why? He owe you something?"

"No, I was just hoping to talk to him." Priscilla hoped she could get some information from this friendly woman. "Has he ever gone away like this before?"

"Oh, sure. He disappears for a few days here and there, but this is longer than usual." The woman took a drag on the cigarette, and the smell of smoke wafted toward Priscilla. She forced herself not to wrinkle her nose. "Have to say, I don't really mind when he's gone. No more people coming in and out at all hours. Though you all don't look like his typical visitors."

"Oh?" Rachel said. "What are his visitors usually like?"

The woman shrugged and lowered the cigarette. "Big guys, mostly. He was in the military at some point, so I think they're friends from there, maybe."

"Have you ever talked to him about his military experience?" Priscilla asked.

"Nope. Just seen the sticker on his car."

"What sticker?"

"He's got an air force sticker on the back of his car. My dad was in the air force, so I know it when I see it." She took another drag of her cigarette. "Plus he's got that big, buff look like all the military guys have, and the tattoos."

Priscilla glanced at Rachel. She wasn't sure everyone in the military had muscles and tattoos, but neither said so.

"What kind of car is it?"

"Toyota Highlander. Black." She blew out a puff of smoke. Priscilla took a step back. "We share a driveway—" She used her cigarette to indicate a narrow cement strip on her side of the house.

"So I'm always having to go around it. Don't know why he can't get a smaller car so's it'd be easier for me."

"Is the car here?"

"Nope. Been gone since Monday too."

Priscilla made mental notes. "What's he like as a neighbor?"

The woman shrugged. "Quiet, mostly. Keeps to himself, like I said. Except for the people coming and going at all hours, he's fine. Better than the couple that was here before. The baby screamed all night, and the parents didn't do a thing about it."

Priscilla gave what she hoped was a sympathetic smile. "Do you know what he does for a living?"

She knew from his online profile that he worked in IT at a local company, but she wanted to hear what this woman said.

"I think some kind of office job. Not sure."

"Do you know if he ever flew a small plane?" Rachel asked.

The woman laughed, a phlegmy, coarse laugh, and then coughed for a minute. She pounded on her chest and shook her head. "No, I'm afraid there aren't many of us around here who can afford a private jet these days."

Priscilla thanked the woman and reached into her purse to pull out a pen and a small notebook.

"If you do hear from Ryan, or if he comes back, I would really love to speak with him." She ripped a paper from the notebook, scribbled her name and phone number on it, and handed it to the woman.

"All right." She looked at the paper dubiously. Priscilla doubted she'd actually get a call, but thanked the woman again anyway.

Then she headed back out to her car and sat in the driver's seat for a moment, considering her next step.

It all checked out. The time he'd been missing; the experience as an air force pilot; the people coming and going at all hours. What else could that mean, aside from selling drugs?

"Do you have time to make a stop?" Priscilla asked.

"Sure." Rachel shrugged.

Priscilla set her GPS to lead her to the New Bedford airport again. This time, she drove directly to the small parking lot. She took a ticket from the automated machine in the entrance booth and drove around the lot, searching for a Toyota. There, at the end of the first row, she saw it. A black Toyota Highlander. With a sticker on the back window. She put her car in Park, and she and Rachel climbed out to take a closer look. She quickly saw that the sticker showed the familiar air force insignia.

"This is his car, isn't it?" Rachel said.

Priscilla nodded. This was it. This had to be it. She walked around to the front of the car and looked at the small piece of paper on the dashboard, the same kind she'd taken from the machine when she pulled into the lot. This one was stamped on Monday at 11:17 am. Ryan's car had been parked there since Monday.

Priscilla felt a rush of adrenaline. It was Ryan. The pilot *had* to be Ryan. She climbed back into her car, paid the seventy-five-cent fee, and made her way out of the airport. But instead of heading back toward the Cape, she typed another address into her GPS. It was shocking how easy it was, nowadays, to find personal information about people online. Since it was a Sunday, she figured he wouldn't be at the college, and she decided to try her luck here. A few minutes later, she pulled into the parking lot of a newer apartment building that overlooked the New Bedford waterfront.

"Nice place," Rachel said.

Priscilla agreed. It was all glass and steel, and even though it wasn't Priscilla's style, she could imagine it was popular with the younger crowd.

Once upon a time, New Bedford had been one of the biggest whaling centers in the world, Priscilla remembered as she made her way toward the door of the high-rise. She wondered what those old whaling captains would think of this place now.

Glass doors led into the lobby, where they found a panel of buttons with names and numbers. They found the name they were looking for toward the bottom of the panel. There was a little fish-eye camera monitoring the small lobby.

Priscilla groaned when she saw the camera. "He's not going to let us in."

Rachel shook her head. "We're not going to call his apartment."

"But how are we going to—"

"Just watch."

They waited by the glass exterior doors until someone came out. Rachel caught the door and gestured for Priscilla to go through.

"See?" Rachel said. "Now, what apartment?"

They took the elevator to the third floor. Apartment 3J was at the end of the hallway, which was carpeted in gray and painted a soft shade of white. Priscilla pressed the doorbell and waited. A moment later, the metal door opened, and Eric Ivans stood there in jeans and a T-shirt. "You're not the pizza guy."

"No, I'm Priscilla Grant. We met the other day. And this is my daughter, Rachel." Priscilla stepped forward into the doorway so he couldn't shut her out. She watched his face change as recognition dawned.

"What are you doing here?" He looked from Priscilla to Rachel and back again.

"We came to find out why you said you didn't know who took your plane when we both know it was Ryan Reid," Rachel said.

For a moment, he didn't seem to know how to respond. He opened his mouth and then closed it again.

"I assume you must get a cut from whatever he gets paid from smuggling, right? Or are you more involved than that?" Priscilla said.

Part of Priscilla couldn't believe the words that were coming out of her mouth. A glance at her daughter told her Rachel must be having the same reaction. When did she get so bold? But at the same time, she recognized what it was that was making her brave—anger. He'd lied to her. He'd lied to the FBI. She had known he knew more than he'd said, and the look on his face now told her everything he hadn't. He knew what was going on, and yet he'd kept his mouth shut, and she wanted to know why.

He looked up and down the hallway, and then stepped back. "Why don't you two come in?"

Priscilla hesitated. Was this a trap? Did she really want to be three stories up inside an apartment building with this man? He was ex-military. He was strong, and he knew how to use weapons.

How thick were these walls? Would the neighbors even hear her scream? There were two of them, but could Priscilla really put her daughter into this kind of danger?

"I'm not going to hurt you," he said. "I just don't want the neighbors to hear you talk about smuggling and get the wrong impression. I'll sit on the other side of the room, and you both can sit here, near the door. You can even leave it unlatched if it would make you feel safer."

Priscilla agreed and stepped inside, Rachel just a step behind. She looked around. To her left was a small kitchen with chiseled wood cabinets and stainless steel appliances and marble counters. Beyond the breakfast bar was the living room, lined with floor-to-ceiling windows on one end, with a breathtaking view of the harbor. To the left was a short hallway that she assumed went to the bedroom. The furniture had an almost Scandinavian simplicity, all wood and white fabrics, and the apartment was meticulously neat. There was a college basketball game playing silently on the flat screen hanging on the wall.

"This is really nice," Rachel said.

"Thanks." There was no emotion in his voice. And then, "Where is he?"

"Where is who?" Priscilla couldn't have heard that right.

"Where is Ryan?" Eric asked. "Do you know?"

If Priscilla didn't know better, she would say he almost sounded...worried.

"Surely you know the answer to that," Priscilla said. "You tell me. Where is he?"

"You don't know, then." Some kind of energy seemed to drain from him. She realized, with a start, that it had been hope.

"No, I don't know where he is," Priscilla said. "I was assuming you did."

He lowered himself onto one of the stools at the breakfast bar.

"You told me you didn't know who took your plane," Priscilla said. "But it sounds like you knew all along who it was."

Eric looked down at the counter for a moment, and then he shook his head.

"Who are you again?" he said quietly.

"Just a person who's concerned about Ryan. I'm afraid he might be hurt and unable to get help." While she feared this might cause Eric to clam up, she decided honesty was the best policy. It always was.

"And I'm her daughter."

Priscilla was glad Rachel didn't mention that she was engaged to the FBI officer investigating the case.

"I saw the plane going down, and I called it in," Priscilla said. "No one believed me, so I went out and looked for it, and I helped find it. So you might say I'm personally invested in the outcome, though I'm not connected to law enforcement."

He didn't say anything for a moment. Then, he took a deep breath.

"I didn't know the plane was gone until the FBI showed up at my office asking about it." He ran his hand through his hair and looked at her. "Can you imagine? I'm at my desk, working on my lecture, and the FBI shows up, and they want to know why my plane is nose-down in a forest on Martha's Vineyard?"

"So you had no idea how it ended up there?" Rachel said.

"Not at first, no. I was completely blindsided. But once I had a moment to think about it, I realized there was really only one possibility."

"Ryan," Priscilla said.

"Ryan." He pointed to the other stools, gesturing for them to sit down. Priscilla had lost her wariness, and she nodded at Rachel. They perched on the stools, putting their purses on the counter.

"I assume you've tried calling his phone?" Priscilla said.

"It goes straight to voice mail." He shook his head. "Which either means it's been destroyed or he turned it off because he doesn't want to be found."

"Maybe the battery's dead?" Priscilla suggested.

"We grew up together. Best friends all through school. Joined the Air Force together. We ended up in the same squadron, but different flights. We both ended up getting certified to fly. We got out around the same time and both moved back to the area."

"When did you get a plane?"

"A few years ago. My dad was an aircraft technician—he fixed planes—so I was around them my whole life. I've always loved them, and I'd always wanted to have my own someday."

"Why didn't you become a pilot when you got out? Like, for an airline?" Rachel said.

"Oh, those jobs are awful. You're traveling all the time, always sleeping in some hotel room, always dealing with cranky passengers. I didn't want that. I just wanted the freedom to fly when I wanted, where I wanted. Just to get up into the sky and go. Have either one of you ever been in a small plane?"

They both shook their heads.

"There's nothing like it. The freedom, the control…The sky just opens up, and the world is spread out before you." He shook his head. "It's what freedom feels like."

"It sounds wonderful." Actually, small planes sounded like death traps to her, especially after seeing the wreckage in the forest, but, hearing him describe it, Priscilla could see why people seemed to find them appealing.

"Anyway. My dad passed away a few years ago, and I knew I should do something more practical with the inheritance he left me, but I also knew what he would have wanted me to do with it."

"You bought a plane."

"Not just any plane. A new Cirrus SR22."

She could see she was supposed to be impressed by this.

"You don't know airplanes," he said.

She shook her head.

"It's a good plane. A great plane. The best for the price. It was beautiful."

Priscilla nodded. She'd seen it in the air. "It was nice."

"Yeah. Well." He let out a long breath. "'Was' is the operative word, I suppose." He didn't say anything for a moment. "But he must be okay, right? He walked away from the crash?"

"We assume he must have been well enough to leave the crash," Priscilla said. She didn't mention the other gruesome possibility—that someone had removed him.

"And there's been no sign of him?" Eric knew the answer, she could see, but still held out hope.

"I'm afraid not." Priscilla watched as a player dunked the basketball on the muted television screen. "Had Ryan flown your plane before?"

"Yes, although always with my permission. Well, at least he got my permission every time that I know of."

"Did you go with him? Or did you just let him borrow your plane?"

"At first I would go with him." He shrugged. "But a few times he wanted to go while I was teaching, or I didn't have the time, so I let him use it. He's a pilot. He knows what he's doing. He doesn't need me making sure he's all right." Then, after a moment, "Well, at least I didn't think he did."

"They think it was mechanical failure that caused the plane to go down," Rachel said. "It wasn't anything he did wrong."

Eric nodded, but didn't answer.

"Do you know where he went?" Priscilla asked gently. "When he flew your plane in the past?"

"He always told me where he was planning to go."

The way he said that made Priscilla wonder.

"But you had doubts?"

Eric stretched his legs out in front of him. "The last time I used the plane, the navigation system told me the previous flight had been to Martha's Vineyard. Ryan told me he'd gone to New Jersey to see his dad for the day."

"So he lied to you about where he'd gone."

"He insisted it was a glitch in the system. But those systems don't mess up. Not like that."

"Do you have any idea what he was really doing on Martha's Vineyard?"

"No." He shook his head. "He denied everything. So I said he couldn't use the plane again."

"Ah." Priscilla saw what had happened now. "So this time, he simply took it without asking."

"It would appear so."

"And could he really just walk into the airport and take off with it?"

"I guess. I would have thought security would be tighter at the hangar, but it appears he was able to. It does make me wonder if I might have to move the plane to a different hangar." He gave a sad sort of laugh. "Well, actually I guess I won't have to worry about that now."

"But wouldn't the airport have to give him permission to take off?"

"Oh sure. They did. But that doesn't mean they know who is flying the plane."

On the screen, there was a shot of the crowd cheering as a player dribbled the ball down the court.

"Do you know if Ryan has ever taken prescription painkillers?" Rachel asked.

"The FBI was asking about that too. The answer is yes, but it was a while ago. At least I thought it was."

Priscilla said nothing, and just as she thought he would, he elaborated.

"He started taking them after he hurt his back when we were in the air force. I know he was still taking them after we got out, long after his back was healed. But he'd been to treatment. I thought he was past all that."

"There was a pill bottle in the back of the plane. It had his grandfather's name on it. It was a prescription for OxyContin."

"He could have taken it from his grandfather. I don't know." Eric shrugged. "I know the FBI were poking around, trying to figure out if he'd ever transported 'goods' on board the plane." He used his fingers as air quotes. "They mean smuggling, of course."

"What did you tell them?"

"That I wasn't aware of it. But it seems there's a lot I wasn't aware of."

Priscilla paused, thinking for a moment about how to ask her next question. "The pill bottle wasn't the only thing that was in the plane." She pulled her phone from her purse and swiped to the picture of the first page of the notebook she now assumed to be Ryan's. She handed the phone to Eric. "Can you tell me if anything you see here could give us clues about what Ryan was doing in Martha's Vineyard?"

Eric brought the phone close to his face and studied the picture. "I can't make out very much of the writing," he said.

"We couldn't either," Rachel said. "We worked out 'necklace' and 'bronze and gold' and 'tablet.' Not much else."

Priscilla thought she saw...something...flit over Eric's face. But just as quickly, it was gone. He handed the phone back to her. It was clear to her that Eric didn't know where Ryan was or why he'd taken the plane. She felt bad for him. He hadn't asked to be dragged into all this.

She stood, and a second later Rachel did the same. "You'll let someone know if you hear from him?"

He nodded. "Those FBI agents who were here left their card." He gestured at the refrigerator, which was clear except for a small white card attached to the front with a round magnet.

Priscilla tried to figure out how to get him to let her know as well, but she left it at that.

"Thank you for your time." She headed toward the door, and he walked her to it. She glanced at the fridge on the way out and saw A.J.'s card.

She smiled, thanked him again, and walked out, just as a man carrying a pizza box stepped out of the elevator.

"You finally have a name," Rachel said as Priscilla merged back onto the highway.

"Yes. That's more than I knew yesterday."

"Do you think the FBI has figured that out yet?" Rachel asked.

Priscilla flipped her turn signal on. "I don't know," she said.

"You know you have to tell A.J., right?" Rachel said.

"Yes, I figured I would have to." She needed to let them know about the paper she'd found anyway.

She glanced over at her daughter's profile, silhouetted against the clear blue sky. Rachel may be headed back home tomorrow, but A.J. wasn't leaving Martha's Vineyard yet.

"I'll tell him tonight at dinner," Priscilla promised.

"I will if you don't," Rachel said.

"You don't trust your own mother?" Priscilla pretended to be offended.

"Mom, I know you too well," Rachel insisted. "I know you like to be the one to solve these mysteries. But this one is not something to mess around with. They're smuggling drugs here. The FBI is involved. You don't want to get in their way."

Priscilla didn't have anything to say to that. Rachel wasn't wrong, about any of it.

"You'll tell him, right?" Rachel asked again.

"Yes. I promise I will."

CHAPTER FIFTEEN

Priscilla and Rachel had time to thaw some homemade chicken soup in the microwave and stick some garlic bread in the oven before A.J. arrived Sunday evening.

"Hey." Rachel pulled the door open and ushered her fiancé inside. It still gave Priscilla a thrill to see the way her face lit up whenever she saw him. "Come in. Warm up."

"It smells amazing in here." A.J. slipped off his coat and let Rachel hang it by the door.

"Don't be fooled. It's leftovers from the freezer."

"But made with love nonetheless," Priscilla shouted from the kitchen.

"Thawed with love," Rachel confirmed. "Come in. Your hands are so cold."

"Did you hear it's supposed to snow this week?" A.J. followed Rachel into the kitchen and leaned in to give Priscilla a hug.

"What?" Rachel's indignation was clear from the tone of her voice. "It's almost April. That's ridiculous."

"Sadly, it's not all that uncommon around here," Priscilla said. She turned off the burner and poured the soup into the bowls waiting on the counter. "As long as it's done before Easter. I can't handle snow after Easter."

A.J. grabbed two of the bowls and carried them to the table. Priscilla loved how he never waited around to ask what needed to be done. He always seemed to know how to help and was always ready to jump in and do it. Rachel pulled the cheesy garlic bread from the oven and sliced it before she tossed it into a basket, covered it with an embroidered tea towel, and carried it to the table. Priscilla carried the green salad to the table and set it down. After she'd said grace, A.J. ladled up a spoonful of the soup.

"So, you'll never guess who Mom and I talked to today," Rachel said.

A.J. raised his eyebrow and waited for her to go on.

"Eric Ivans." Rachel glanced at Priscilla. Priscilla hadn't planned to dive into it quite like this. She shoved a piece of bread into her mouth to give her time to think about how to respond.

While Priscilla was chewing, Rachel filled the silence. "We asked him why he was lying, since we know it was his friend Ryan Reid who was flying that airplane."

A.J. choked on his soup. Priscilla shoved his glass of water toward him, and Rachel leaned over and patted his back. He coughed a few times, and then he used his napkin to wipe his face. He shook his head.

"How..." He took a swallow of the water and seemed to gather his thoughts. "How did you come to that conclusion?"

"Mom figured it out," Rachel said.

"That's one of the things I wanted to talk to you about tonight," Priscilla said. She went on to recount how she'd found his name in the obituary and researched him, and how she'd realized he was connected to Eric Ivans.

"And Eric...said he'd let Reid use his plane?" A.J. said.

"No. Ryan took it without Eric's permission," Rachel said. "He didn't even know it was gone until you all showed up at his place."

Rachel was clearly delighted to be delivering the news, but A.J. looked stunned. Priscilla wasn't sure whether it was because he hadn't known, or because he had but didn't think Priscilla would have figured it out. She tried to read his face, but it gave nothing away.

Priscilla and Rachel recounted the day's adventures, and A.J. shook his head.

"You shouldn't have done that, you know," he said. "He could have been dangerous."

"But he wasn't. Besides, he ended up telling us what we wanted to know," Rachel said. "The missing pilot is Ryan Reid. He was the one smuggling the stolen drugs off the island. Now all we have to do is find him."

A.J. looked like he wanted to bolt from the table—to report back to his colleagues?—but good manners kept him in his seat.

"There's one more thing," Priscilla said. "I knew the plane was going to be removed today, so Rachel and I went out there this morning. Just to take another look, you know?"

A.J. watched her.

"I know it's silly, but since I saw the plane going down, and then Gerald and I found the crash site, I feel a little...well, it's a bit personal."

"We got up super early," Rachel said. "To get out there before you all took the plane away. That's dedication, I'd say."

"Well, anyway, while we were out there, we saw something. I'm not sure it means anything at all, and it's probably nothing. But, well, we found this caught in the branches of one of the trees a little way from the crash site."

Priscilla stood and retrieved her purse. She rooted around in it until she found the piece of notebook paper.

"Here," she said, holding it out. "I meant to give it to you earlier, but between church and our trip to New Bedford, I didn't have a chance."

A.J. had taken the paper and was staring down at it.

"Where did you say you found this?"

"It was caught in one of the trees, way up in the branches." Priscilla sat back down. "That's probably why no one noticed it before."

"How did you get it down?" A.J.'s eyes were wide.

"She climbed the tree." Did she imagine it, or were Rachel's eyes shining with pride?

A.J. stared at Priscilla, openmouthed.

"I climbed many trees in my day," Priscilla said. "You don't need to look so stunned."

"I'm not.... It's just..." A.J. shook his head. "Really?"

"Yes, really." Priscilla tried to put an edge of finality into her voice. "It wasn't graceful, but I did it. Now." She pointed to the paper in his hand. "I don't know if it's at all useful. You can see—"

But A.J. was already pushing his chair back. "I'm really sorry to do this, but I need to run." He clutched the notebook paper in his hand, and there was a wild, determined look in his eyes. "I hate to be rude, but I need to report this right away."

"Of course." Priscilla was stunned by the speed with which he kissed Rachel goodbye and made it out the door.

"I guess that paper was important after all," Rachel said, shaking her head.

"I guess it was," Priscilla said. But why? What in the world had it meant, and why was he so excited about it? She sighed and looked at A.J.'s half-eaten dinner. "I'm sorry to ruin your dinner with A.J."

"You didn't ruin anything," Rachel said. "It looks to me like you made A.J.'s night. Whatever you discovered must be a big breakthrough in the case."

"I guess so," Priscilla said, shaking her head. But what was it?

CHAPTER SIXTEEN

Rachel took the first ferry back on Monday. Priscilla spent the morning cleaning and running errands, but her mind was elsewhere, thinking through yesterday's conversation with Eric, and the way A.J. had bolted after she'd shown him the paper. Wondering where Ryan Reid was now, and whether he was still on the island—whether he was even still alive. She itched to call A.J., but she knew he wouldn't be able to tell her anything, and it would put him in an awkward position if she insisted on asking.

A bit before noon, she got into her car and headed into town to meet Gerald for lunch. Usually the prospect of seeing Gerald filled her with excitement, and she *was* excited, she supposed, but also, there was trepidation. She needed to talk to him about how she was feeling. Rachel had told her that again last night, when they were talking before bed, and the unsettled feeling in her gut made Priscilla think her daughter was right. She wasn't sure how she would bring it up, but she knew she should.

She easily found a spot on Main Street and parked her car, and then she headed up the steps of the Colonial Inn. The gracious old Victorian home overlooking the harbor was one of the best spots in town for lunch, and as soon as Priscilla stepped inside, Tilly Snyder greeted her.

"Hi, Priscilla. I hear you're collecting gift certificates for an Easter egg hunt."

"That's right, I am," Priscilla said. "Though right now, I'm just here for lunch. But if you're interested in donating one—"

"Of course I am." Tilly put her hands on her hips. "Don't you think people would want to come here?"

Priscilla laughed at the indignation in her voice.

"Of course they would. I'd be honored if you'd be willing to donate a gift certificate."

"I'll bring it by your table," Tilly promised, and then directed her to the booth near the side window, where Gerald was already waiting.

"Hello," Gerald said, standing as she walked up to the table.

"Hi, Gerald." Despite her nervousness and her complicated feelings, her heart still fluttered at the sight of him. "It's good to see you."

"You look lovely, as always." He leaned in and gave her a peck on the cheek, and they both sat down.

Priscilla set her napkin in her lap and opened the menu, even though she already knew she would get the crab salad. It bought her a bit of time to figure out how to bring up what she wanted to say.

"You sure created quite the stir last night," Gerald said.

Priscilla looked up. "What?"

"Finding the identity of the pilot like that. You made the police and the FBI look like slackers."

"Oh." She had? She hadn't intended to do that. She tried to read his tone. He seemed…Well, he seemed relieved, honestly, but could he really be happy, given how strongly he'd felt about her staying out of it? "Do you mean they didn't know who he was until I told A.J.?"

"They did not," he confirmed. "But once you told A.J. what you'd figured out, they went into high gear."

"Really?" Could it be true? Could she really have figured it out before they had? "What do you mean?"

Just then Hilda came up to take their order, and Gerald ordered the grilled salmon and Priscilla the crab salad before Gerald continued.

"I was chatting with Hank Westin this morning, and he said they were going to try to get in front of a judge to get a search warrant. And the FBI sent a team out to New Bedford to talk to the plane's owner, the one who cracked talking to you but not the FBI. They really need to ask you about your interrogation technique."

Priscilla wasn't imagining it. Gerald seemed almost pleased. After all his moaning about her staying out of the mystery behind the plane crash, he was happy now that she'd actually uncovered something useful.

"He didn't 'crack,'" Priscilla said. "And I didn't interrogate him. Honestly, I think he was just worried about his friend. He was hoping I had information about where Ryan is. Ryan may have taken his plane without permission and crashed it, but they've been friends their whole lives. He wanted to know if Ryan was okay."

"Well, whatever you did, it was better than what the police and the FBI were able to do," Gerald said. "There's now a full-out manhunt for this guy. And you even told them where he was try-ing to go when the plane went down." Again, he shook his head.

"I did what?"

"Didn't you?" Gerald cocked his head. "I got the impression that you figured out where the plane was going to land."

"No." Priscilla had no idea what he was talking about. "What made you think that?"

Gerald frowned. "Hank wouldn't tell me where it was, but he said they had officers on the way there."

"Where?" Priscilla tried to understand what he was talking about. "I have no idea where the plane was headed." She picked up her glass.

"Hmm." Gerald took a sip of water from the icy glass in front of him. "I got the impression you'd handed them the location. Literally. Not on a silver platter, but on some kind of paper you'd found."

"Wait." She set her glass down hard. "The paper had nothing but numbers on it."

"Really?" Gerald pursed his lips. "Hank gave me the impres-sion it was more than that."

"Here." Priscilla dug in her purse and pulled out her phone. "See?" She pulled up the picture and enlarged it.

Gerald leaned in and looked. His eyes widened.

"What?" Priscilla could see that the numbers meant something to him. "What is it?"

"You found this *where*?"

"It was caught in a tree near the crash site. What does it mean?"

"Let me check something." He pulled out his phone, swiped it, and then he typed something onto the screen.

"Gerald, you're making me crazy," Priscilla said. "What does it mean?"

Something changed on his phone, and a slow smile spread across his face.

"I think I know where the plane was headed."

CHAPTER SEVENTEEN

Gerald didn't exactly toss the bills on the table as they ran out, but they didn't linger. They had taken their food to go, and a few minutes later they were headed to an address on Chappaquiddick Island. Chappaquiddick, or Chappy, as the locals liked to call it, was a small island next to Edgartown. Priscilla hadn't spent much time on the island, but it was known to be peaceful and largely undisturbed, with few homes, one paved road, and several large nature preserves.

"So explain to me how the numbers on that paper led you to here?" Priscilla asked.

"They're coordinates. Longitude and latitude," Gerald said.

"No." She shook her head. She had learned this in high school. "When you write down longitude and latitude, there are degree marks, and you have to say north or south and east or west."

"You're dating yourself," Gerald teased. "For navigation these days, this way is more standard. Most of the GPS systems recognize this method."

Priscilla tried to absorb this. If the numbers on the paper she'd found represented coordinates on a map...And if she'd recognized them for what they were... "How would the pilot have been able to use them, exactly?" Priscilla had a vague understanding of the lines on the globe, but she didn't have a good grasp on how it all worked.

"Pilots navigate using longitude and latitude," Gerald said. "And in the old days, they used various systems, including decimal or degree minutes and seconds. But in most planes today, you would probably just punch the location into a GPS, and it would give you these GPS coordinates. Which is exactly what I did."

"And when you use those coordinates, what do you find?" Priscilla asked.

"You find a spot on the map, which happens to be on Chappaquiddick Island," Gerald said. "And if you found this notebook page in the area close to the plane, it makes it seem very likely that this is where the pilot was heading when the plane went down."

"But what's there? What's at that spot on the map?"

Gerald shrugged. "I guess we'll find out."

They drove through the historic village of Edgartown, past small shingled homes set close to the road and beautiful Victorian homes dripping with gingerbread trim and surrounded by wide lawns, and through narrow streets of the quaint downtown. They passed clothing stores and high-end art galleries and restaurants, and even Micawber Books, run by Gail's daughter Sara, before they left the main part of town and approached the small parking lot for the Chappaquiddick ferry.

The little boat didn't run on any set schedule but went as needed back and forth across the narrow waterway that separated the island from the bigger island of Martha's Vineyard. After Gerald's car was loaded onto the small flat boat, there wasn't much room left, but the ride only lasted about two minutes, and soon they emerged and drove off along the paved road, following the directions on Gerald's GPS. The island was serene and still, and they caught glimpses of the sparkling blue seas beyond the sandy shores. After a few minutes' drive, they turned off the main road—a funny way to think about this two-lane road—and onto a dirt road. They drove past large homes set back from the road and surrounded by walls of shrubs.

"It must be so isolated living out here," Priscilla said.

"I think that's what you're hoping for when you buy a place out here," Gerald said. "Peace and quiet. Privacy."

"Privacy for what?" Priscilla asked.

Gerald shrugged. They turned off onto a smaller dirt road, and then one more. A small wooden sign on the corner identified it as Pin Oak Lane. At the end of the road, there was a house surrounded by a wall of tall hedges. On the other side of the road, the land sloped down toward a ridge and then dropped into the sea. They drove up to the break in the hedges and found a locked iron gate.

"Wow." Gerald let out a low whistle. Through the gate, they could make out a large shingled house, three stories tall, set off with black shutters and white trim, across a long, perfectly manicured lawn. From here they could see a separate garage with—how many doors was that? There had to be at least eight, Priscilla thought. A fence at the side of the property looked like it might surround a pool, though it was impossible to see from this distance.

"That's a big house," Priscilla said.

"Surrounded by a large property," Gerald said.

They found an intercom on a post next to the gate. Priscilla waited for Gerald to roll his window down and push the button, but he sat for a few moments and then put the SUV in Reverse and backed away from the gate. That's when she saw a fish-eye lens watching them.

"You're not interested to see if someone answers the intercom?" she asked him, disappointed.

"Not with you in the car," he said grimly. "I'm not going to put you in danger, or myself, for that matter. This isn't a job for a Coast Guard captain and his favorite amateur sleuth, even if she is the sharpest tool in the shed."

Priscilla felt herself blush. "Do you think there's anyone in there?"

Gerald nodded and gestured down at the ground.

"It looks like the FBI wasn't issued an invitation either," he said, and it took Priscilla a moment to see what he meant. There were fresh tire tracks on the dirt around them, but they didn't go beyond the gate. The cars—no doubt belonging to the FBI—had reversed out of the small area and turned around without making it past the gate.

"Can they say no to the FBI?" Priscilla asked. "I thought that if the FBI wanted to come in, you had to let them."

Gerald shook his head. "Not if they don't have a search warrant, you don't. The Fourth Amendment protects against unlawful search and seizure." He nodded toward the house. "But it sure looks shady if you don't let them in."

Gerald sat looking at the house for a moment more, and then he turned the SUV around. But instead of turning back onto the road, he went the other way, following the wall of shrubs. Privet, Priscilla thought, trimmed to create a tall fence. The densely grown plant was almost impossible to see through, even at this time of year, when only the very first fresh green leaves were poking out.

"What are you doing?" Priscilla asked. The ground was bumpy and uneven, but the SUV handled it just fine.

"I have an idea," he said. At the corner of the hedge, he turned the SUV and continued driving. The privet along this side seemed to go on forever.

"This property is huge."

"It is. Which is exactly what I was hoping for."

"Why? Priscilla tried her best to see in through the shrubs, but they really were quite a good privacy fence.

"We're looking for a place where a plane could have been aiming to land, right?" Gerald asked as they bumped along the grass.

Priscilla nodded.

"If this is the place, it would only make sense if the yard were big enough for a landing strip of some kind."

Priscilla saw what he was getting at now.

"If we want to get a judge to approve a search warrant, my guess is it's going to take more than a scrap of paper with some numbers on it. We need hard evidence that the plane was headed here."

"And how are we going to get that?"

Gerald stopped the car and put it into Park. "Watch this."

He hopped out of the car and walked around to the back of the SUV, where he opened the hatch.

Priscilla climbed out and followed him, and got there in time to see him taking what looked like a small robot out of his car. She knew immediately what it was.

"You brought a drone?" Priscilla couldn't believe it. It was a small quadcopter—a machine with four legs, each topped by a small propeller, with a camera attached to the bottom.

"I didn't bring a drone on purpose. I thought I was just coming to have lunch with you. But it was in the back of my car," Gerald said.

Priscilla had a hundred questions and an uneasy feeling in her gut, but it was overlaid with a feeling of excitement. What would they find?

Gerald switched the drone on, and it started to hum. He set it on the ground, pulled a handheld remote control from his car, touched a few buttons, and then the propellers started to whir.

"Do you think it'll work?" Priscilla asked.

"I don't know." Gerald shrugged. "I guess we'll find out." He touched the remote control again, and the drone took off. Priscilla was surprised by how quiet it was as it rose into the air. Aside from a low humming, you'd never know it was there. She watched as it soared right over the hedge and kept going, up and over the house and yard. Priscilla watched in awe as Gerald flew the drone all around the edges of the property, and then over the house again. He sent the drone way up high, and then brought it back lower again. As Priscilla watched, the feeling of unease came back over her. How could it be this easy to take videos directly over someone's home? It was invasive, and even if it was legal—which she assumed it was, if Gerald was doing it—then at the very least it was an ethical gray area. What about that Fourth Amendment right to avoid unlawful search and seizure? How was this any different from entering the house without consent?

Priscilla tried to push the thoughts down. What if something illegal was happening inside this house? What if this is where those hundreds of thousands of dollars' worth of prescription medication was stored, waiting for a plane that had never arrived to take it off the island? In that case, it would be perfectly fair to use the technology to find the culprit. But what if the drugs weren't here? How could you know when it was ethical to use a drone like this and when it was not? It was complicated, more complicated then she'd thought at first.

Priscilla's musings were cut short when Gerald brought the drone back and landed it in front of them, just a few feet from where it had taken off.

"Now what?" Priscilla asked.

"Now we get out of here before someone comes out to find out what all that was about," Gerald said. He ran forward to get the drone and scooped it up, and then he pulled something out of it and set it in the back of his car. He slammed the rear door and gestured for Priscilla to get in. He started the engine, executed a sharp U-turn, and headed back to the dirt road. No one followed them as they made their way to the main paved road and back to the ferry. They only had to wait a few minutes for the ferry, but while they waited, Gerald reached for a laptop that was on the back seat of the car. He opened the lid and inserted what looked like a small square of plastic into a slot on the side of the computer.

"What's that?"

"It's the SD card from the drone," Gerald said, as a window popped open. "Like the card that would be inside a digital camera."

"So that will play the footage you just took?" Priscilla asked.

"That's the hope, anyway," he said. A blurred image appeared on the screen, brown with tints of green, but when he pushed play, the image crystalized into the ground underneath the drone as it rose into the air.

"Oh my." It was amazing how clearly it could look right into the yard. It was amazing, really—it was as if she were looking down at it from above, because, through its lens, she basically was.

"Look at that pool," Priscilla said. "And how huge that hot tub is."

"There's a whole pool house," Gerald said.

"Tennis courts too."

Priscilla knew some lived an ultrarich lifestyle, but it was striking to see it so clearly now.

"And check out that garage," Gerald said.

Priscilla whistled. "Could you fit a small plane inside there?"

"Easily," Gerald said. "Probably more than one."

Priscilla watched as the camera zoomed all over the property, taking in the many peaks of the endless roof and the broad expanse of lawn. And then...

"What's that?"

"It's very interesting, isn't it?" Gerald said, pausing the video. It just looked like a patch of the lawn that had been worn smooth and flat. "It could be..."

He started the video again, and the camera moved away from the stretch of grass, but then, toward the end of the footage, it rose way high into the air, and you could see the whole property at once.

And from that angle, it was perfectly clear what that stretch of grass was. A long, flat, straight patch of grass with no obstacles around.

"That's a runway, isn't it?" Priscilla said.

He nodded. "A private airstrip, built right into the backyard." He smiled. "I think we found our evidence."

CHAPTER EIGHTEEN

Priscilla didn't want to go home, but there wasn't much else she could do. Gerald had already sent the drone video footage to the police and the FBI, and he explained that they would use it as further evidence to try to get a judge to issue a search warrant. Until then, he insisted, all any of them could do was wait.

Priscilla didn't like it. In fact, it really rankled. If she'd sat around waiting like they all wanted to, they wouldn't know the identity of the pilot, and they wouldn't have that paper that gave them the coordinates and led them to the house on Chappaquiddick. She couldn't just sit here. But she honestly couldn't think of how she could get answers at the moment, short of heading directly back to the house with the airstrip and demanding answers. And that seemed foolhardy enough that she wasn't about to do that. Not yet anyway.

In the end, she decided she couldn't just sit around the house, and called Joan to see if she wanted to ask some more businesses to donate to the egg hunt. Chloe had requested even more gift certificates, and as annoying as that was, Priscilla was actually glad for the chance to get out and do something useful. Priscilla had also agreed to pick up flyers for the event from the copy shop in town and post them wherever she could.

"I'm sorry, I'm afraid I can't come," Joan said when Priscilla called. "I promised to go sit with Uncle Hugh so Gail can go out for a while this afternoon."

"Well, I suppose I can't argue with that," Priscilla said.

"Try Trudy. She might be around," Joan said. Priscilla thanked her and called Trudy, and when Priscilla explained what she was going to do and invited her to come along, Trudy let out a "Woo-hoo!"

"I'm so tired of sitting inside all the time," Trudy said. "In the fall, I'm always like, 'I love sweater weather!' But by the time mid-March rolls around, I'm so sick of all my sweaters. I'm ready to get out and garden and get some exercise and not be stuck inside but it's still too cold."

"So should I take that as a yes?" Priscilla asked.

"I'll meet you on Church Street in twenty minutes."

Half an hour later, Priscilla had parked in Tisbury and she and Trudy had a stack of colorful flyers in hand and were headed toward the information board at the end of Church Street. There was a map there, as well as a corkboard where people posted information about upcoming events.

"She really went over the top with the graphics, didn't she?" Trudy was trying not to laugh but mostly failing.

"If it were me, I would have stuck to one," Priscilla said. "But I wasn't the one who volunteered to design the flyer, so I guess I can't complain."

"Prizes! Prizes! Prizes!" Trudy hooted.

"That word does show up a lot, doesn't it?"

"It will certainly get people's attention."

"And that's exactly what it's supposed to do." Priscilla took one of the flyers and stapled it to the corkboard.

"Now." Priscilla looked around. "How about we start at Maypop?"

"Do you really think kids will want to win a gift certificate to an antique shop?" Trudy asked.

"I don't think kids will want many of the prizes except the candy," Priscilla said. "I guess the idea is that the lure of prizes will get parents to bring the kids out to the event."

"Ah." Trudy nodded, but she still looked dubious. "Well, here goes."

They walked inside. A beautiful Edwardian satinwood armoire with beveled mirrors stood by the door, next to a display of records and a turntable that looked just like the kind Priscilla's parents had owned. They threaded their way through displays of vintage clothing and furniture and eventually made it to the back, where Jack Ehrman stood behind a full-on carved mahogany bar.

"Hi," Priscilla said. She'd met Jack a few times around town. He was a big, burly man who looked like he should be out chopping trees or wrestling sharks, and Priscilla always thought it amusing to find him arranging dainty displays of Depression glass and polishing sets of silver.

"Hi, Jack." Trudy waved. "How do you like this weather?"

"I'm ready for summer," he said. Today he wore a button-down shirt rolled up at the sleeves and jeans, and a beautiful necktie in shades of blue and green. "How about you?"

"You know what I'm excited about?" Trudy said. "Easter. And you know what I'm most looking forward to?" She pulled a flyer out of her bag. "Have you heard about the Easter egg hunt at the Coast Guard station?"

It took Trudy less than a minute to get a gift certificate and a promise from Jack to display the flyer, and soon they were on their way to Ortmann's. Trudy was very good at this, Priscilla had to admit. She'd soon talked her way into gift certificates from the grocery, as well as Murdick's Fudge and Tisbury Pharmacy, which had an old-fashioned soda shop that was very popular with the tourists.

"How about we head to Mocha Motts next?" Trudy asked.

"I think Chloe was going to ask them for a gift certificate," Priscilla said.

"I didn't mean for a gift certificate. I mean I'm ready for some coffee."

"Say no more."

A few minutes later they were seated at one of the small wooden tables near the door. Trudy cradled a mocha in a huge ceramic mug, while Priscilla had a latte.

"So, what's the update on that missing pilot?" Trudy asked.

"We know who he is," Priscilla said.

"Really?"

Priscilla explained how she'd figured it out. "I don't know why the police around here don't have you on the payroll," Trudy said, taking a big sip of her drink.

"Oh, don't be silly." Priscilla laughed. "But get this. The really exciting part is that we know where the pilot was headed."

"What?"

Priscilla explained how she'd found the paper—"Please tell me someone has photographic evidence of you up in that tree!" Trudy laughed—and her trip to Chappaquiddick with Gerald.

"That's a funny place," Trudy said.

"What do you mean?" Priscilla asked.

"I don't know. Something about it being an island, all isolated like that. The people who choose to live out there are all a bit off, you know?"

"Um…" Priscilla didn't know how to break it to her. "You do realize you live on an island too, right?"

"Well, right, but that's different," Trudy insisted. "Martha's Vineyard is a real place. Chappy is so quiet. They have like, one store. Maybe two roads. I don't know. It's different."

She took a long sip from her mocha and got a bit of whipped cream on her nose. She used a paper napkin to wipe it off and then continued. "It is beautiful out there though."

"It is," Priscilla had to admit. "The property we tracked the plane to was gorgeous. The house was huge, and had a pool and a pool house and a tennis court and everything, and it was surrounded by an enormous lawn with a landing strip built right into it."

"Wait. The one right by the beach?"

Priscilla cocked her head. "Aren't most of the houses there right by the beach?"

"Yes, but I mean, how many of them have runways? It has to be the same one. The one I was at has a tennis court and a ten-car garage and an airplane hangar and everything."

"This house was on Pink Oak Lane," Priscilla said.

Trudy shrugged. "I have no idea what street the house was on. But it was way off the main road. Like, you had to really want to get there."

"What were you doing there?"

"It was a fund-raiser. This was years ago. Maybe five, or maybe even more. But it was this big shindig. Something about saving the sea turtles or something. I don't really remember. I got the sense it was something the wife was into."

"How did you end up at the fund-raiser?" Priscilla knew there were plenty of people on Martha's Vineyard who went from one charity gala to another, but that wasn't really Trudy's world.

"Dan's work bought a table, and we got picked to go."

Ah. That made sense, then.

"Dan was annoyed about it, but I was thrilled to dress up and go to a fancy party."

"I bet." Trudy did love a good party. "What was it like?"

"It was amazing. The house was huge—like, multiple wings huge—and they let us walk out into the gardens and around the grounds. He had a bunch of antique cars on display on the grounds, and Dan spent the whole evening nerding out about them. I was more impressed by the art, myself."

"The art?"

"The owners of this place, whoever they were, had an amazing art collection. I saw a Rothko and a Koons, and a drawing of Picasso's, and there was a Calder out in the yard, and a ton of other artists. There were paintings and statues everywhere. Some dusty old manuscripts too, but I didn't really spend much time on those."

Priscilla recognized the name Picasso, and assumed the others Trudy mentioned must be famous artists too. Smuggling drugs must pay well.

"Do you know anything about the owners of the house?"

"Not really, I'm afraid. Someone told me that it was the wife who was into the turtles. She was on the board or something. But that's all I really know about them. I probably could have paid more attention, but I was having too much fun pretending to be rich for a night."

"Do you remember their name?"

Trudy shook her head. "Sorry. Unless their name was Picasso, I wasn't paying attention."

"Would Dan remember?"

"Let me find out, just give me a second." Trudy took her phone out of her purse, swiped to a screen, and typed a message. "There," she said. "He usually answers a text pretty fast, if he's not in the middle of a project or something."

Sure enough, after a couple of minutes, Trudy's phone vibrated. She picked it up and read the screen. "Richard and Emily Leonard."

Priscilla took a pen and jotted the names on her napkin. "I don't know if that helps, but thanks for finding out." It was more than she'd known before.

"So you think the missing pilot was planning to land the plane there, on the grass runway in the yard?" Trudy said.

"That's my theory." Priscilla folded the napkin and put it in her purse. "I think he was going to pick up the drugs that were recently taken from the hospital to sell on the mainland."

"Huh. It is the kind of place where no one would really ask questions about what's coming in and off the planes." Trudy sipped her drink, made a face, and reached for the container of sugar on the nearby drink stand. She dumped in some sugar and used a wooden stirrer to mix it in. "But didn't you say there were marks in the mud near the downed plane? Like someone had dragged something away from it?"

"Right."

"Was he going to unload something at the house on Chappy, then?"

"I guess he must have been." Priscilla hadn't really thought that aspect through. If he had been coming to Chappaquiddick to pick up a load of stolen goods, what did he drag *away* from the plane?

It didn't make sense. Now that Trudy pointed it out, none of it made sense.

She was missing something.

CHAPTER NINETEEN

After they finished their coffee, Trudy said she had to head home, but Priscilla decided to make one more stop before heading back. She was feeling pretty guilty about how she'd treated Gerald the past couple of days, especially after he took her with him to check out the house on Chappaquiddick and let her in on the drone adventure. She figured Candy's double-chocolate-chip cookies would go a long way toward repairing any breach, so she hurried to the bakery before it closed at five.

Candy was wiping down the counter when Priscilla rushed through the door. "Candy, I won't keep you, I just wondered if you had any double-chocolate-chip cookies left?"

Candy tossed her rag in the sink behind her and smiled at Priscilla. "I have about a half-dozen left. How many do you want?"

Priscilla breathed deep to catch her breath. "All of them, please. Whew! So glad I caught you!"

Candy emptied the coffee carafe into the sink. "I still have a few chores to finish up before I head out. Tuesday mornings Harper takes the early shift, so I don't have to be here at the crack of dawn tomorrow."

Priscilla thought she might as well kill two birds with one stone. Or was it throw everything against the wall and see what sticks? Well, whatever the metaphor, she had a question to ask. Candy had lived on the island all her life. "Have you ever heard of Richard and Emily Leonard?"

"Who hasn't?" Candy shrugged. "They've probably been featured on *Lifestyles of the Rich and Famous* at one time or another. That's how wealthy they are. Wait...I think..."

She went to one of the tables in the back of the bakery that held magazines and newspapers for patrons to browse while they drank their coffee, and dug through them until she found the one she was looking for. "Here we are...I think...yup, here it is."

She brought the open magazine to Priscilla and showed her the two-page spread with the headline "Leonards Host Fund-Raiser for Literacy in Hyannisport." "I saw this when I was looking through magazines for wedding ideas. Then I ended up not needing any at all." She giggled and handed the magazine to Priscilla.

The pictures that accompanied the article showed a man and woman who looked to be in their late fifties. Richard Leonard was tall and had snow-white hair combed back from his forehead. Emily Leonard, wearing an obviously expensive designer gown, had her long dark hair piled on her head in an elaborate style and crowned with a tiara. Priscilla skimmed the article and found out that Richard was a retired hedge fund manager, and Emily was on several prominent boards in Boston. They owned homes in New York, Malibu, Aspen, and...Martha's Vineyard, more specifically, Chappaquiddick. Bingo. Trudy was right. These were the people who owned the house on Pink Oak Lane, whose private landing strip Ryan Reid had been aiming for.

But all this didn't get her any closer to figuring out where Ryan Reid was. Priscilla sighed, closed the magazine, and returned it to the table.

"Did you find what you were looking for?" Candy asked.

"Yes and no." Priscilla sighed again.

"Is there any way I can help?" Candy pulled on her coat.

Priscilla didn't even know where to start. "I don't think so," she said, and Candy gave her a smile.

"Well, maybe the double-chocolate-chip cookies will help you feel a little better." She took her keys from her purse.

"I'm sure they will." Priscilla smiled, said goodbye, and headed to her car. When she got home she made a quick dinner of chicken quesadillas and, after a walk on the beach with Jake, tried to figure out what to do for the rest of the evening.

Now that she'd bought the cookies for Gerald, she wasn't sure how she should proceed. Invite him over? Go to his house? Obviously, she hadn't thought this through. They never did have the talk she was hoping to have. Maybe it was best just to table the whole thing for the evening and think about it tomorrow. There was that book she wanted to finish, or she could catch up on some of her favorite shows. She could watch them while she worked on that baby blanket. But even though she was exhausted, she was antsy, and she had a thousand questions swirling through her head.

What did Richard Leonard know about the missing pilot? About the missing drugs? Had Gerald's drone video led to a judge granting a search warrant for the property? Had the FBI turned up anything at Ryan Reid's home?

Priscilla had just bitten into one of Gerald's cookies—after all, he didn't know how many she'd bought, now did he?—when her phone rang. She looked at the caller ID and frowned. She didn't recognize the number. She swiped the screen. "Hello?"

"Priscilla Grant? This is Eric Ivans."

Priscilla's jaw dropped. She recovered before her silence became awkward and stammered, "Y-yes? How can I help you?"

"I can't stop thinking about Ryan, and I'm really worried about him. I'm afraid he might be somewhere where his well-being isn't a priority for the people he's with." He took a deep breath and let it out. "I've decided that, for his own protection, I need to tell the rest of what I know about him . . . about his activities of late."

Priscilla asked the obvious question. "Why aren't you calling the police? Why call me?"

"Because if and when Ryan is caught and sentenced, I want to be able to go and see him. He's going to need me, and I want him to let me come. When the time is right, I'll tell him about my part in this. But until then, if he asks me if I went to the police, I can honestly say no."

Priscilla thought a moment. "I don't know if I can promise not to let the police know where I got the information. I can do my best, but—"

"I understand. Can you meet me tomorrow at one o'clock at Offshore Ale in Oak Bluffs?"

"I'll be there," Priscilla said. "You're doing the right and loving thing, you know."

"I know," Eric said. "And one of these days I hope I believe it."

A half hour later Priscilla backed out of the driveway and headed into town. The sun was dropping over the horizon, casting the whole area in a beautiful golden light. She stole a glance at the passenger seat at the plate that held five double-chocolate-chip cookies. A.J. had said he and his fellow agent were staying at the Mansion House, one of the larger inns in Tisbury. Surely after a long day of work, he wouldn't turn up his nose at a plate of cookies from his future mother-in-law. And if she managed to get some information out of him about whatever he'd turned up today, well, what could that hurt?

A few minutes later, she had reached the Mansion House hotel, which was situated, appropriately enough, in a large old house overlooking the waterfront. The building had a restaurant on the first floor and several porches offering views out over the harbor. She stepped into the lobby, clutching her plate of cookies, and pulled out her phone. She dialed A.J.'s number and looked around. She'd been past this place a thousand times, but she'd never been inside before. The lobby had wood floors and big windows and plush couches.

"Hi there, Priscilla," A.J. said on the other end of the line.

"Hi, A.J." Priscilla took a deep breath. She had to phrase this carefully, or she could come off as a bit mad. "I stopped by Candy's this afternoon and picked up some cookies. I wanted to share them with you."

"Oh wow." He laughed. "That's so nice."

"And I was in the neighborhood, so I brought them to your hotel. Are you around? Or should I drop them off at the desk for you?"

"You're here?"

"In the lobby."

"Okay then. I'll be right down."

A moment later, he was stepping out of the elevator and crossing the lobby. He was wearing black pants and a light blue polo shirt, which was what he often wore while he was on duty.

"Don't tell me you're still working?"

"Oh yeah." He nodded. "It's going to be a late one. Which is why your dropping off cookies is the most amazing thing." He smiled, and she felt a surge of affection for this man who had won her daughter's heart.

"You must have had a busy day," she said. A.J. nodded and took the plate of cookies from her. "Did you find anything at Ryan Reid's apartment?"

He peeled back the plastic wrap. "You know I can't tell you that." He picked up a cookie. "These look amazing."

Priscilla tried to keep a smile on her face and her voice light, as if these were just casual questions and not the whole reason she'd come here. "How about the house on Chappaquiddick? Were you able to get a search warrant for that property?"

"We're still waiting on a search warrant for the house in Chappaquiddick. The judge didn't think even the runway was enough evidence to grant that. So we're digging for more. Congratulations on asking me a question that didn't have a classified answer." He grinned at her and took a bite.

Priscilla tried not to let her disappointment show.

A.J. stacked the cookies in his hand and handed her the plate. "Look, I'm sorry to do this, but I have to get back upstairs."

"Wait. Is there anything else? Anything at all you can tell me?"

A.J. shook his head. "Honestly, Priscilla, I've told you everything my integrity will allow. Surely you don't want me to violate my professional ethics."

Priscilla sighed. "Of course I don't. You wouldn't deserve my daughter if you did."

He ducked his head in thanks. "But I sure do appreciate these." He held up the cookies, turned, and she walked with him to the elevator. "I'll be in touch, okay?"

"That sounds good," Priscilla said. She smiled at him and gave him a hug. "If you talk to Rachel tonight, tell her I said I miss her."

"Will do. Goodnight, Priscilla, and thanks again for the cookies."

He entered the elevator and Priscilla stood for a moment, thinking. The drone footage hadn't gotten a search warrant from the judge. She wondered if what Eric would tell her tomorrow would be enough to convince him.

The next day Priscilla arrived in Oak Bluffs and made her way to Offshore Ale. Although she'd had pizza from here before—they

made an amazing mashed potato pizza with scallions and pep-
pered bacon—she'd never been inside the restaurant itself. The
first thing she saw when she walked in was the gleaming wooden
bar that took up one side of the room. In the wall behind the bar
was a large sixteen-pane window that looked into a room with an
enormous bright copper vat, which she assumed was the "ale" part
of Offshore Ale. She knew this particular establishment was very
Coast Guard friendly, and regularly donated to the cause.

She found a table in the corner and settled in to wait for Eric.
A few minutes after one, he walked through the door, looked
around, and saw her wave at him. He strode to the table, took off
his jacket and hung it on the back of his chair, and sat down.

"Thank you for agreeing to meet me, Priscilla," he said.

"I'm very happy to help you in any way I can," Priscilla assured
him.

Eric picked up a menu. "I almost didn't come. I even turned
around once, but then I remembered how concerned you were
about Ryan. We just have to find him."

The waitress came to the table. Eric ordered a Pulled Pork
Quesadilla and Priscilla ordered—what else?—the mashed potato
pizza. The waitress brought their iced teas, and Priscilla squeezed
her lemon slice into hers while she waited for Eric to begin. When
he did, she had to lean forward to hear his words.

"Did you ever read about what happened to the Iraq Museum
in the days after the US invasion in 2003?"

Was he speaking a foreign language? "Not really...I mean, I
don't think so." She shook her head. "No."

"In April of 2003, before US forces advanced on Baghdad, looters broke into the National Museum of Iraq. The museum staff, fearing for their safety, vacated the building, and with the museum standing empty, thieves came in. Thousands of priceless artifacts were taken from the museum's collection."

Priscilla could tell that she was listening to someone who was used to giving lectures to students. He was a professor, after all. He took a sip of his tea and continued. "Some of the more than fifteen thousand stolen artifacts taken were thousands of years old, some from before the time of Christ. Some of the earliest artifacts and records of civilization were taken, as well as some of the earliest examples of Middle Eastern art. The plunder of the museum was considered the largest museum theft of all time and one of the worst acts of cultural vandalism in recent times, robbing the country of its history and culture. And because it was one of the most ancient civilizations in the world, the loss went well beyond one country—all of humanity had lost its history in the theft."

Priscilla couldn't imagine it. She tried to think of what would happen if people broke into the Smithsonian and walked away with the American flag that had flown over Fort McHenry and inspired the national anthem, or Abraham Lincoln's top hat, or the *Spirit of St. Louis*. Or if the National Archives were looted, and the original Declaration of Independence taken. She thought about what it would be like if looters entered the Louvre and walked off with da Vinci's *Mona Lisa*, or broke into St. Peter's and left with Michelangelo's *Pieta*. It would be a tragedy. An entire culture's heritage...just vanished. Stolen, overnight. It was unthinkable. And she hadn't even *heard* about it.

Eric broke into her thoughts. "Some of the most important pieces still missing are a bull from the face of a temple built by the King of Ur, from around 2400 BC, and an eighth-century BC ivory plaque covered in gold, *Lioness Attacking a Nubian.*"

Priscilla finally found her voice. "What does this have to do with Ryan?"

Eric continued, as if she hadn't spoken. "The people who looted the Iraq Museum haven't been caught, and most of the treasures quickly vanished underground, changing hands in the black market antiquities trade. The artifacts taken included vessels, cylinder seals, amulets, and jewelry. There were also early manuscripts, gold and silver coins, and...*clay tablets* inscribed with some of the earliest known human language."

Priscilla gasped. "Tablets? Did you say 'tablets'?"

Eric sighed. "Yes. As soon as I saw Ryan's writing on your phone, I knew that what I'd suspected, what I've been afraid of, is true. Ryan has been smuggling Middle Eastern artifacts, not prescription drugs."

CHAPTER TWENTY

Priscilla looked up from her computer screen when the little clock on the mantel bonged. Could that be right? She squinted at the hands on the clock, trying to make sense of them. It couldn't possibly be midnight, could it? Jake stirred beside her, awakened by the noise. She patted his head, then turned back to her computer screen.

Just a bit longer, she promised herself. She was almost finished with an article—one of dozens she'd read tonight—about what had happened in Baghdad in the shadowy days after the city fell in 2003. She'd had no idea. None at all.

Priscilla read that in the years since the looting, more than 7,000 artifacts had been recovered, but the rest had disappeared—mostly into the hands of private collectors. She read that the illegal trade in looted antiquities was growing, and that most of the extremely valuable and recognizable pieces that had vanished from the museum were thought to be in the private collections of very wealthy individuals. Priscilla couldn't believe it. How could a person think it was ethical to buy artifacts that had been stolen? But apparently it was not all that uncommon. An American museum had recently gotten in trouble for purchasing a large number of ancient artifacts and manuscripts—early copies of scriptures—that, unbeknownst to them, turned out to have been looted from the museum.

The worst part of all was that many of the artifacts had ended up in the hands of terrorist organizations. The trade in these stolen artifacts was made even more unconscionable by the fact that it was groups like ISIS and Al Qaeda that were getting rich off the sales.

That explained why A.J. and his counterterrorism team had gotten involved, then. This was not about prescription medicine. This was about something so much bigger than that. This was, Priscilla was now almost sure, about a wealthy art collector purchasing stolen artifacts from the black market. She suddenly understood why Ryan didn't call for help, even as the plane went down. Whatever cargo had been on board that plane, he could not be caught with it. Eric wasn't sure if he was involved in the illegal artifact trade itself or whether he was just a pilot for hire, making a delivery for a fee; in any case, when that plane went down, he was in a bad spot. She had found that he'd joined the air force in 2005, so he couldn't have had anything to do with the thefts themselves, but he was very clearly caught up in their resale somehow. The FBI believed that stolen artifacts had been on that plane, and judging by what she knew of the plane's destination and what Trudy had said about Richard Leonard's art collection, she was pretty sure they were right. And that explained why whatever artifacts had been on board that plane when it went down had to disappear, and quickly, before the wreckage was discovered.

The only question left was, had the artifacts—and the pilot charged with getting them there—ever made it to the house on Chappaquiddick?

Priscilla wasn't sure. But, she thought, there was really only one way to find out.

CHAPTER TWENTY-ONE

Priscilla slept deeply Tuesday night, and when she woke up Wednesday morning, she almost couldn't believe that any of it was true. She couldn't believe that Ryan Reid had been smuggling stolen antiquities when the plane went down. But she had a hunch that she knew where both Ryan and the stolen artifacts had ended up.

The air was just a few degrees warmer today, just barely hinting at spring, but it was still windy down by the water. As she walked along the beach with Jake, Priscilla thought through her plan. As of Monday night, the FBI hadn't gotten a search warrant for the house in Chappaquiddick. Since she hadn't heard anything from A.J. or Gerald, she was willing to bet they still hadn't gotten one. Which meant that as of this morning, they still had no way to get onto the property and search for evidence of stolen artifacts, or Ryan, or anything.

Overnight, Priscilla had developed her own theory about what had happened after the plane went down. She figured Ryan must have called Richard Leonard, or someone at the house on Chappaquiddick, to let them know what had happened. Ryan somehow managed to drag his cargo out of that forest and make it to the road, where someone picked him up and most likely took him to Chappaquiddick to recover. Given the extent of the injuries that must have resulted from such an accident, it didn't seem crazy that he would still be recovering a week later. Then again, Ryan could have left Martha's Vineyard altogether days ago. There was really no way to know without more information.

But they didn't have that yet. And it was already more than a week after the plane crash. If Ryan was still on Chappaquiddick, he couldn't stay there forever. And if there was anyone at the house, surely the parade of government vehicles and the drone flight Monday must have alerted them that the authorities were narrowing in on them. Which meant that someone needed to get to the house to search right away.

The police and the FBI wouldn't be able to access the house without a search warrant.

But a concerned citizen didn't need a search warrant, did she?

"Jake, leave that poor bird alone," she called as he started to chase a seagull down the sand. The bird flew off, and Jake ran off down the beach.

Priscilla stood still, looking out into the waves. As she stood there, a plan formed.

Theoretically, it could be dangerous, she knew. More likely, it would be a colossal waste of time. But still. What if it did pan out?

She thought for a moment, trying to find the holes in her logic. She knew what Gerald would tell her to do. He'd tell her to stay out of it. A.J. would no doubt say the same thing.

But she couldn't just sit here and hope. She couldn't just pray that the authorities would find the answers. So far, all the big breaks in this case had come when she'd done something bold or brave.

She knew Gerald and A.J. just wanted her to be safe. But she also knew no one had believed that she'd seen a plane, and she'd been right about that. She'd been convinced to listen to the experts, with their radars and records, and she'd even started to question her own mind, but she'd been right in the end. She had to trust her own instincts. She had to trust the voice inside of her that told her to be brave, not the voices around her telling her to be careful.

"Come on, Jake."

As the dog bounded back to her, his tail bouncing, Priscilla knew what she needed to do. If there were answers in that house, she wasn't about to just sit around and wait for someone else to find them.

Priscilla found the hedge fence that surrounded the house easily, and she drove carefully to the gate. She put her SUV in park and hopped out of the car. She had made sure to make herself look as harmless and unsuspecting as possible, wearing a sweater with lavender and pink bunnies on it over light purple slacks. The whole getup was a touch too pastel and grandmotherly for her, but she was going for innocent, and nothing said innocent like a bunny sweater. Now she walked up to the camera with a huge grin.

She pushed the buzzer and waved at the camera. "Hi," she said. "I'm Priscilla Grant. I'm organizing a free Easter egg hunt for the families of Martha's Vineyard, and I'm going door to door looking for support." She sounded like a kid selling candy bars for her basketball team, but she didn't care. Her only hope of getting inside that gate was to appear unthreatening, so she was shame-lessly playing the clueless-old-lady card.

"See?" She flashed one of the flyers Chloe had made to the camera.

"You're doing what?" a voice on the other end said.

"Organizing an Easter egg hunt for the families of Martha's Vineyard." She left off the part about the Coast Guard, suspecting that any mention of the government organization would erase any chance of getting inside those gates. And judging by how skeptical this voice sounded, her chances were slim enough as it was. "We're soliciting donations. I was hoping I might be able to talk to some-one about it."

There was a pause, and then the voice said, "Hang on."

Priscilla didn't know if that was good news or bad news, but she kept a smile pasted on her face and tried her best to look inno-cent and helpful. A moment later, the voice came back on the intercom.

"Come inside the gate and park in front of the house. Some-one will come out to meet you."

Priscilla thanked him, then she hopped back into her car, and a moment later the gate opened. She drove inside, and the gate closed behind her. She tried not to let that worry her as she drove slowly down the long driveway toward the house, which looked even more impressive than it had seemed from the drone video. From the driveway approach, the home was tall and imposing, and the wide expanse of lawn on either side was stunning, even in its current mostly brown state. There was a circular driveway, and she parked in a spot marked for guests. She climbed out, clutching the flyer for the Easter egg hunt in one hand and her purse in the other.

She stood by her car uncertainly, but then the front door opened, and a man in black pants and a blue button-down appeared.

"This way, please."

Priscilla walked toward the house and up the front steps. She was ushered into a soaring entryway with a glossy black-and-white tile floor and large windows that went all the way to the second story. A staircase with an iron railing curved up to the left, and a series of rooms branched off in every direction.

"If you'll just wait in here." The man gestured toward a room with a huge marble fireplace and gray couches. Priscilla thanked him and stepped into the room, which was beautifully decorated with tasteful muted fabrics and a plush Oriental rug. But what really caught her eye was the art. Hanging over the mantel was a painting of purple and green water lilies in Claude Monet's distinctive impressionist style. Could that really be ... But then, Trudy had said this house was full of art. She walked closer and looked at the painting. She could see the individual brushstrokes and the way the paint was layered on the canvas. It was stunning. And if it really was a Monet, it was priceless, though she guessed someone had paid an impressive price to acquire it.

Priscilla noticed another, smaller painting on another wall. This one had a blue background with two green squares painted on it. She didn't recognize the artist, but guessed it was someone famous. And there in the corner, on a small round stand was—

Oh. Oh my. Priscilla's breath caught. That couldn't be what she thought it was. She crossed the room in a few long strides and stood in front of the piece.

It was small, but it was unmistakable. Underneath a glass display case, the small tablet showed a lion or a large cat of some kind biting the neck of a woman. It was carved into some hard material—ivory, she knew—and covered in gold. She'd seen this sculpture just last night, on her computer screen. This was *Lioness Attacking a Nubian,* that had been plundered from the Iraq Museum. This was one of the world's oldest missing treasures. It was priceless. It was stolen. And it was here.

Priscilla looked around and, seeing no one, quickly pulled out her phone and took a picture of the sculpture. She immediately sent the photo to both A.J. and to Gerald, along with a text: *At Chappaquiddick. Look what I found.* Then she moved away quickly, both to avoid drawing attention to it and because she was afraid she would somehow break it.

She moved over to the green and blue painting and studied it. It just looked like someone had painted squares on a canvas. She didn't get modern art. Maybe she had no culture, but she didn't see what the big deal was. She started to move toward another painting on the far wall when something out the window caught her eye. She sent another text to both men: *There's a small plane here coming out of the garage.*

That couldn't be—

"Hello."

Priscilla whipped around and was surprised to find Emily Leonard standing in the open archway. She looked just the same as she had in the photos online, only her dark hair was now pulled back into a smooth low ponytail and she wore dark-rimmed eyeglasses.

"Hi," she said. She tried to regain her balance, but what she'd seen out the window had rattled her. "My name is Priscilla Grant."

Priscilla's phone vibrated in her purse, but she didn't move to answer it. Emily waited for her to go on, and when she didn't, Emily said, "They said something about an Easter egg hunt."

It wasn't until this moment that Priscilla realized how flimsy this excuse had been. When she'd gone to visit Michelle, at least she genuinely had been interested in getting her to do an art demonstration at the egg hunt. But what could she ask Emily for? She doubted the woman would be up for donating a Monet.

"I'm organizing a community Easter egg hunt next weekend, and we're trying to spread the word." Priscilla held up the flyer.

"You're going door to door telling people about an Easter egg hunt?" Emily cocked her head.

"We've also been soliciting donations," Priscilla said. "For prizes. To get more people to come out."

"Okay." Emily shifted her weight. "So . . . What are you look-ing for, exactly?" There was a look on her face that Priscilla couldn't read. Priscilla's phone buzzed again.

"Some businesses have donated gift certificates," Priscilla said. "And we have an artist donating her time to demonstrate painting to the kids, and some musicians donating their time to provide music, and a pastor who will share about the true meaning of the holiday." She was flailing, and she knew it. "If there's anything that you could donate, we'd be happy to take it, otherwise I'll leave this flyer so you have the information..."

Priscilla held out the flyer, but Emily didn't move to take it.

"What are you really doing here?"

"What?" Priscilla's stomach dropped. "What do you mean?"

"You were here yesterday, with that Coast Guard officer. The one with the drone."

Priscilla didn't know how to answer. If they knew Gerald was with the Coast Guard, why did they let her in?

"We saw you on the security camera with him. Imagine our surprise and delight when you showed up again today...alone."

Oh, no. This wasn't going the way she planned, not at all.

"We don't love having people take videos of our place, but it's not like we have anything to hide." She shrugged. "But I am curious about what you were looking for."

"I—" Priscilla didn't know what to say. "My friend is really into his new drone." She tried to play it off like this was a totally normal scenario, though she was starting to sweat. "He took all kinds of videos all over the island. Did it end up over your house for a while?"

"For quite a while," Emily said. She had rings on several fingers— a large ruby one, and some kind of pink stone on another. "It was a very thorough look. But I don't understand what you were looking for. I was hoping you might be able to enlighten me."

"I don't—" Priscilla's phone was blowing up in her purse, buzzing again and again. "I'm sure I don't know." She thought quickly, and tried a new tactic. "This is a lovely home. Wasn't this where the fund-raiser for sea turtles was held a few years ago?"

Emily narrowed her eyes at Priscilla.

"My cousin was here," Priscilla explained quickly. "She told me your home was lovely, and it turns out she was right." Then, before she could get herself into any more trouble, Priscilla started for the door. "Well, I should be going. I have lots more houses to deliver these flyers to."

Emily moved to block the archway.

"Oh surely you're not planning on leaving yet," she said. Her voice was calm and even, but her meaning was clear.

"I really do have to get going," Priscilla said. This had taken a bad turn. She needed to get out of here, quickly.

"Not yet." The man who had answered the door stepped into the room, a nylon rope in his hands.

"Oh surely we don't need to resort to that, Jerome," Emily said. "I'm sure our guest will be perfectly willing to play nicely."

"Mr. Leonard insists," the man said, and stepped up next to Priscilla.

"What are you doing?" Priscilla's heart was pounding. She couldn't believe it. Were they seriously going to tie her up? Was Emily really going to allow this? She cared about saving the sea turtles but didn't mind tying up her guests?

"Don't worry. This won't hurt." The man gestured for her to put her hands out in front of her. He took her purse, her phone buzzing away inside. Priscilla didn't know what to do other than comply. Slowly, reluctantly, she held out her arms.

From where she was standing she could see that the small plane was now taxiing out onto the grassy yard. It was similar to the plane that had crashed, but this one had propellers on both wings and was white, with a black underbelly.

"What's going on with that plane?" Priscilla asked.

"My husband is just taking a little flight," Emily said evenly. "I have to go out there with him in a moment. But don't worry. Jerome will make sure you're okay."

Jerome, whoever he was, was yanking her hands together, and she felt the smooth rope coil around her wrists.

Priscilla knew she only had a few moments. And, well, after all, she was already being tied up. It wasn't like things could really get worse. She might as well ask at this point.

"Is Ryan Reid still here?"

"Ah. You know Ryan, then. Is that what this is about?" Emily had moved away from Priscilla and was taking a metal case out of the drawer in a cabinet on the far wall.

"Is he okay?" Priscilla asked.

"He's recovering. He was comfortable here. But he was in no shape to travel." She set the metal case on a desk and opened it. "But he's doing better, so he'll be heading home today."

"Can I see him?"

"I'm afraid not. He's already on board." She used her head to gesture toward the plane outside. Then she reached into the drawer and pulled out a pair of white cotton gloves. "He really has caused quite a bit of trouble this time, I have to say."

She moved to the stolen artifact, lifted off the glass cover, and carefully picked it up. She placed it into a cloth bag and gently laid it inside the case, which Priscilla could see was lined with foam. She closed the case and used a small key to lock it, and then lifted it up. Priscilla couldn't believe the nonchalance with which she hefted one of humanity's oldest treasures.

"I'm afraid I must be going as well."

"You're all leaving?" Priscilla's mind was racing. They were leaving, with the treasure. Taking the evidence away with them and leaving her behind. She had to stop them. If they left, that treasure might never be recovered again. It belonged in a museum, and it was about to vanish underground again.

"Don't worry, you won't miss us for long." She gave Priscilla a look that Priscilla couldn't read, and then she shook her head and walked out of the room, carrying the case with her.

Priscilla watched her go, mind racing. She was the only one who would be able to prove that the stolen artifact had been here at all. As Jerome tightened the ropes around her wrists, she got a sinking feeling in her stomach. There was no way he was going to simply let her go after that plane was gone. She was the only one who could prove that they were connected to an international crime. She was the only one who could tell the FBI how they left and what to look for. Jerome was hardly likely to simply set her free.

She thought quickly. Maybe she could pretend she had no idea what she'd witnessed. Would he buy it?

"What was that?" she asked. "What was she putting in that case?"

Jerome laughed. "I have a feeling you know exactly what it was."

Well, that hadn't worked how she'd hoped. She tried a different tactic. "I took a picture of it, you know."

Out the window, Priscilla could see Emily marching across the lawn toward the waiting plane. The metal case was tucked under her arm.

He shrugged. "Remind me to destroy your phone."

She didn't think it was a good idea to point out that she'd also texted the picture to the FBI. Now he was taking something out of his pocket—a long piece of cloth. What in the world?

"Where are they going?"

"That doesn't concern you." Jerome moved toward her, and she realized he was intending to put the cloth over her mouth. It was a gag. What was he going to do to her?

Emily was now scrambling into the plane through the door just over the wing. Jerome was slipping the gag over Priscilla's mouth. She didn't know what to do or how to stop him, and she felt the fabric press hard against her mouth as he pulled it tight around her head.

Please, Lord, she prayed. *Please send help.*

She watched as the plane door shut, and the plane started to roll over the grass. She tried to watch as it went, but it quickly disappeared from her view. It was headed, she was certain, toward the grass runway in the yard. It would take off and vanish, going who knew where, and the ancient treasure might never be seen again.

Please stop them, she prayed.

She couldn't see the plane, but she could hear the noise of the engines growing louder.

"Sit." Jerome was now gesturing for her to sit on the couch. She didn't know what to do aside from comply, so she sat down, and he took another rope from somewhere and started to tie her ankles together.

The engines were growing louder, but there was another noise too. A sound she recognized. She held her breath, praying she was hearing it right. A few moments later she was sure—helicopters. What sounded like a whole fleet of helicopters was moving toward the house, and quickly.

Priscilla couldn't help the relief that washed over her. She knew she was still in a dangerous situation, and she had no idea if the helicopters would be able to stop the plane, but she also knew that their arrival had just made it more difficult for the plane to take off.

"What on earth…" Jerome walked to the window and looked out. He muttered something under his breath and ran out of the room. He hadn't finished tying her feet, so Priscilla worked her way out of the rope and walked toward the window. There were one, two, three… at least four Coast Guard helicopters circling the property. The sound of the blades was deafening. Could the plane still take off? She didn't know. Maybe if the pilot timed it right.

Priscilla looked around. Where had Jerome put her purse? She spotted it on the far side of the room on the floor. She made her way over to it and knelt down. Her wrists were still tied together, but she was able to move her hands inside the purse. She felt for her phone and found it, and picked it up with one hand.

There were at least a dozen messages. Gerald asking her if she was crazy. A.J. asking what in the world she was doing there. Then, when he'd registered what the photo she'd sent him was, A.J. promising to get in front of a judge immediately. But it was when she'd sent the text about the plane that things got really interesting. Gerald saying he was sending helicopters out now. A.J. saying agents were on the way.

Now, she sent one more message, typing as best she could with one hand.

Tied up inside. Plane on runway, tablet on it.

The helicopters were still circling overhead. She assumed the plane hadn't left the ground—yet. What would happen if it did? She was pretty sure planes were faster than helicopters. Would it be able to get away? Would the helicopters give chase? But how far could they go before the plane outpaced them?

But surely the plane wouldn't get very far, Priscilla thought. The FBI could track it. Wherever it landed, there would be agents waiting, wouldn't there? Priscilla didn't know. But something outside had changed. Suddenly she could see black SUVs streaming into the driveway, sirens blaring. Priscilla's heart raced. The FBI was here.

She couldn't see much of what happened outside next. All she knew was that the front door opened and three men in black raced into the house holding the biggest guns she had ever seen.

She quickly recognized one of them as A.J., and after securing the room, he rushed to her and used a pocketknife to cut the gag and the rope.

"Thank you," she said. "The plane. The tablet is on the plane."

A.J. shook his head. "I don't know whether to hug you or strangle you." The other agents were rushing through the house, searching room by room, but A.J. sat with her.

"Just stop that plane from taking off," she said, pointing out the window.

"Oh, don't worry." He smiled grimly. "That plane is not going anywhere." He gestured for her to follow him to the window. She stood up, her legs shaky, and A.J. held out a hand to steady her. She leaned against him, and he led her across the room. She saw that the plane was now surrounded by FBI vehicles, with two directly ahead of it, blocking the runway. The choppers were still circling overhead.

"How did you get here so quickly after the Coast Guard sent the helicopters?"

"We were already here, a half mile away, waiting for the judge to approve the search warrant," A.J. said. "Once you said you were tied up, we had a hostage situation, and we were able to come in right away."

Priscilla held her breath and watched, waiting for something to happen. An FBI officer was using a megaphone to tell the Leonards to come out with their hands up.

Nothing. Were the Leonards going to ignore the FBI? But where could they go? There was nowhere for them to run to. No way to escape. They were surrounded. But still, there was no movement from the plane.

Finally, slowly, the door of the plane opened. Agents moved closer, guns drawn, as Emily climbed out, clutching the metal box. As soon as her feet hit the ground, agents had the box in their custody and her in handcuffs. An older man that Priscilla recognized as Richard Leonard stepped out next, followed by a younger man. His arm was in a sling, and she could see the bruise on his cheek from where she stood. Ryan Reid. He was alive and safe after all. The agents slapped handcuffs on him as well, and all three were quickly escorted to a waiting FBI vehicle.

"You do know that coming out here like that was really stupid, right?" A.J. said to her. Then he turned and looked out the window again. With the suspects now in custody, the Coast Guard choppers were starting to land on the big expanse of lawn.

Now that the danger had passed and the Leonards were in custody, the fear that had flooded Priscilla was giving way to relief tinged with a bit of giddiness. "Yes, I know."

"I mean it. You could have gotten yourself killed or worse."

"I know you do." Priscilla smiled. Because while he was right, they both knew that if she hadn't come out here the Leonards and Ryan Reid would have gotten away with *Lioness Attacking a Nubian*, and there would have been no way to prove they were ever connected to the piece at all. "By the way, what would be worse than getting myself killed?"

A.J. didn't answer. Instead, he just shook his head. "I'm just glad you're okay."

"Thank you for coming." Priscilla meant it. He had risked a lot to come save her.

"Are you kidding?" A.J. laughed. "Do you know how mad Rachel would be if I allowed you to get yourself hurt out here?"

Priscilla had to smile. Having an FBI agent for a son-in-law just might come in handy.

But then her gaze was caught by something outside the window. Someone, really. She recognized Gerald as soon as he stepped out of the closest chopper and watched as he hurried to the house. And despite everything—despite the frustration of the last week, and the doubts she'd been having, and the hurt she'd held on to, her heart swelled at the sight of him. He was here—her boyfriend was here, had come, alongside men and women decades his junior, to make sure she was all right. She found tears welling up, and she realized she couldn't wait to wrap him in a huge hug.

She and Gerald may have some issues to work out, Priscilla realized, but she loved him. She loved him, and he was worth the difficult conversations that needed to be had. She would worry about those later, though. For now, all she wanted to do was run out and meet him.

"He's a good man, you know," A.J. said, nodding his head toward the window.

"I know," Priscilla said. "Believe me, I know."

CHAPTER TWENTY-TWO

It wasn't until she was wrapped in a blanket on her couch that evening, sipping a cup of tea, that she got the full story of what had happened that afternoon.

"I just about fell out of my chair when I got your text," Gerald said. He was seated in an armchair by the fireplace. A fire crackled in the hearth, casting a cheerful glow over the room. Priscilla hoped there wouldn't be too many more evenings this spring when a fire would be necessary, but for tonight, it felt cozy and comforting, and that was exactly she needed.

"I'm glad you got it," Priscilla said. "Those helicopters arrived just in the nick of time. Another minute and the plane would have been gone."

"I got there as soon as I could," Gerald said. "I figured helicopters were the quickest way."

Priscilla laughed. "Yes, I suppose they were." The warmth from the mug felt good in her hands. Gerald had explained how he'd already been informed what the FBI thought was inside the house, so he'd recognized the sculpture immediately, but like A.J., his hands had been tied in terms of venturing onto the property. Still, that hadn't stopped him from rushing to help. "As soon as I realized you were inside the house, I knew there was going to be trouble," Gerald said. "And when I saw the picture of the plane, I knew we didn't have any time to waste. I just grabbed my crew, and we flew there as quickly as we could. There was no way I was going to let that plane get off the ground."

"I'm glad you didn't," Priscilla said. "If the plane had gotten into the air, that artifact could have been lost forever instead of on its way back to the Iraq Museum."

Richard and Emily Leonard were still in custody, though all indications were that they wouldn't be charged for the theft of the artifact. They insisted they'd had no idea the piece was stolen, and maybe they were telling the truth. Based on the way Emily had taken the piece with her when she realized the Feds were onto her, Priscilla very much doubted that, but it was theoretically possible, she supposed. In any case, they hadn't taken the piece themselves, just purchased it on the black market, so in all likelihood, the piece would be returned, and that would be that. There was still the matter of their kidnapping Priscilla. That was something they might not be able to get out of as easily, although Priscilla had no doubt they would have the best lawyers money could buy. Ryan Reid might be in more trouble, depending on how much they determined he knew about the cargo he'd been hired to haul. He insisted he was just supposed to make the delivery and hadn't known what was inside the plane, but the search history on his laptop indicated otherwise. Priscilla was pretty sure Eric wouldn't add to his friend's troubles by pressing charges for his stolen plane.

Gerald studied her for a moment, as if thinking through what she'd said. "Yes," he finally said. "You're right, I suppose, but the artifact didn't even enter my mind at the time." He hoisted the mug of hot chocolate she'd made for him. "I thought there was a good chance they had taken *you* on board the plane," he said. "That's why I was so determined it wasn't going to get off the ground."

Priscilla felt her belly warm. She hadn't even thought about that possibility. Thankfully, it hadn't come to that, but the idea was chilling. There was a moment of uncomfortable silence while they both considered what might have happened. Then, to lighten the mood, she asked, "Will you get in trouble for using the Coast Guard helicopters to rescue your girlfriend?"

Gerald laughed. "Oh, I don't think so," he said. "One of our jobs is to combat smuggling, so I think I can make a case for this being legit. Granted, usually there are boats involved in our operations, but I think it's close enough." He took another sip of his hot chocolate. "Besides, Coast Guard helicopters swarming in to stop the smugglers and rescue the damsel in distress? Think about how good that's going to be for PR."

Priscilla laughed. "Yes, it probably will help with that. Nice work on that one." She pulled the blanket up higher on her lap. "I must admit, I was a damsel in distress."

"That's true." Gerald sighed. "But then, I have to admit that we never would have even found the piece, let alone recovered it and found the missing pilot, if it hadn't been for you."

"They wouldn't have known who the pilot was or where to look for him, either," Priscilla said. She hadn't meant to whine, but if she was honest, there was probably some petulance in her tone.

"True enough." Gerald sighed. "Look, I know I made some mistakes this time around, and I misled you about some things. I know I don't always give you enough credit. I really do think you're one of the smartest people I've ever met."

Priscilla tried to keep her voice level. This was her chance to speak up. To say all the things that had been banging around in her mind for the past couple of weeks. "So why do you treat me like I'm not smart, then?"

He looked down at his lap for a moment.

"You didn't just ask me not to investigate this one. You actively tried to keep me away." He nodded, so she continued. "You didn't believe me when I said I'd seen a plane going down, even when I was sure of what it was. Instead of listening to what *I knew* I'd seen, you tried to convince me of what *you thought* I'd seen."

He ducked his head again but didn't say anything.

"You also made it seem like you had to look up the plane's owner in some official database," Priscilla said. "When I'm sure you knew that's all public record."

"That's true," he said. "I did. And I'm sorry."

He'd admitted it. He'd apologized. In her old life, maybe this would have been enough for her. Maybe she could have gone ahead, content to know that he'd acknowledged the truth. But then she thought about what Rachel had said about how she'd never spoken up for herself to Gary. She thought about Joan, urging her to tell Gerald how she really felt. Summoning their supportive voices within her, she found herself speaking words she never imagined she'd have the courage to say.

"You tell me you think I'm great at figuring things out, but then you try to keep me from doing anything about it," Priscilla said. "It's frustrating to be treated like a child, when you yourself admit I've got a knack for putting clues together."

Gerald didn't say anything for a moment. Priscilla could hear the crackling of the fire, and underneath that, the low, rhythmic pounding of the waves against the rocks below.

"I can see why you'd find that frustrating," he finally said. "But in my mind, I'm trying to protect you."

"I do believe that," Priscilla said. In her gut, she knew what he was saying was true. But that didn't change the fact that it wasn't okay. She took a deep breath. "Please, listen to what I'm telling you. I know you want me to be safe. I love that. But at this point in my life, being safe is not all I care about. When it comes to you—when it comes to us—I also want to be *heard*. I want to be believed. I want you to trust me to make my own decisions instead of trying to make them for me."

Gerald didn't say anything for a good while. She waited. Finally, he opened his mouth tentatively.

"I'm sorry," he said. "I truly am."

She nodded.

"I guess..." He faltered. "I guess I don't really know any other way to act with a woman. That was always how it was with me and Cathy. I made most of the decisions, and she was happy with that. She was thrilled to not have to think about our finances or where to go on vacation or anything, really. She was happy to let me take on the role of the man in charge, and I lived up to that. I got used to it."

Priscilla waited for him to acknowledge the obvious.

"But, you are not Cathy," he said, echoing exactly what Priscilla was thinking. "Maybe I need to listen more to what you're saying instead of assuming I know best."

Priscilla nodded gently. "When it comes to dangerous situations, you probably do know best," she said. She also knew she had a confession of her own to make. "When I feel that you don't trust me, when I feel like you're hiding things from me because you think I can't handle them, I start to want to prove myself to you. I take risks I wouldn't normally take. I realize now that I should have shared with you what I discovered from talking with Eric and Michelle and from going to the nursing home to find Dennis Reid. I should have been the one to tell you that the pilot's name was Ryan Reid. I should have told you about the paper Rachel and I found." She was the one looking down now. "I'm sorry I let my hurt and frustration influence the way I treated you."

Gerald reached for her hand. "Apology accepted." He rubbed small circles on the back of her hand with his thumb. "I can't promise you I'll be perfect," he said softly. "But I care about you, Priscilla. I care more about you every day. The thought of losing you or having to live without you is enough to make me crazy. I want to spend the rest of my life with you. So I can promise you this: I will try as hard as I can to do a better job."

"Thank you," Priscilla said. She appreciated that he'd acknowledged her concerns and offered to address them. But she also played the last few sentences over in her mind to make sure she'd heard them right. Could he mean . . . ? Was he thinking about—

"And Priscilla?"

She looked at him, waiting. Something in his tone was deathly serious. What was he... Was he going to—

"I also promise not to foist Chloe on you ever again."

Priscilla couldn't help it. Even as she felt a twinge of disappointment, she laughed out loud.

"You know, I agreed to help with the Easter egg hunt because I thought I was going to be working with you," she said when she'd recovered.

"I know you did." He shook his head. "And I'm sorry. But then Chloe volunteered, and I—" He grimaced. "I just can't handle all that energy."

"She is a bit much," Priscilla admitted. "Don't get me wrong. She's great. She's working really hard. But— "

"But she uses so many exclamation points," Gerald said.

"And so many emojis." She laughed.

"After our very first conversation about it, I knew she was going to drive me completely bonkers."

"So you left her for me to deal with!" Priscilla was still a tiny bit annoyed, but mostly she was relieved he was admitting it to her.

"I thought you'd do a great job with it," he insisted. "You're so good with people. And I'm... not. I thought you'd get along with her, or at least, not be driven nuts by her."

"She's... young," Priscilla said. "And very... enthusiastic. But she really is good at organizing things. Maybe she should be steered into a role where she's responsible for more organization."

"And has less interaction with people," Gerald said.

Priscilla laughed. "She's got some growing up to do, but she's a good kid," she said. "I do think the hunt is going to be fun. I think people are going to enjoy it."

Gerald looked at her over the rim of his mug. She couldn't see his mouth, but his eyes told her he was smiling. "As long as you'll be there, I can't wait."

CHAPTER TWENTY-THREE

The promised snow had dusted the island on Thursday, but it melted quickly, and Saturday morning dawned bright and sunny. The weather forecast promised temperatures reaching into the low fifties. Practically balmy. Priscilla arrived at the Coast Guard station early, and she enlisted a whole crew of helpers to hide the colored plastic eggs around the lawn.

Chloe had arranged for a group of food trucks to line one side of the parking lot, and they'd set up a tent where a band would be playing children's music and where Michelle Goldstein would be giving painting lessons. There was a photo area with a man in an Easter bunny suit, as well as a photo booth where adults could pose with props. Pastor Curt was ready under a tent off-site to give a short message to anyone who wanted to hear it, and Coast Guard officers had volunteered to give tours of the cutters and the smaller rescue boats, and even one of the helicopters.

Now, just a few minutes before the hunt was supposed to start, dozens of families stood around, holding paper bags and plastic baskets, waiting to collect the eggs. Some of the little girls were in frilly pastel dresses, some of the boys were in tailored shirts with bow ties, while some were in jeans and T-shirts. All wore winter jackets and hats.

"Ready?" Chloe was wearing a set of bunny ears and had spent most of the morning talking at light speed. But, Priscilla had to admit, she had managed to pull it all together.

It was nothing at all like the Easter egg hunts she'd arranged back in Kansas. Not even remotely.

But, she thought, looking around at the happy families gathered together enjoying the day, that was okay. Martha's Vineyard was nothing at all like Kansas anyway. And here they were, families gathered around, spending time at the Coast Guard station, learning about the men and women who served the public.

This may not be at all what she'd had in mind when she said yes to the Easter egg hunt, but that was the way life worked. She never would have been able to picture any of this—her home, her relationship with her cousins, her church community, her growing feelings for Gerald—when she'd decided to make the move to Martha's Vineyard all those months ago. Living here was nothing like she'd imagined it would be—but that didn't make it any less wonderful.

They still hadn't figured out who had taken the medication from the hospital, but the police continued to investigate. Joan found out that Michelle had been retrieving sample medication at the request of one of the doctors when Joan had seen her. Who knew? Maybe Priscilla would look into the medication theft next. But for now, she had her hands full. Her hands, and several Easter baskets.

"I think we're ready," Priscilla said.

"Awesome-sauce," Chloe said, and then sounded an air horn. All around her, hundreds of kids sprang into action, searching for plastic Easter eggs.

No, Priscilla thought, watching them scurry. This was nothing at all like she'd imagined, but it was exactly what God had had in mind. She'd just keep trusting in Him, and everything would work out fine.

AUTHOR LETTER

Dear Reader,

The idea for this book occurred to me when I was sitting on my parents' couch in Cape Cod writing, and a small plane flew low over their house and vanished behind the trees over the marsh across the road. That plane didn't crash—I have no idea where it was heading, and I think it made it there safely—but I started to wonder what would happen if it had vanished.

The premise seemed intriguing, and when I began this mystery, it only seemed to be a minor problem that I knew absolutely nothing about small planes. As I got into the story, I started to get really tripped up, trying to figure out who had access to radar data and whether every flight was tracked and how in the world pilots figured out where and how to land. I am grateful to several pilot friends who served as consultants for me and talked me through it, and any errors are mine alone.

Another thing I knew nothing about? Drones. But I included them after one of the Guideposts editors mentioned a controversy in her community surrounding the use of drones by the police. Where is the line between protecting and encroaching on privacy? I was intrigued by the ethical questions drones raise as much as the practical uses for this story.

And I'm sorry to say that the looting from the National Museum of Iraq was very real. In the shadowy days surrounding the invasion of Iraq in 2003, more than fifteen thousand pieces were taken from the museum, some by what were surely professionals who knew exactly what they were looking for, and some by less organized looters. More than seven thousand ancient artifacts—some of them representing the earliest known works of human civilization—are still missing, sold on the black market, possibly gone for good. *Lioness Attacking a Nubian* is one of the most famous pieces still missing in what is considered to be one of the largest museum heists of all time.

Despite the difficulties, writing this book was really fun, and I so enjoyed returning to the island and getting to visit the characters I've grown to love. I hope you enjoy reading it as much as I enjoyed writing it.

Best wishes,
Beth Adams

ABOUT THE AUTHOR

Beth Adams lives in Brooklyn, New York, with her husband and two young daughters. When she's not writing, she spends her time cleaning up after two devious cats and trying to find time to read mysteries.

AN ARMCHAIR TOUR OF
MARTHA'S VINEYARD
Chappaquiddick

Chappaquiddick is an island just off Martha's Vineyard, and though the ferry ride only takes about two minutes, it is a world apart. The island has two paved roads, one store, a lighthouse, and acres and acres of land preserves. Most visitors come to the island for hiking, biking, and birding. There are homes and beaches and plenty of stunning natural beauty—and, according to Google Earth, at least one private runway. The island was once the home of Wompanoag Indians, but European settlers claimed the territory and started building homes in about 1750.

Chappaquiddick is probably most famous for an incident in 1968 involving the late Senator Ted Kennedy, who drove off the single-lane Dike Bridge, which connects the main part of Chappaquiddick with a barrier beach. When Kennedy's car landed in the water, he was able to swim free, but his passenger, Mary Jo Kopechne, was trapped inside the car and drowned. Kennedy left the scene and didn't report the incident for nearly ten hours. The incident was a tragedy, and is often the first thing people think of when they hear the name Chappaquiddick.

SOMETHING DELICIOUS FROM
OUR SEASIDE FRIENDS

Bakewell Tart

Priscilla bakes this tart based on a decorated version she saw on
The Great British Baking Show, but this is a simpler version of the
traditional British treat, drizzled with a basic icing.

Ingredients for dough:

1½ cups all-purpose flour

6 tablespoons butter,
well-chilled

2–3 tablespoons ice
water

Ingredients for filling:

1¼ cups almond flour

½ cup all-purpose flour

1 teaspoon baking powder

¼ teaspoon salt

1 stick unsalted butter,
very soft

½ cup sugar

2 large eggs, lightly beaten

½ teaspoon almond extract

1 cup raspberry jam

⅓ cup sliced almonds

Ingredients for icing:

½ cup confectioners sugar

½ to 1 tablespoon water

Instructions:

Preheat oven to 400 degrees. Make piecrust by cutting the butter into the flour until it resembles bread crumbs. The easiest way to do this is to pulse a few times in a food processor, but you can do it by hand too. Add just enough water to make the mixture come together. Wrap in plastic wrap and chill for 30 minutes. Roll out the crust to about ⅛ inch thick. Carefully place onto a 9-inch pie plate. Gently press the pie dough down so that it lines the bottom and sides of the pie plate. Prick the dough all over with a fork, cover with buttered foil, and line with baking weights. Bake for 15 minutes. Remove the foil and weights and bake for three minutes longer, and then set aside.

For the filling: reduce oven to 350. Combine the flours, baking powder, and salt in a medium bowl. Using a mixer, beat butter and sugar together for three minutes or until pale and creamy. Beat in eggs one at a time. Beat in almond extract. Turn mixer to low and add half the dry ingredients. When fully incorporated, add the rest of the dry ingredients and beat until just mixed.

Spread the jam in the cooled piecrust and top with the filling. Sprinkle with sliced almonds.

Bake for 40 to 50 minutes, or until firm all the way through. Allow to cool completely.

To make icing: mix confectioners sugar and as little water as possible to make a glaze and drizzle it over the cooled tart.

Read on for a sneak peek of another exciting book
in the Mysteries of Martha's Vineyard series!

Sheeps Passing in the Night
by Elizabeth Ludwig

A glimpse of bright orange peeked through a fluffy blanket of clouds, the first patch of sunlight in over a week. Priscilla peered through her kitchen window at it and smiled. Winters on the Vineyard could be hard, but now it looked as though the cold and rain would finally make way for spring.

She reached for the leash on the counter and held it up for her dog to see. "What do you think, Jake? Should we risk a walk today, or do you think it's going to rain again?"

Catching sight of the leash, Jake barked and jumped up to rest his front paws against the countertop, his nose and tail twitching eagerly. Priscilla laughed and snapped the end of the leash to his collar.

"Okay, but maybe not the beach. That salt spray is going to be frigid, and I'd rather not get wet. How about we head to town and check out the preparations for the Lambapalooza?"

Jake quirked his head and stared at her as though to say, *Lamba-what?*

She knew exactly how he felt. The first time she'd heard about the event, she had been just as confused as he appeared to be. Spread over four days, Lambapalooza was a local festival designed to help the island's sheep farmers welcome spring and prepare their flocks for warmer temperatures. Of course, it wasn't just the farmers who enjoyed the festivities. Besides the standard carnival-type rides, there was also sheep shearing, wool carding, knitting classes, and plenty of food and entertainment. There were activities for people of all ages to enjoy, and Priscilla was looking forward to it.

Giving a whistle to Jake, she climbed into the car and set off. Wilson's Wool Ranch, the farm where the Lambapalooza event was held every year, was just a short car ride from Misty Harbor. Normally it was sheep who roamed the acres and acres of green pastureland, but in just a few short hours, it would be crowded with children and families hungry for some homespun fun.

Jake's wet nose left streaks all over the passenger side window. Giving in to his whimper, Priscilla rolled it down so he could stick his head out and soak in the sun and salty sea breezes.

"We've been cooped up inside the cottage for quite a while, eh, boy?" she said, reaching out to ruffle his fur.

As if in agreement, Jake strained farther out the window, his tongue lolling out of the side of his mouth and his jowls flapping noisily. Priscilla laughed. Oh, to be a dog!

Spying cars winding slowly up the gravel driveway leading to the farm, Priscilla slowed and turned her attention to picking out a spot to park. Vendors had already begun setting up tents. She spotted an assortment of handcrafted goods alongside the wool products the island was known for. Volunteers manning the sheep-related stations were also hard at work putting up tables and spreading hay and sawdust to help with the mud. She was amazed by the amount of activity.

"Wow, Jake. Looks like there's quite a bit going on."

Slipping her keys into her purse, Priscilla reached for Jake's leash and climbed from the car. The second his paws hit the ground she felt a tug.

"Whoa, now, Jake. Wait for me. There's a good boy."

Looping the leash over her wrist, Priscilla set off down the hill toward the closest row of barns. Bright banners with the words *Come Meet Our Lambs* flapped a welcome. She steered Jake that way, ducking in and out between rumbling wagons stuffed with feed bags. Soon, Jake's happy bark blended with the overall melee and Priscilla was glad she'd decided to come. It seemed they both needed some time out of doors.

"Priscilla!"

Hearing her name called, Priscilla looked this way and that and finally spotted one of her cousins a few yards down near the sheep pens. She raised her hand in greeting and gave the leash a tug.

"C'mon, Jake. Let's go see Gail."

Gail was dressed like a farmer from a storybook in overalls and a plaid shirt. Rubber boots hit her mid-calf, and on her head she wore a floppy hat with frayed edges that said it had seen better days. She grinned as Priscilla approached and hunkered low to give Jake a good rub behind the ears.

"Hey, buddy. What are you two doing out and about?"

Priscilla pointed to the bright spots of sun poking out from behind the clouds. "Enjoying the sunshine, finally. What are you doing? Didn't you have to work today?"

Gail rose and hooked her thumbs in the pockets of her overalls. "Haven't you heard? I'm a sheep farmer now." She laughed. "At least, I am for the weekend. Derry Wilson is a patient of mine. He stopped by last week and said they could really use a few extra hands setting up for the Lambapalooza so, voilà!" She held her hands wide and smiled wider. "Here I am, a regular farmer in the dell."

"Well, you certainly look the part," Priscilla said, laughing as she pointed to Gail's rubber boots. "Where on earth did you find those?"

"They come standard with the hat." Gail pulled it off of her head with a flourish. "I know where you can get one if you're interested."

"Actually, I think I'll pass."

"I don't blame you," Gail said, slapping the hat against her thigh.

Priscilla chuckled, then raised her eyebrows. "Hey, have you heard from Trudy? Isn't she supposed to be back this week?"

Another one of her cousins, Trudy, was the most flamboyant. She was also very active in her church and other fund-raising events, so Priscilla had been glad to hear that she and her husband Dan were taking some time for themselves. They had left several days ago for a week-long cruise to the Bahamas.

"Other than her posts on Facebook?" Gail shook her head. "By her pictures, it sure looks like she and Dan are having a great time. They should be back in a few days."

"Well, I'm glad they were able to get away. And speaking of that..." Priscilla gave a nod to Jake, who had begun tugging anxiously on his leash. "This one is more than ready for a little romp. I think I'll take him over by the pasture so he can run a little."

"Oh, okay. But listen, we're breaking for lunch in about an hour. How about we meet up near the big barn and grab a bite to eat? They're bringing in a food truck from the Red Cat Kitchen." She rubbed one gloved hand over her belly. "I can already taste those hush puppies."

"Sounds good." Priscilla checked her watch and then bent to give Jake a pat. "Okay, boy, let's go. See you, Gail."

"See you." Gail gave a wave of her hat, then plunked it onto her head before turning to go back into the pen.

"She's a better gal than I am," Priscilla said to Jake, as Gail sloshed through mud up to her ankles. This rainy weather had certainly made working the Lambapalooza difficult. No wonder they were having trouble rounding up volunteers.

She tapped her chin, thinking as she walked past the sheep-shearing pens. It might be fun to help. She paused to watch a couple of volunteers pouring fresh water into troughs. She could certainly feed sheep or empty trash cans as well as the next person—

Interrupting Priscilla's musings, Jake lunged toward a flock of sheep grazing in a nearby pasture. The move was so sudden, he jerked the leash completely out of Priscilla's hand.

"Jake!" She scrambled to step on the end of the leash as it skittered across grass and stones. "Stop. Jake, come back here."

He ran on, oblivious to her cries. The sheep, however, were not oblivious. Hearing his bark, they scattered in panic.

Huffing, Priscilla rushed toward the fence where Jake stood barking, the hair on his neck standing on end.

"Jake, come here," Priscilla said, reaching for the leash. He dashed under the fence before she could grasp it and took off after the closest sheep.

"Jake, no!" She watched in horror as he nipped at the sheep and then turned and began chasing the rest toward the far end of the pasture. They leapt wildly over one another in their rush to escape.

Her frustration growing, she shouted Jake's name over and over. Of course, he would eventually tire, but in the meantime, the entire flock of sheep was bleating and scurrying as fast as their little legs could carry them.

"Priscilla? What's going on?" Gail joined her at the fence. "I heard you yelling."

Priscilla pointed. "It's Jake. He pulled the leash out of my hand and now I can't get him to come back."

"Oh no." Gail added her voice to Priscilla's. "Jake, bad dog! Come here, boy."

More barking. More bleating. This was rapidly becoming ridiculous.

"I've got to get him," Priscilla said, looking over her shoulder for the owner of the farm. He certainly wouldn't appreciate having his sheep terrified by a naughty dog. She ducked under the top rail of the fence then swung her leg over the bottom rail and wriggled through to the other side.

"I'll help," Gail said, joining her. "Maybe if you circle one way and I go the other?"

"Good idea." Priscilla pointed. "I'll go that way, and for goodness' sake, let's hurry before he hurts one of those sheep."

"Right." Her hat flopping, Gail ran, her boots sucking loudly in the mud. Priscilla ran the opposite direction, trying desperately to keep her shoes on her feet while she dodged sheep and hollered for Jake. Finally, she was able to corner him near the fence, thanks to Gail. Mud dripped from his fur as he sat in a puddle, panting.

Priscilla grabbed the leash and wrapped it around her hand twice before leaning back against a fence post to catch her breath. Jake wasn't the only one covered in mud. She had splotches of the stuff clear up to her knees, and there would be no saving her shoes, she thought angrily, staring at her feet.

"Thank goodness," Gail said, propping both hands on her hips. Her breath puffed from her reddened cheeks and sweat trickled from her brow. "I'm getting too old for chasing dogs."

"You and me both." Priscilla ran the back of her hand over her forehead then scowled down at Jake. "That was very naughty. Look at us. We're both heading straight for the tub the moment we get home."

Not to mention that Jake had more than a bit of wool clinging to his jowls. Apparently, he'd gotten a little too close for comfort to more than one of the sheep.

"Hey, you there!"

Both women looked up at the angry male voice.

"Uh-oh." Gail bumped her hat back from her forehead and pointed to the owner of the farm. "Here comes Derry, and he doesn't look happy."

A NOTE FROM THE EDITORS

We hope you enjoyed Mysteries of Martha's Vineyard, published by the Books and Inspirational Media Division of Guideposts, a nonprofit organization that touches millions of lives every day through products and services that inspire, encourage, help you grow in your faith, and celebrate God's love.

Thank you for making a difference with your purchase of this book, which helps fund our many outreach programs to military personnel, prisons, hospitals, nursing homes, and educational institutions.

We also create many useful and uplifting online resources. Visit Guideposts.org to read true stories of hope and inspiration, access OurPrayer network, sign up for free newsletters, download free e-books, join our Facebook community, and follow our stimulating blogs.

To learn about other Guideposts publications, including the best-selling devotional *Daily Guideposts*, go to Guideposts.org/Shop, call (800) 932-2145, or write to Guideposts, PO Box 5815, Harlan, Iowa 51593.

Sign up for the
Guideposts Fiction Newsletter
and stay up-to-date on the books you love!

You'll get sneak peeks of new releases, recommendations from other Guideposts readers, and special offers just for you . . .
and it's FREE!

Just go to Guideposts.org/Newsletters
today to sign up.

Guideposts®   Visit Guideposts.org/Shop
or call (800) 932-2145

Find more inspiring fiction in these best-loved Guideposts series!

Secrets of Wayfarers Inn
Fall back in history with three retired schoolteachers who find themselves owners of an old warehouse-turned-inn that is filled with hidden passages, buried secrets and stunning surprises that will set them on a course to puzzling mysteries from the Underground Railroad.

Sugarcreek Amish Mysteries
Be intrigued by the suspense and joyful "aha" moments in these delightful stories. Each book in the series brings together two women of vastly different backgrounds and traditions, who realize there's much more to the "simple life" than meets the eye.

Tearoom Mysteries Series
Mix one stately Victorian home, a charming lakeside town in Maine, and two adventurous cousins with a passion for tea and hospitality. Add a large scoop of intriguing mystery and sprinkle generously with faith, family, and friends, and you have the recipe for *Tearoom Mysteries*.

Mysteries of Silver Peak
Escape to the historic mining town of Silver Peak, Colorado, and discover how one woman's love of antiques helps her solve mysteries buried deep in the town's checkered past.

To learn more about these books, visit Guideposts.org/Shop